Hostility
and
Heartstrings

E.G. Verot

HOSTILITY AND HEARTSTRINGS

E.G. VEROT

BLURB

Our story begins in England during the early 1800s, or as it is more commonly known, the regency era.

Marriage is common amongst the residents of England, love is a rarity.

Margo began her journey in society as a teenager, inconsiderate and so consumed by her own fears that she was unaware of the hurtful affect her words had on someone very important to her. She now finds herself nearly a decade older and is just now realizing the error of her ways. When she meets a young friend who finds herself in a similar situation upon entering society, Margo tries to share her mistakes in the hope that another will not repeat them. Will she be able to save a valued friendship once lost?

Edward however had a very different outlook on love when he was younger. So much so that he made himself vulnerable to utter heartbreak...a devastation he has never recovered from. Now, he is forced to come face to face with the woman who broke his heart when his sister decides to spend her summer holiday at Margo's country estate.

To those who have convinced themselves for one reason or another that you will never find love, it's out there. Perhaps where you least expect it.

AUTHOR'S NOTE

Please note this book contains adult themes and situations. There are some sensitive themes in Hostility and Heartstrings that readers may find triggering.

This book contains mention of the death of a loved one and physical violence (not done to a main character).

You will also find tension, spice, and a happy ending!

Thanks for reading!

-E.G. Verot

PROLOGUE

8 YEARS EARLIER...

I hold out my hand in a gesture to finalize the agreement. This may be the most important moment of my existence.

That's a lie.

It is the first of many essential pieces that will need to fit together perfectly to lead me to the one thing I want most in this life.

The dark walls of this office have surely been witness to many conversations over the years, both of business and personal matters, I assume. Parchment, letters, and quills cover the wooden desk that separates us. I can only assume there is a personal order to it all that only the powerful man who sits behind it can understand.

He accepts.

"Thank you, sir!" I shout in a poor attempt to contain my relief.

Quickly, I turn and walk out of his office to avoid any further possible embarrassment. The entirety of the meeting is replaying in my mind as the fresh air fills my body. I did not expect him to turn me away, but one can never be too sure with these matters. The first task of the day is completed, now onto the far more intimidating part.

The walk back through town feels more vibrant than it has recently. I have walked these streets my entire life, and yet, this week, everything appears brighter. Hope is in the air as the early signs of spring are starting to show in the landscapes separating the townhomes from the sidewalks and streets.

Thankful for the short journey to my home, I am anxious to begin preparations for this evening. Upon my approach to the front entrance of my family's townhouse, a familiar voice draws my attention. I am greeted by my mother and younger sister, who look to be returning home from another day of shopping.

"Edward..." My mother calls from the top step, "Where have you been this morning?" My mother may be smaller in height, but her strong disposition makes up for it. She is as beautiful as any of the other mothers in our social circle, yet her face has a younger appearance than most. Even the slight breeze never fails to mess with her blonde hair, styled high and away from her shoulders. When her eyes meet mine, I recognize the meaning immediately. She does not want a lie. I can respect that, but I'm not going to give her the details either.

"Out." A simple yet accurate answer as I wish to avoid sharing too much. She has a tendency to try to influence my decisions based on the path she would prefer, motivated purely by social reasons. My father, a good businessman, has perfected the art of appeasing my mother while keeping her influence out of his business dealings. Unfortunately for me, there are different expectations for her husband than for her son.

"Hello, Eddy!" My adorable younger sister Evelyn runs to my side to hug me at the hip. Her dark brown hair bounces off her shoulders as her hair ribbon becomes even more crooked than it already is. Only two people use that nickname for me, both of whom I love very much. I can still remember the day my sister was born. She is an exuberant ten-year-old to my age of twenty. In society's eyes, it would be normal for me to take little notice of Evelyn, with her being younger and a girl. But she always manages to hold my complete attention when we are together.

"Good day, Miss Evelyn. How was your morning?" I ask as I kneel to eye level with her. As I await her answer, I take it upon myself to straighten the ribbon and pull her bangs away from her eyes.

"It was spectacular! Many people were out today." Evelyn squeals with such enthusiasm. I detest how much my mother keeps her boarded up in the house. I try to take her out when I have the chance, but lately, those chances are less often than I'd like.

"We spoke with quite a few young ladies and their mothers during our travels today, Edward," my mother interrupts. "Evelyn, do tell Edward about the lovely young ladies who were curious about his possible attendance at the Parker family's ball this evening."

"Do not be an accomplice to our mother's unrequited interference in my love life, Evelyn," I say to my sister with a pointed finger before she can answer. "The day will come, my dear sister, when you will be on the marriage market, and I have a feeling that you will not care for my interference."

"I am going to marry a prince," Evelyn declares with her chest puffed and her chin held high.

"Well, that should keep you plenty busy, Mother," I say as I kiss her cheek and hold out my arm, directing them to enter the townhouse. Once inside, I inform them, "I will be attending the ball this evening. Now, please excuse me while I get ready." I continue directly up the stairs before my mother's shock can subside and more questioning begins.

EXCITEMENT IS BUILDING THROUGHOUT LONDON. The social season commences with the ball at the Parker Estate this evening. Young ladies will make their official entrance into the marriage market. How stressful it must be for these girls. I barely allow myself the thought of Evelyn being among them. I wish to keep her the innocent, sweet, and sometimes terrifying child she is right now.

One young lady in particular comes to mind whom I doubt is feeling any concern while preparing for this evening, Miss Margaret Eton. Thoughts of Miss Eton can be consumingly distracting, her beauty and intelligence are equally matched.

My chest begins to tighten when I think of the last time I was in her company. It was at an art gallery, and she was accompanied by a family friend, Lady Calderwood, I believe. Her friend was gracious enough to give us some privacy as we explored the various paintings. Not only did Margaret have a quick wit when it came to business, but she also had a great appreciation for art.

When I express my admiration for a particular painting of the English countryside and the artist, I share quietly that I would have liked to learn to paint.

Margo turns to me, "You are not dead, Eddy. You still have plenty of time to learn. I recommend purchasing paint and brushes as soon as you leave here."

When I laugh at her jest, she rests her hand on my shoulder. With a reassuring voice, "I'm not joking, Eddy. If you want to paint, paint."

Margaret has an extraordinary gift of making me feel invincible with her support.

I imagine seeing her this evening, her smile that I have longed to witness again. I can only hope Evelyn will find herself with the same abundance of integrity, honesty, and confidence that Miss Eton displays in all aspects of her life.

Being raised as the only child of the Eton family would be difficult for any child, let alone a daughter. In society, a woman is rarely able to consider herself an heir, but that is how she has always been referred to and treated by her parents. Lord Eton has allowed Margaret to attend all functions that men typically were accompanied by their sons, causing quite a stir. Most young girls would cower in a room full of gentlemen and their sons, yet she was anything but shy.

Margo took her role more seriously than most of the children in attendance at those events, at times more seriously than even myself. She tried on numerous occasions to add her thoughts to the conversation, but the gentlemen did not see any value in an opinion coming from a young girl. Margo would share her thoughts with me, encouraging me to share them. She had great instincts far beyond her years, but I could not take the praise from her and did not believe these men were worthy of her astute perception.

A smirk forms on my lips when I think of Margo scolding me for making her laugh during these meetings. It never took much to earn a smile on her face, a simple note usually disclosing the location of the pastries that were to be served after the meetings or a joke about the older gentlemen snoring on the opposite side of the room. In hindsight, she understands better than I do that sitting in the back giggling can get her removed from the meetings. That was never my intention. It was selfish to crave her attention. Tonight at the ball will be nothing compared to the situations she has grown up in.

It has been a little less than a year since I have had the pleasure of being in her company. Every day for the last year, I have thought about seeing her again. Recalling every moment we shared since childhood over in my head, each of those memories fresh in my mind. My reflection in the mirror alerts me to the change in my appearance; my face is slightly blushed, and my chest is moving more forcefully. Typically, I make every possible excuse to avoid these events, but nothing can stop me from attending this evening.

These matchmaking events hold little interest for me, having no reason to attend them before tonight. But my father and colleagues have made it clear that being present is advised throughout the season. Sure, I have attended many in the last two years, but barely did I dance. It would have been quite dishonorable to give a young lady the wrong impression that I may be interested. I believe it is a display of poor manners for me to take up a spot on their dance cards that could be saved for an actual suitor.

Tonight is different. This will be my first night as a serious suitor. A distressing thought comes to mind, one I have not considered until this very moment. Other men throughout London may be preparing for the evening, intending to declare themselves serious suitors for the very woman I plan to charm. I have never cared for any girl who attended these events, which meant I never thought of the other gentlemen as competition in the marriage market. My stomach starts to knot as I finish buttoning my cufflinks and do a final appraisal of my appearance.

With a deep breath, I smile back at the handsome young man in the mirror. Why should I be worried about competition? I am by far one of the best-looking gentlemen in my acquaintance and young enough to still have smooth skin, full dark brown hair, and the posture of a statue.

~

HOURS LATER, I find myself at the entrance of the ball. I look up at the front of the exquisite exterior, take a deep breath, and—

"Edward Riley!" a voice calls from behind me. It sounds familiar, and I turn to discover its owner.

"Albert Berry! Fancy seeing you here. Did not think you would show your face in society for a few more weeks."

Albert Berry, a gentleman, only two years my senior and, like me, enjoys life with minimal responsibilities until he inherits his father's titles. The Berry family estate, Greenbrook Manor, is a sight to behold, yet Albert has only invited me there once. I do not believe he visits often. It seems the young ladies who pay him endless compliments are far more interested in the great estate. Unfortunately for them, Albert has made no secret of his distaste for society and these "arranged marriage parties," as he refers to them. He is not ready to settle down and has a horrible view of marriage. I always believed it was because his parents were the furthest thing from a love match, and he assumed his fate would be the same.

"Yes, I have a new plan to combat the social season this year, chap," he says as he catches up to me. "I'm going to get in all my socializing at the beginning of the season."

He leans in and lowers his voice as if he is sharing a secret. "At the beginning of the season, the mothers are still optimistic about their daughters finding a husband. They are less pushy, do you not agree?"

I nod, and he continues. "Then I will have satisfied my social obligations and no longer attend the balls when they are absolutely desperate for their daughters to marry."

"A true genius you are, my friend." Clapping his back,

"Shall we get this over with then?" I say as we both make our entrance.

I withhold my intentions for this evening from Albert. He is so pessimistic about marriage and the idea of love that he couldn't understand how I feel about her. I can only hope one day he will find someone who will turn his world upside down...

PRESENT DAY LONDON, 1815...

I hardly recognize the woman in the mirror.

A deep exhale leaves my body as I look at society's idea of perfection with the exception of my age of six and twenty. The beautiful white dress complements my womanly figure and tall height, my black curly hair pinned up off my face in the latest style with sparkling jewelry placed throughout my body. It is all perfect, aside from the disgust painted across my face. My fascination with London society faded years ago. Now, this is simply a duty I am required to serve if I want to protect the other life I lead in the country. That is the part that I genuinely enjoy, and this is the agreement I made with my parents.

My mother, motivated by social reasons, and my father, motivated by financial reasons, are the developers behind our agreement that finds me preparing for my third ball this week.

My mother, Lady Eton, is only concerned with one

thing: maintaining society's high regard for her and, in turn, her offspring. She had very little instruction for me in life, but what she has passed down is how to make sure everyone is envious of me. Her dream is to see me as coveted in the marriage market as she was in her youth.

My father, Lord Eton, exclusively saw a child as a piece of his legacy. Unfortunately for him, he has no male relatives. In fact, he does not have any relatives left. I am the last in his family line.

Upon reflection, I have found it interesting that he never tried for a son, and I was left as an only child. The only reasonable explanation I can assume is that my parents could not stomach the idea of repeating the process to produce another child with no guarantee of a son.

Lord Eton's good standing was enough to convince the Crown that when I am married, my husband will inherit everything. My father does not appear to care who will fill this role, just that it will not be forfeited at his death. He pointed out once, in a rather cold way, that this will secure my future as well, but that will only be true if I marry someone who will allow it. While it is required that I eventually take a husband, my father has yet to put a time limit on our arrangement.

Tired of looking at my reflection, I turn my attention to the beautiful mirror. The frame is gold with arms that replicate vines growing up the side. Fitting for the room in which it lives. My room at Lady Lily Calderwood's townhouse in London looks as if it belongs to royalty. It is even more spectacular than my room at my parents' townhouse. This is not a guest room. I imagine it would be the room occupied by Lady Calderwood's first child if she ever had children. When I first stayed with her, she insisted I stay in this room and spent months decorating it for my arrival, days before I was to make my first appearance in London Society.

"Margaret!!!" my mother shrieks. Her black gown rustles as she elegantly sweeps into the room, the white jewels sparkling like little stars on her skirt. There's not a hair out of place, the dark locks swept to the side. She is dressed in her usual formal evening dresses and excessive makeup. I imagine tonight she will be off to the opera.

"There is my daughter! I barely recognized you when you arrived. That country living does you no favors, dear. You always come back looking so...*plain*," she says with a sour face.

Of course, she does not recognize me. We spend so little time together it is a wonder she remembers what I look like under any circumstances.

Lady Eton closes the space between us and grabs my hands in hers. "But now, Margaret, you look exquisite. I do hope you enjoy tonight's festivities and be mindful you are representing the Eton legacy."

"Yes, Mother," I reply with every effort to hide my disgust. My mother makes no notice, but Lady Calderwood knows me much better and quickly joins us. She stands at my side, opposite my mother. It is a subtle but comforting show of solidarity for me. I turn and give her a discreet, thankful smile.

"Well, I must be off. Thank you, Lady Calderwood, as always, for looking after my sweet Margaret at these balls. They never could hold my attention after I was married."

Nothing had held my mother's attention once she was married, at least not her husband or her daughter.

I do believe my parents' union was a matter of convenience on both sides. My father had a fortune many could only dream of, and my mother had a wealth of beauty. They are both competitive and cold individuals. They each saw the marriage as a victory among their peers. I have never witnessed them share an affectionate look across the room or share a dance in all my years.

"It is my pleasure, Lady Eton. I love Margaret as my own, almost as much as I love a reason to continue attending the balls," Lady Calderwood responds with a wink in my direction.

"Better you than me," my mother calls with a wave to both of us and exits the room.

I let myself exhale as soon as the door closed behind her. Lady Calderwood and I both share a quiet laugh.

The door opens slightly. I worry my mother has returned, but it is just word that the carriage is ready for us.

THIS IS the third ball this week. Within the agreement with my parents, I must attend at least twenty balls in town each year. I tried to squeeze as many into each visit to London as possible. Thankfully, I am able to stay with Lady Calderwood at her townhouse rather than the Eton family townhouse.

My parents and I have never been close, and at the age of six and twenty, I am starting to truly appreciate our separate lives. I am the person I am today, a person very unlike my parents because of those who raised me, including Lady Calderwood. She is a widow who lived near my parents' estates, both in town and the country. The Calderwood Estate neighbors Eton Cottage in the country. I always wandered about her land as a child.

I remember Lord Calderwood fondly. He was an extremely kind man who loved his wife deeply. I was younger when he passed away, after which I spent many nights with her to console her in his absence. Their love story is better than any I could read about in a novel. She still talks about him with a look of love in her eyes. I cannot imagine most finding a love like that. I know my parents certainly never did.

Lady Calderwood is not like most women in London society; she enjoys the country just as much as I do. She has a close friendship with my country home's caretakers, Mr. and Mrs. Landon, who have acted as my caretakers for most of my childhood and still do.

As I got older, Lady Calderwood insisted I start calling her Lily. She explained close friends do not refer to each other by their titles, at least not in private. Lily was there to teach me the rules of society and what was expected of me due to my family's standing, but more importantly, that there was much more to life than London society.

I met Lily when she first married, and I recall thinking of her as an adult, but the older I grew, the less the age difference seemed to be. She was a little over ten years my senior. I always thought her beautiful but in a much different way than my mother. Lily has light blonde hair and a smaller figure. Her light skin is flawless, and her blue eyes are always so bright.

The carriage ride to the ball is filled with laughter and discussion regarding my mother's visit. My friendship with Lily has always come easy to me. We can talk for hours and never get tired of hearing the other's voice. Yet, we can also sit quietly, each reading without awkward silence. Tonight, we discuss returning to the country. As the weather is warmer, we will be able to enjoy more time outside in the country fields, on walks, and swimming in the lake. How I long to be home in the country, away from this busy city life.

Edward

"Will you be riding with us tonight, Edward?" My mother, Lady Riley, inquires with a pointed glare. I straighten my jacket in the window's reflection as we wait by the front entrance of Riley House, our family's home in London.

"I am not about to allow my sister to attend her first ball without an escort, Mother," I reply dryly, already tired of her games. My mother is well aware I want to be there, especially when she and I so strongly disagreed on this matter.

She is determined to have Evelyn marry in her first season. It appears my mother and her friends are in a competition, who can secure an offer for their daughters first.

I expressed my disagreement to my parents on multiple occasions in the month prior but was never taken seriously. I personally believe Evelyn is too young to get married, but that may be due to the reason I still see a child when I look at her. As her brother, it is my job to watch over her tonight. It is no secret how Evelyn feels about this. She has been unable to keep food down all day due to nerves.

"Perhaps you should be more concerned about gaining attention yourself this evening instead of bothering with your sister's prospects. You have avoided attending all events this season. I imagine there are many new young ladies who would love a chance to dance with a man as handsome as you." My mother was not always as insistent as she is now about my taking a wife, but as I grow older and less interested, she is becoming increasingly concerned.

I will eventually take a wife, but I prefer to enjoy my freedom a little longer. Accepting long ago that a love match was not an option for me...not anymore.

Memories flash in my mind of the one who was responsible for that. I rub my chest, trying to soothe the slight pain I have ignored for years. So young and foolish, my broken heart was partially my own fault, but it was she who left it beyond repair.

Looking toward my bleak future, I prefer to put off an unhappy union as long as possible.

"Eddy!" my sister screams from the top of the stairs. I move to reach her, and my mother blocks my way.

"Mother." Failing to hide my exasperation in my tone.

"What can she need from her brother when she is dressing for a ball?" With a look of disgust, she turns and yells up the staircase, "What do you need Evelyn?"

I have always sensed jealousy from my mother when it came to my relationship with my sister. They do care for one another, but my mother has continually pushed for Evelyn to be more like her, more excited about marriage at her age. When, in truth, out of her two children, it was I who was far more excited about marriage at Evelyn's age. I just did not share it with my parents. It is difficult for my mother to hide her disappointment around Evelyn. It is no surprise she was asking for me at this moment.

"I am requesting *Eddy*!" With a snide look, I step around my mother and run up the stairs.

"Yes, sister?" I call from outside her closed door. Evelyn only opens the door enough to push her arm through, grab my jacket, and pull me into her room then slam the door behind me.

"This was just pressed," I scold her while trying to smooth out the now wrinkled area of my coat.

Looking at her, it is abundantly obvious that my sister is no longer a schoolgirl but a beautiful young woman. Her blue dress complements her skin tone perfectly, and her bangs are pinned to the side to show off her deep blue eyes. "Evelyn...you look beautiful." Feelings of pride fill my chest.

"Yes, thank you, Eddy. That is what everyone is telling me, but I'm more uncomfortable than when I fell in the lake last summer."

She is angry. If I could take her away, we'd already be gone, but there is no possibility we would get past our mother. Her ridged shoulders start moving quickly up and down,

"I cannot breathe," she yells in my direction. "I cannot breathe!" she repeats, rushing the words out quicker than before.

I place my hands on her shoulder to steady her. "Trust me, I do not want to go tonight any more than you do."

She opens her mouth to speak, but I cut her off. "There is no getting out of this, sister. I promise to not leave your side the entire evening. I will monitor any gentleman that asks for a dance."

I lean closer and down to her eye level, still holding onto her shoulders, and make her a promise. "You will not have to do anything you do not want to do this evening... aside from attending." With a weak smile, I give her a moment to gather her thoughts.

She takes two long, deep breaths and straightens her spine. "The sooner we arrive..."

"The sooner we leave," I reply as I hold out my arm for her to take. She slips her arm in and gives my arm a squeeze.

We leave her room and descend the stairs where our mother is waiting with her hands on her hips. Without stopping, we walk directly out of the house and into the carriage.

HOLDING Evelyn's hand as she exits the carriage and gazes up at the entrance to this evening's event, I give it a tight squeeze, reassuring her. She enters with me on her right and our mother on her left. It is a nice enough ballroom; already, it appears to be at capacity.

My next matter of business is to take inventory of the guests in attendance. There are two people I search for when I arrive at these events, one a dear friend whose company I would quickly search out if he were here, the other a not so dear enemy. Enemy is a strong term, but how else would I describe the person I would do my best to avoid if she were in attendance?

Neither seems to be here, and I am equally relieved and disappointed. The disappointment does not last long as shortly after we make our way about halfway through the ballroom, I am greeted with a slap on the back by my dear friend, Mr. Albert Berry.

"Edward! How nice of you to escort your sister during her first night in society as an eligible young lady."

Then, turning to my mother and sister, "Lady Riley," he gives a bow and another to my sister. "Miss Riley, I must say you look delightful this evening."

Albert's attitude about such events has drastically improved over the years. Yet, he never seemed to dance much or show any interest in the eligible young ladies in attendance.

"Thank you, Albert," Evelyn says with a friendly smile, which fades quickly when my mother elbows her in the side to correct her address.

"*Mr. Berry.*" My mother corrects my sister as she leans closer to Evelyn, "You are no longer a little sister who is acquaintances with her brother's friends, Evelyn. While out in public, you must address everyone who is not your brother by their formal title. Calling a man by his first name in a crowded ballroom is the quickest way to spread rumors." Evelyn's shock is clear on her face as our mother continues to scold her. "You know better."

Evelyn pushes her lips together as if trying to hold in the argument building in her head, but she stops and turns back to Albert. "My apologies, Mr. Berry."

"Not a problem, Miss Riley." He lowers his voice so only our group can hear, "I promise you will encounter me far more informally as your brother's mate than you will see me at formal events." He winks at her and then turns back to me.

"So, Mr. Riley...any ladies in here grab your attention tonight as a possible Mrs. Riley?"

I laugh. Albert is well aware of exactly where I stand in the marriage market. He has been supportive without ever questioning my reasoning. Albert continues, "Well, seeing as you are on guard duty for your sister now, I do not see how you could find the time to look for yourself."

It happens between songs; more and more guests turn their attention to the entrance of the hall. As if royalty is walking through the doors, women point and whisper between themselves, and men stand taller and try to fix their appearances.

"It is her..." Evelyn whispers to herself and then continues, "...she is so beautiful."

Positioning myself to stand behind Evelyn, I look over her head.

Who could she recognize and remark so kindly toward?

When I see her, I feel my back go straight, not in hopes of impressing her but to raise my defenses.

Turning back to Albert, he understands immediately and tilts his head in the opposite direction.

I lean down to my sister and whisper, "Try not to get into too much mischief. I'm going to step outside for some air." She nods without even looking back at me. Unable to take her eyes off the woman.

Albert and I make our way outside at the opposite end of the room.

3

As I enter the ball, the countdown to when I can leave begins in my head. I must dance with five gentlemen and spend at least two hours here. A condition in the agreement my father insists upon.

I can admit to myself that it is a shame that I have become so exasperated with London balls that I am no longer intrigued by the beauty and work put into each ball. During my first season, I enjoyed admiring the decorations and trying to determine the theme before speaking with the host. Lily and I would attempt to smell each and every flower, admire the chandelier, and try to see as many rooms as possible.

Now, I can barely find joy in it. Nothing compares to the country. The flowers aren't as bright, the food not as rich, and, most upsetting, the conversations are always shallow and meaningless.

Taking a quick glance around the room, only familiar faces look back at me with smiles that are as delicate as they are untrue.

While the majority of my female peers have been long married, most of my male peers are in a similar situation as mine. We have enough money to enjoy the freedom of a single life until we choose to marry.

My eyes travel the room, receiving a few barely contained male sneers along with some quickly upturned noses. Sure, I have more freedom than the typical lady in this society, but a shiver of enjoyment steals down my spine at those resentful looks.

Lady Calderwood stays close by while a few brave gentlemen line up to request a dance from me. Unfortunately, it is only three and I will have to catch the eye of two more by the end of the night to meet my requirement of five.

I am interested in eventually marrying, but I want it to be for love and not the financial security that will be guaranteed to my future husband. It has been my greatest regret that I was not able to stop Lord Eton from making our arrangement public. It might have provided me a real chance to find love if they hadn't. Now, it is next to impossible to trust any of the kind smiles or sweet words delivered by the gentlemen offering their attention.

THE FIRST DANCE is with a young man, Mr. Oxworth, who was introduced to me by his mother—a woman whom I have overheard voicing her unpleasant opinion of me multiple times this past year. It seems that is not enough to stop her from presenting her son as a competitor to become the next Lord Eton.

"Are you new to town?" I ask the young man, and he simply shakes his head no as he stares down at our feet. I would not consider him a particularly poor dancer, but I feel that if he looked up that would change his abilities drastically.

"Did you just finish your schooling recently?" He nods in reply, with his head still facing the floor.

There is a good chance he is counting in his head, and if I keep interrupting, I may end up getting stepped on. I remain silent for the remainder of our dance.

The next dance is with a gentleman named Mr. Harold Grange. He is a regular dance partner of mine, over twenty years my senior, and a second son who is known for fortune-hunting. As everyone knows, there is no bigger fortune to be found than mine.

Mr. Grange has made every attempt to claim a courtship between us while staying within my father and his associates' good graces. If I am ever questioned about a possible courtship between us, I simply act surprised and fabricate a lie that he mentioned interest in another girl. In the past, I have provided a fictitious name, and other times I gave the name of a girl who has been particularly cruel to me.

On occasion, during our dances, he leans in closely, whispering words he believes to be tempting, promises of pleasure and delights that only a man of his mature age could give me. While I have no interest in dreaming of the pleasures he believes he can provide, I find it difficult to believe anything can be pleasurable when his breath alone stinks with a mixture of tobacco, coffee, and bourbon. I truly loathe that my numerous exposures have allotted me the ability to identify each of those scents.

He makes quick, polite conversation and moves directly on to his inquiry about my family, specifically about my father and his health. He must be aware of his apparent questions, it is clear he was hoping to hear my father is falling ill, assuming that would force me to pick a husband sooner than later.

Typical Mr. Grange.

As the music ends, he grabs my hand while bowing. "It was a great pleasure, Miss Eton."

I respond curtly, "Thank you, Mr. Grange," purposefully, not to reciprocate the sentiment.

He continues, "I look forward to dancing with you at each and every ball for the rest of my days."

Revolting.

I ignore his reply, quickly turning and walking away. I have no intention of marrying Mr. Grange. I would gladly take Mr. Oxworth before ever considering this awful man.

The third dance is quiet as Mr. Woohurst is a fine dancer, especially considering he is able to keep his steps precise, all while only meeting my eyes twice and spending the remainder of the dance with his eyes on my chest. Although, if I had to choose, I would far prefer a man after my physical attributes than my money.

This next dance partner is more than welcome. It is someone I consider to be a good friend, Mr. Albert Berry. He is kind, funny, and handsome, with brown locks that fall to his shoulder, and has a smile that only a few have the pleasure of witnessing.

We have a terrible habit of sharing gossip via whispers

during our dances. He is just over the age of thirty and comes from an equally wealthy family. We bonded over society's mutual frustration with us, as we are both known for our minimal interest in settling down. He is an excellent dance partner and always makes me laugh. Albert calls on me regularly while I am in London with Lady Calderwood, and we are grateful to see him rather than other suitors, such as the ever-persistent Mr. Grange.

I would be lying if I said I had not thought of marrying Albert. I often wonder if the thought has also crossed his mind. Of all the conversations and dances shared between us, it always feels like a friendship. Never a flirting comment or a longing look to be shared between us. No rush of excitement or flutter of the heart. However, we have shared many smirks and eye rolls from across a ballroom to each other. I suppose if it came down to marrying Mr. Berry, it would not be a love match, but it would be a strong and trusting friendship.

"Dear Miss Eton, how splendid you look this evening." Mr. Berry takes my hand and leads me to the dance floor.

"Mr. Berry, you look rather charming yourself. Thank you for once again permitting me the joys of being your dance partner." I do love dancing with him. It is one of the rare things I enjoy during my time in London.

"Of course. So, how much longer must you endure London's society before you can escape to the country?" Mr. Berry asks in a soft tone as both of us have agreed to keep our fondness of the country quiet. Would not want too many of tonight's attendees to catch on. While they all have been known to enjoy a holiday and most even have their own country home, it is typically frowned upon to voice a preference for anything other than the excitement of life in the city. More than that, I prefer to keep the country and my love of it as a secret shared with only those close to me. These people here make clear their dislike for me each time I am in their presence. They do not deserve to know my personal feelings.

"Just through the end of the week, then I will resume my life of tranquility," I say with a smile I am unable to mask.

"That sounds relaxing. I, too, am planning to travel soon. I am considering Greece. I find myself exhausted by the countless balls and longing looks of desperation from the unwed onlookers in town." Looking around the room, it is easy to notice the many looks of longing he is getting from the young ladies. Any of them would love to become Mrs. Berry, but he never seems to give anyone much of a chance at his attention, nonetheless his title.

"Safe and prosperous travels to you, sir. Greece, I have heard marvelous stories! You must write to me and share every detail." To travel to Greece, I would give anything to go with him.

He laughs and answers, "I promise to write, darling. Yet, I cannot guarantee every detail, what a scandal that would be for me to share all the intimate details with a lady such as yourself." Leaning in, he gives me a wink and smile. "What would people say if my letters fell into the wrong hands?"

"You need not worry about scandal. At this point, I doubt there is any scandal I can be involved with that would outweigh my fortune to any suitor." That is proved by the consistent attention I have received from Mr.

Grange since my father announced my husband would inherit our family title and estate.

Mr. Berry nods while observing the room with distaste clear on his face, knowing that statement would be true of most gentlemen in attendance. "Unfortunately, I think you are correct."

"So please, do me the favor of sending the most scandalous stories." I offer him my most pleading look.

"All right, my dear. I'll try to get into the most precarious situations possible only so that I can write to you about them!"

"It is much appreciated, Mr. Berry." Giving him a genuine smile, most likely the only one I will share tonight.

"Who else is on your dance card tonight? Any actual prospects?" He asks this at every ball, but the answer is always the same.

"None at all, but I still have one space free. Maybe that will be the man to sweep me off my feet."

"That would be lovely," he remarks sarcastically. "Well, best of wishes to your final dance partner, and thank you for this dance. It will certainly be my favorite of the evening."

I am so thankful for Mr. Berry's presence at these events. He always provides a brief sense of calm and sometimes even joy during such stressful experiences. I remember the first night we met eight years ago. I was less skilled at hiding my emotions upon my entrance into society. I think that was what caught his eye.

"This is torture.." I say in a not low enough voice to Lady Calderwood.

She turns to me with a wicked look in her eye. "You may complain all you'd like in the carriage this evening and into tomorrow, but you must keep these comments to yourself in public." She is right. I know I am acting like a brat, but being thrust into society is not an easy transition for me.

She purposely clears her throat and then turns her attention to an approaching gentleman.

He bows. "Hello, Lady Calderwood, it has been too long. How are you doing this evening?"

"Mr. Berry, the evening is much improved with your company. Let me introduce you to my young friend, Miss Eton."

I smile at the handsome gentleman.

"Miss Eton, it is a pleasure to make your acquaintance. I would be remiss if I did not ask for a dance this evening."

"Yes, Mr. Berry, I would be honored."

The musicians began picking up their instruments to resume playing.

"What luck, I think we can head out now," he says as he holds out his hand for me.

As soon as the music starts, our conversation begins.

"Counting down the minutes until you can leave, Miss Eton?" Mr. Berry says quickly to me with a friendly face. Terrified I have offended him, I trip over my words trying to apologize.

He lets out a quiet laugh. "No offense taken, my dear. I was simply making an observation. I recognized your disgust tonight because it is a feeling I am more than familiar with when attending these events."

My breath catches; could it be? Am I not alone in my

morose feelings about these events, which most of the town favored above all else?

"Lady Calderwood will be sure to lecture me in the carriage this evening if my dislike was so obvious."

"It was not extremely obvious. I only noticed because I feel the same," Mr. Berry says politely.

I can not help my curiosity and blurt out, "Then why are you here? As a gentleman, it is not your priority to marry, so I do not believe you are being forced to attend."

"While you are partly correct, I am not being forced by anyone to attend. I have found it is overall beneficial for my business to blend in with society rather than exclude myself from such happenings."

It made sense. People would be far more likely to talk about him if he avoided society completely than if he simply did not appear to enjoy the spectacle.

"Am I correct to assume you are not eager to find a husband this evening, Miss Eton?"

"Yes, you would be correct. I am not opposed to marriage. I would simply prefer to do so without everyone's eyes on me and the pressure to please my family. I'm afraid I am not even sure what I want in a husband yet. It would be nice to have more time."

"I wish you all the time you need, sweet girl." With the music ending, Mr. Berry bows and kisses my hand before leading me off the dance floor. "I look forward to commiserating with you in the future. If you need anything, a dance, a distraction, or a friendly conversation, please never hesitate."

I'm pulled out of my memories as we walk off the

dance floor and are approached by a friend of Mr. Berry's, Mr. Edward Riley.

Edward Riley is someone I once thought of as a friend… but that was a long time ago. Our fathers had much-shared business, and we found ourselves at many of the same meetings as children. Most fathers brought their sons, who would eventually inherit their titles and duties, but as my father's only heir, I was the only girl in attendance.

Eddy, as I called him, was different then, before we had any expectations of adulthood thrust onto us. Beyond being a companion in many games of hide and seek, he was funny and caring. He was carefree and kind, but that all has changed. We grew apart as we got older, and with each passing year, we've become crueler to each other. He is among the gentlemen that like to voice their severe distaste for the way I chose to live my life, by refusing to immediately marry.

How dare he think that he has a right to have an opinion, let alone voice it aloud, about my life?

He nods politely at Mr. Berry and then meets my gaze. At the same time, our faces fall into a look of disgust at one another. He bows politely, only out of societal rules, and says dryly, "Miss Eton." I give a brief curtsey and return the greeting in a similar tone, "Mr. Riley."

It is Mr. Berry who breaks the silence. "You two are adults. You need to act as such." He has always found himself in the middle of our feud, trying to mediate with very little success.

"If *Miss* Eton were acting like an adult, she would be married by now," Mr. Riley spits cruel words in my direction. If he is going to insult me, he really should attempt to be more creative.

"Cannot the same be said for you, sir?" Defending myself in a hushed but angry tone. He hates it when I compare the two of us. As if he can not stomach the thought of us being equals.

The man who stands in front of me is so different from my childhood friend, Eddy. Years have been wasted, wondering what had changed in Eddy. I am not exactly sure when it began. It was a slow pull away, like a fern frond curling into itself to avoid an unwelcome touch. He started cutting our conversations short, then began avoiding me altogether.

My heart still aches at the memories of the nights spent crying over the distance my friend put between us —at least, I believed him to be my friend. Before long, he would no longer make eye contact with me. How I wish the strain between us had stopped there. But no, Eddy soon started openly mocking me for not being married. That action, that betrayal, pushed me past the etiquette of polite society. I pushed back. I defended myself, thus fueling the rumors he was spreading—that I am an undesirable prospect.

Again, Mr. Berry must intercede. "Enough! We are in public, and god knows the two of you always have eyes watching. Miss Eton, if I should not see you again this evening, I will call on you tomorrow morning."

"You must be joking, Albert. Why would you want to waste your morning on the persistent spinster?" Edward questions.

Mr. Berry turns to his friend. "I do not inquire who you

will be spending your morning with, so please hold your tongue about my whereabouts."

How I would like to stick my tongue out at Edward, but I settle for a smirk. Serves him right.

Mr. Berry turns back to me. Grabbing my hand and placing a kiss on my knuckles. "It was a pleasure, my dear. Enjoy the rest of your evening." He does not have to say it, but this is his way of letting me know it is time for me to leave the conversation. I bow, then smile at Mr. Berry and let my face drop to a scowl toward Mr. Riley before I take my leave.

4

It only takes a moment to find Lady Calderwood seated at a table with two widows. I am familiar with her company but would not consider us friendly. Joining them would mean finding myself inundated with questions regarding when I plan to take a husband. I catch Lily's eye. Nodding my head toward the veranda, she gives a swift nod of understanding. After finding the best spot to admire the night sky, I enjoy a few moments to myself.

The silence is short-lived as an exasperated scream comes from down the hall.

"I know, Mother! You are not listening to me. I have no desire to be here." Whispering follows. I am unable to make out the words, and soon the screaming resumes.

"You knew this would happen. I begged you to delay my coming out for at least a year. I would prefer two." More whispers, which I can only assume belong to the girl's mother, who is trying to stop her daughter from causing a scene.

"You do not care about how I feel." Whispers resume. "Fine! Just give me a moment, and I will rejoin you in the ballroom."

Heels clink on the floor, and I move to hide myself from the surly, furious mother.

The faint sound of sniffles hit my ears. I feel my heart breaking for this young girl and decide to join her in the hallway. I find her curled up on a bench with her forehead resting on her knees as she cries.

"Hello, are you all right?" I try to keep my voice soft.

The young girl jumps, startled despite my gentle tone. When she looks up, I notice tear-filled blue eyes that match the color of her dress perfectly. Her features seem familiar, but I cannot place the resemblance. She has a simple beauty similar to Lily Calderwood, but that is the only likeness between the two. The young lady immediately begins to apologize for her appearance and her crying.

"No need. I have spent many balls crying in various locations over my frustrations." The young girl looks up at me.

"I'm Mar—"

"I know who you are, Margaret Eton. Everyone knows who you are," the girl says with wide eyes.

"Everyone may know my name, but I would argue almost no one in that room can really claim to know me. Here's a secret—those who know me well call me Margo," I say with a smile. "May I ask what your name is?"

"Evelyn."

"That is a beautiful name. Tell me, what is your least favorite part of tonight's festivities? I have many complaints, and I would love to know if they match any of yours." It is my attempt to soothe her worries in the same way Albert did for me so many years ago.

"You do not wish to be here? But why not? Every man in the room would give anything at a chance to be your husband." I almost laugh at the obvious confusion on her youthful face.

With a soft smile, I explain, "That is true, but those gentlemen who are interested are only after my family's fortune. I can promise that they would not be interested in me if they truly were to know me." I pause to shrug. "It no longer offends me, as I have long since determined that I am not interested in any of them."

"But your mother, she must be encouraging you to socialize, is she not?" Evelyn asks, her brow still scrunched in confusion.

"Technically, she is, but she is not in attendance this evening, so I will not concern myself with it at the moment," I say with a wink.

"The dancing. Well, no, that's not true. I do not hate the act of dancing itself. I hate that I am required to dance with people...men that I do not even know. I am not ready to marry yet, but my attendance tonight gives everyone the opposite impression. It feels as if I am living a lie. And I worry that I am one dance away from becoming someone's bride before my next birthday." The words fall out of her mouth so quickly that it seems she is afraid her mother will return before she can finish the sentence.

My heart breaks at that moment. Nervous tears are welling up in her eyes. Before I can find the right words, she looks back up at me. "How have you managed to stay unwed *all these years*?" Internally, I groan. She makes it sound like I'm dozens of years older than her.

"All these *years*?" My attempt at making her laugh. "Well, if everyone assumes I am as old as you do, I guess it could be my senility that keeps the men uninterested."

We both begin to laugh.

Lowering my voice, I share with her some of my best tricks for discouraging unwanted attention. "There are some things I rely on when at these events I could share with you. Although, they might be useless in the presence of your persistent mother."

"I will take any advice you have," Evelyn pleads eagerly.

"Okay, do you remember all of the things you've been taught to do that would appeal to a man?"

"Yes, how can I forget?" Evelyn confirms as she rolls her eyes.

"Well, do the exact opposite. Appear uninterested in anything he has to say. Stay quiet, or if you truly are not interested in the man, disagree," I say with a sarcastic gasp and my hand over my mouth.

"How brilliant. I am disappointed that this never occurred to me." She throws her hands up in frustration.

"Well, Evelyn, this knowledge is now yours to wield whenever you see fit." Smiling, I follow her gaze back in the direction of the party. "I'm afraid we should be getting back now before someone comes looking for either of us."

"Evey, please call me Evey. And I will need to call on you for the remainder of your advice."

"Then you must call me Margo, and I'm sure we will see each other at the remaining balls this week. Then we can meet to discuss more ways to avoid the undesirable bachelors of London." I give her a wink and stand, holding out my hand to her. We walk back into the main ballroom, still talking closely with one another.

I quickly notice Lady Calderwood standing in hushed conversation with a few women, including Lady Riley, Edward Riley's mother. I never know if I should pity her for having such an awful son or scold her for raising one.

"Evelyn!" Lady Riley shouts at Evey.

No, that cannot be... It cannot.

"Mother, I was just getting some fresh air with Miss Eton."

I am not sure who looks more shocked, Lady Riley or myself. While none would ever say it to my face, I know my reputation with most of the ladies in town is not very positive. I am seen as a horrible young woman who laughs at the tradition of marriage and being a mother. They view my actions as disrespectful. While that does not stop them from pushing their sons at me and my fortune, they are always sure to keep their daughters far away for fear I could change their minds with my carefree beliefs.

I place a friendly smile on my face to save any hope of having an actual acquaintance with Evey in the future. Bowing politely, "Lady Riley, it is a pleasure to see you again. I just met Miss Riley on my way back into the ballroom." Yes, minimize our interactions. Hopefully, this will save Evey from a sure lecture she will get from socializing with the likes of me. "What a beautiful and well-mannered daughter you have. London society is lucky to have her included this year."

"Yes, thank you for the compliment, Miss Eton. Come,

Evelyn. Mr. Richmond was asking after you while you were gone. I think he is interested in a dance." Lady Riley leads Evey by the elbow to the opposite side of the room, where Mr. Richmond is speaking with Edward Riley. Watching Evey being dragged toward an unwanted dance makes my stomach sink. Then I notice Lady Riley whisper to Edward and look back at me. She then turns her attention to Mr. Richmond and Evey.

Lady Calderwood clears her throat and breaks my focus to remind me to paint the smile back on my face. As I sit down next to her at the table, the questioning begins, "What was that about? Recruiting the young Miss Riley to your cause?"

"Evelyn Riley is a sweet young girl who is suffering from the stress of coming out in society when she is not ready. What did you want me to do? Let her cry alone after being berated by her mother?" I defend myself.

"It was kind of you to console her. Yet, you would be wise to remember that you are not her mother. It is not your place to interfere with another family's business." Lily is right; I should not have interfered, but I still do not regret my decision.

I open my mouth to defend myself again but stop as I notice Lady Calderwood's gaze looking over my shoulder.

"Miss Eton, may I have this dance?" I recognize the voice before I turn my head to see Edward Riley standing over me. Letting out a low chuckle.

I turn to Lady Calderwood and roll my eyes at her without answering his request. She raises her eyebrows and lifts her open hand, holding up all five fingers, and she mouths the word "five" to me, indicating that if I accept this dance offer, we can leave immediately after.

"Miss Eton?" Edward says with frustration and pushes his hand out further in my direction. This would not be the first time I have shared a dance with Edward, but it only happened on rare occasions. I do want to leave...

"Thank you, Mr. Riley." I take his hand and walk to the dance floor. Regret floods through me for not securing a fifth partner earlier in the evening. If I had, I would have had the pleasure to turn down this dance and save myself this mix of emotions attempting to overtake me.

Edward holds my hand firmly in his, but not too hard. As much as I would like to pull it away, I find comfort in the familiarity of his touch. Before I can torture myself with longing for my childhood friend, I turn and begin to count the windows in the room as a distraction. I catch Mr. Berry's eyes and notice the look of surprise on his face. I shrug at Albert before turning to face my dance partner.

We stay silent as the music begins. Never would I voice these thoughts aloud, but Edward is a very skilled dancer, more than most gentlemen I have danced with this year—or any season prior. He is also handsome. Unfairly handsome. If only the outside matched his ugly personality. But no. He grows more striking with each passing year. His large build is intimidating to most of the delicate ladies, but I find it enticing. I despise how attractive I find him. I would never admit it to another, but I can never seem to deny it to myself. With any luck, we will stay silent the entire dance, and I can pretend he is someone with a more appealing personality.

My gaze holds on our hands clasped tightly together

until his other hand touches my hip to pull me into our opening stance. As the music continues, he slides his hand to the small of my back and I find myself melting into his touch.

What is wrong with my body?

What is this need for more contact?

I feel myself flush at thoughts of his hand continuing to move across my body. My back would be just the beginning of his exploration. My breath quickens as I run my eyes from his arm up his shoulders and return my left hand to his shoulder, his very solid shoulder.

Enough of this.

I will just enjoy this dance in silence and not think about my handsome yet dreadful dance partner.

I spin out and turn back to him with his arm crossed around mine and my back against his chest. He leans down, and I feel his breath on my ear. While I am facing away from him, I can forget his true identity. I can pretend...

As if he senses I am beginning to enjoy myself, he reminds me who I am dancing with by softly saying, "I want to know what you are playing at, Miss Eton," in my ear.

Turning my head toward him, "Excuse me, sir?" We are too close. This position allows me to feel the rise of his muscular chest against my back. His body is warm, even as his attitude grows colder with each passing moment.

I spin back out and I am able to breathe a little easier with the space now between us, slight as it is. He gives me a scowl. "With my sister. Is there a reason you have decided to befriend her out of all the other young ladies in the room? I presume it is due to her young, impressionable mind, or are you simply trying to antagonize me?"

"Ha!" The laugh bursts out of my mouth before I can stop it. It is loud, certainly louder than is polite in the middle of a dance.

Edward leans closer. "Do. Not. Mock. Me." He's getting close again.

Why does this body not belong to someone else? It's a shame it is wasted on such a frustrating man.

With a deep breath of relief, my body begins to have the correct reaction to the self-centered man. It is time to put him in his place. "I am well aware of how little you think of me, Mr. Riley. First, let me clarify—your sister is a wonderful, bright young lady, and I have no ill intentions toward her. I simply exchanged pleasantries with her."

Then, I lean closer to him. Closing the small distance between us, I look directly into his dark brown eyes. I will not be intimidated by him. Not wanting anyone else to overhear, I speak only loud enough for him to hear me. "Do not make the mistake of flattering yourself with the idea that you ever cross my mind, let alone have any influence on my decisions, *sir*."

At that moment, the music ends, and I could not be more grateful. I step out of his embrace, give a brisk bow, and walk away without looking back in his direction. I do not stop while walking past Lady Calderwood. She turns and follows me out the door into the carriage.

5

Margo practically runs out of my arms before the musicians complete their final note. Frozen on the dance floor, I try to process that she is gone, the chill from the empty space she just occupied, and the words she spoke before she left. Letting out the breath I was holding, I allow myself a moment to mourn her absence and scold myself for ruining the dance we shared. Giving into an emotion I prefer to keep locked away.

I miss her.

Enough of that. She behaved poorly and interpreted my concern for my sister as an offense. I do not doubt that the scornful Miss Eton will not try to capitalize on my concerns. The pain in my chest returns. I try to ease the pain by rubbing it after. Margo's declaration that she never thinks of me cuts deeper into the wound that has refused to heal for years.

Moments pass before I realize that I have not moved and am the only person remaining on the dance floor.

Everyone is looking, not that I care. Quickly, I take my leave in search of fresh air.

In an attempt to cool my increasingly excessive body heat, I remove my jacket, never breaking my stride. Only then do I notice Albert following me.

I pass by the front entrance and spot the flash of Lady Calderwood's lavender dress as she enters a carriage. As if Margo needs a chaperone at her age, she should be a chaperone herself. Turning swiftly to the right, I head for the balcony overlooking the gardens, telling myself it's to avoid the possibility of seeing Margo again. But in truth, I am removing the temptation.

A hand grabs onto my arm, and I am forced to stop. I know it is not Albert. He would never put his hands on me in such a manner. Slowly, I turn to see who has idiotically halted my escape. The hand still has a tough grip on me. My eyes meet Harold Grange's incensed gaze. "Take your hand off me," I instruct him with a commanding tone.

He leans in closer and tightens his grip on my arm. "I will let you go when I'm done with you."

Not in the mood to deal with this ignoramus and his antics, I lean back and prepare to slam my fist into his face. Albert must recognize my intentions and intercedes before I make contact. He wedges between us, and Harold drops my arm.

The red-faced Harold has incorrectly estimated he could handle me... He cannot. There is no question he would fall quickly against Albert and me. Albert scowls. "That's enough, Harold. Scurry back to the hole you crawled out of tonight."

Harold backs up, fixes his dress coat, and clears his

throat. "No need to act as momma bear for your cub, Albert. I am simply inquiring as to the reason behind Mr. Riley's dance with my intended. She abruptly left after he danced with her. I was unable to ask for another dance or even bid her goodnight."

I stay silent. It is common knowledge that Harold Grange has long been set on becoming the next Lord Eton. Ever since Margo's father announced her dowry, including his title and estate. It is just as equally well known that Margo is not the slightest bit inclined to marry Harold Grange. His claim to her has no credibility. Still, these words coming out of his mouth cause my jaw to clench.

"Get off it, Harold." Albert shakes his head and tries to suppress laughter. "As you saw tonight, Miss Eton can handle herself when it comes to our dear friend, Mr. Riley. And to that, I'm sure she would be greatly unsatisfied to hear you were trying to insinuate anything less."

Grange looks a tad concerned at Albert's account. Does this fool truly believe he is a serious suitor for Margo? She must see right through him. Taking advantage of his silent contemplation, I turn to walk away. I hear Albert bid goodnight to Harold before footsteps begin behind me.

When Albert catches up, he asks, "All right, Chap?" I'm hunched over, the railing imprinting grooves in my skin from where I grip it so intensely. It takes three breaths to steady myself as Albert shakes his head.

"I am afraid you will not win the battle with the wrought iron, Edward. You'll likely break your fingers in the attempt."

Straightening my stance and releasing the railing, I

began to pace the veranda, still unable to ration my anger into words. Albert has always been the example of a true friend, not forcing me to talk but not leaving my side either. Simply waiting for me to gather my thoughts. Unfortunately, the most I can give him is brief eye contact and various looks of frustration, shaking my head and throwing my hands in the air.

"Stay here," he says. When I do not answer he comes to stand in front of me. "I shall find your mother and let her know we are leaving. We will get them home, and then we will get you sorted out." I meet his gaze and do not answer. "Understand?" I nod, and then he is gone.

ENTERING THE CARRIAGE, it is evident I will not need to avoid questions from my mother or sister. From their silence and refusal to look at each other, it is clear they are in the middle of their own argument. I do not have the capacity for this tonight and decide to deal with them tomorrow.

My gaze remains out the window until we arrive at our townhome. The only words exchanged are wishes of goodnight with my mother and sister as they exit the carriage. I do not move. Albert speaks with the driver, and once he is seated, we begin to move again.

It takes three glasses of whiskey from Albert's personal collection for my lips to loosen. "Arrogant woman."

Albert looks up from his drink with surprise on his face. "I thought you would remain silent for at least the remainder of the evening, old chap. Good to have you back."

Without responding, I refill my glass.

Albert continues, "I have two questions. First, what possessed you to ask Miss Eton for a dance, and second, what could have transpired between you two that could stir...this mood of yours?"

I take a swallow of whiskey, the burn feeble compared to the angry fire that woman ignites in me. "I asked her to dance because I needed to speak with her." He looks at me silently as to suggest my answer was not complete. "She was seen speaking with Evelyn. I needed to know why."

"And did she give you an answer?" he asks.

"She was immediately defensive of my questioning and insisted she was merely being polite."

"Edward, my friend. What you are relaying to me hardly seems enough to throw a man into the state of anger you seem to be in."

Albert is correct, as he usually is. He always has a sense of looking at things from a more rational view than me. It seems I have come to the point where everything Margo does gets under my skin. In truth, the part of the conversation I chose not to share with him is what truly ignited my anger. Anger, if that is even the correct term.

In recent years, I have found every interaction I have with Margo brings out a collection of emotions that leave me without words or the ability to function properly. Her beauty makes it difficult for me to look in her direction for too long in fear that I will fall under her spell once again.

She appeared to care for Evelyn while defending her this evening. Perhaps the girl I once knew is still a part of her, but I know better than to hope. There are vast dangers that accompany remembering that she is a compassionate person or that she once was one.

Allowing myself to hope...that would undo everything.

Dancing with her tonight, before our argument began, felt like one of the many dreams I had long ago. The moment she was in my arms and the music began, my heart raced. It is a rare event for us to dance, but it would be a lie to say I did not cherish it. I cherished it so much that I forgot my original intention of asking for the dance. It was not until she was wrapped in my arms, and I looked up to see Evelyn looking on from the side that I remembered its purpose.

A small part of me is frustrated with myself for ruining the short time we were in each other's arms. She fit so perfectly against me and moved so gracefully. When dancing with Margo, it flows so naturally. We move as if we fit.

We do not.

I stand by my accusation. I was worried to see her interacting with my sister. Evelyn was suffering enough with tonight's events, and I did not want Margo adding to that. I must speak with Evelyn in the morning to see what was said between them. While I am not supportive of Evelyn being married this year, I do not want her to resolve herself to a life without a husband, as Margo has.

How can a single individual inspire such enjoyment and frustration during a single dance?

Margo's presence left my heart swelling in my chest, while her argument left my head pounding. If I could withstand being near her for more than a few moments, I would be able to explain that her stubborn personality has made her blind to the predicament that she has put herself in.

Albert is still waiting for a more extensive explanation, but I am not yet ready to share it with him. I shake my head. "Margaret Eton has ruined enough of this evening. May we not let her ruin any more of it?" Between the drink and the rush of emotions in my head, I no longer trust myself not to admit everything I am feeling for that woman.

"Of course," Albert answers with a pat on my back and standing up from his chair. "Let us find something to distract you, my boy." I nod and stand with him. Taking notice he used the term "distract" meant he is well aware, even without speaking of her, that it will be difficult for me to stop thinking of her for the rest of the night.

We find our way to a favorite tavern of Albert's. It is not as popular with our peers as the local gentlemen's clubs, but here we are granted an enjoyable night of cards with men who live different and much more exciting lives than ours. The air is mixed heavily with tobacco and ale as we approach the entrance. The low-lit interior makes it difficult to navigate the way to our table in the back. Tables are crowded with men leaning into the lantern at the center to prove each of their cards is the winning hand.

The men at our table get rowdy as the barmaid makes her way over to us. She places fresh glasses on the table and turns to leave with a wink in my direction. I end up losing the first game, which I blame on Margo's dress which I cannot stop thinking about. It was white and complemented her black hair very well. All young ladies are wearing similar fashions this season, but Margo's beauty makes her stand out among the others.

Being that I do not wish to lose all of my money, I resolve not to think of that dress again. I win the next game, but then one of the men at the table mockingly refers to me as "sir," and Margo comes back into my mind. Not just the words she spoke but how close her face was to mine when she spoke them. Merely two inches separated our faces while our eyes were locked. This memory is far more challenging to block out of my mind.

After losing the next five games, I thank the men for letting us join their game and take my leave. It may be the drink letting the irresponsible part of my brain take precedence, but I half consider writing to let her know of tonight's activities. She would certainly take great enjoyment in knowing that she has influenced me to the point I lost more money than most earn in a week over the thought of her...and that white dress.

It is only thanks to the large amounts of liquor that I sleep, accompanied by a night filled with dreams of Margo.

6

As I sit at the top of the staircase just out of view of Lady Calderwood's front entrance, I hear the voices below. "I will be sure Miss Eton receives the beautiful flowers you've brought her this morning, Mr. Grange," Lily says in a soft tone.

"Are you sure I cannot speak with her, Lady Calderwood, even for a brief moment?" There is a pause, and before he allows her to deny his request, he continues. "I witnessed her leave in such a hurry last night after her dance with the unreasonable Mr. Riley. I worry he said something to upset her."

Someone clears their throat. "Harold, we spoke on this matter last night. I will not stand by and let you make accusations against either Mr. Riley or Miss Eton without any evidence for your suspicions."

"Albert! Here again?" Mr. Grange sounds taken back. I cannot blame Albert for staying unseen, just as I did when we were notified of Mr. Grange's arrival. "I find it concerning how often I find you in the company of Miss Eton. If I need to make my intentions clear, I will."

A low laugh escapes Albert. I hear Lily's soft voice attempt to calm the situation. "Albert…"

It does not stop him, and he says, "You can make your intentions as clear as you like, as long as you remember it is Miss Eton's intention to stay as far away from you as she possibly can." The next words come out slower and with more power behind them. "The young lady is not available to see you today. Take your leave. Now."

Mr. Grange huffs and begins to address Lily once more, "Lady Calderwood, please stress my disappointment to Miss Eton." I roll my eyes as his footsteps retreat, followed by the sound of the door slamming.

Whatever shall I do? Mr. Grange is disappointed.

After a few moments, Lily appears at the bottom of the stairs, "You're safe to come down now, Margo."

"That was a sight to behold last night, love." Mr. Berry sits across from me in Lady Calderwood's drawing room.

I sit with my arms crossed. My body radiates with anger at the reminder of the night before. "Did you know what he was getting at when he asked me to dance, Albert?" At his request, we've dropped the formalities, calling each other by our first names, if only in the privacy of Lady Calderwood's home and at Eton Cottage.

"Margo, when I spoke to Edward after my dance with you, he made no indication he planned to ask you for a dance. Quite the opposite, honestly. You are both very vocal about your distaste for one another. Then, the next thing I know, the two of you are on the dance floor, looking ready to murder each other. After you practically ran out the door and he...well..." Albert shakes his head and runs his hand through his hair.

"You can take comfort in knowing his attempts at intimidating you backfired, and you left him unnerved throughout the evening. I would not be surprised if he has a similar look this morning as you are wearing."

My emotions got the best of me last night. This is not about Eddy. Prior to the dance with Mr. Riley, I was planning to invite Evey over for tea this week. But now I wonder if her overbearing brother feels he has the right to decide who I invite for tea.

Albert notices my mind racing. "Margo, let it go. If you want to be friends with the young lady, proceed as you want. Invite her to tea. If he causes a problem, I will speak with him."

It is inconsiderate for me to be complaining about not having friends when Albert is a better friend than I could have dreamed of. Again, my mind wanders to the thought of marrying him. I would feel safe and secure for the rest of my life. While there is a lack of romantic feelings between us, he is very handsome, and maybe they would develop over time. "Thank you, Albert. I cannot express how much I appreciate your advice. I will invite her over tomorrow. Enough of my problems. Tell me, how was your night? Any ladies catch your eye?"

"Unfortunately, I spent the remainder of my night dealing with the mess you left Mr. Riley in, love. Not that I minded. It was refreshing to see someone put him in his place."

Lady Calderwood returns to the room and takes the

seat next to Mr. Berry. Society would dictate that I need a chaperone with Mr. Berry, but the three of us are more like family—at least within the privacy of this townhouse. It is also notable that I have not had a caller aside from him in more than a year's time.

"Albert, you are a saint of a man for listening to yet another morning's worth of Margo's tirade about Mr. Riley. I cannot imagine you can take much more."

"Lily, you look beautiful this morning." She smiles at Albert in response. "As for Margo and Edward, it's nothing new to hear them complain about one another. I'm just glad that it is not in public at the moment."

Lily tries to change the subject. "Will you be joining us in the country in a couple of weeks?" she asks Albert. I cannot blame her. I have not stopped talking about my dance with Edward Riley since we entered the carriage last night.

"Sadly, I will not. I plan to travel in the coming months; my destination is Greece."

The remainder of Mr. Berry's visit is spent discussing his upcoming trip. How long he plans to stay, his plans when he arrives, and his travel companions. On his way out, he gives Lily a proper bow, and as he turns to me, I jump into his arms for a hug. "Please travel safely. I need you back here in one piece. And do not forget you promised to write," I say in our embrace.

He pulls back, holding my hands. "I would never forget a promise I have made to you. Do try to stay clear of Mr. Riley if you can, at least until my return, Sweetheart." With a smile, he is out the door.

TWO BORING DAYS have passed when Lady Riley and Evey finally arrive for tea.

"Lady Riley, what a pleasure to have you and Miss Riley over this afternoon. Thank you for accepting our invitation." Lady Calderwood greets our guests upon their arrival. She truly is the best hostess London Society has to offer. I am greatly appreciative of her influence that secured Lady Riley's acceptance of the invitation. I consider this an opportunity to show Lady Riley that I am not the monster that her son has clearly convinced her I am. I need to be on my best behavior.

Though, the idea rankles. Why am I trying so hard?

"Miss Riley, how are you enjoying your first season out in society?" I say with a *play-along look* on my face.

Evey is an intelligent girl and catches on quickly. "Miss Eton, I was a little apprehensive at first, but after we spoke at the ball, I am eager to approach them with a new perspective."

Lady Riley gives a surprised look of approval. Lady Calderwood, knowing I will not be able to keep this I up much longer, offers Lady Riley a tour. She quickly accepts and they are down the hall in moments.

I immediately bounce over to the loveseat and sit next to Evey with a smile. "How are you, darling?" I ask. I enjoy using some of Mr. Berry's terms of endearment for Evey. It makes us feel even closer.

Her mouth twists as if she just ate someone sour. "Still trying to dissolve the bitter taste in my mouth from the words I just spoke to my mother. I fear that will have repercussions for me later."

"How is that going? Is she still persistent that you marry this season? We only have a couple of weeks left." My words offer very little comfort, as it only takes one night for a gentleman to set his sights on her.

"Honestly, with my downright refusal to even attend balls, she has shifted her attention to convincing me that they are enjoyable and speaks less about the marriage market than before," she says before enjoying her cup of tea.

"Well, that is a start, I suppose. Nevertheless, I invited you here with an ulterior motive in mind. What do you say to visiting me in the country at the end of the month? You can stay for a couple of weeks or a couple of months. Whatever your mother will approve of." I am holding my breath, wondering if she will accept my offer.

"The country?" Evey asks with surprise.

"Yes, my haven. Lady Calderwood is my neighbor, but we would spend the majority of our time at my home. It will just be us and the caretakers, Mr. and Mrs. Landon. I promise you will love it. There is no pressure of balls, society, and certainly not marriage. I spend my time reading and painting. I can arrange for dance lessons, or we can spend the warmer days swimming." Any attempts at minimizing my hopes she will agree are gone.

"Dancing? I have had enough lessons to last my life..."

"Not that kind of dancing. We can train in ballet, and it can be done with a partner, but only one who is also training. It's more of an art form than what you are familiar with at balls. Please come visit. If you hate it, you can return at any time." I notice I'm pleading at this point.

"Hate it? How could I possibly hate it when it sounds to be the exact opposite of everything I despise here in town? But what if my mother does not allow it?" Her excitement is overshadowed by obvious trepidation at asking her mother for anything.

"Let Lady Calderwood take care of that. She can work magic. I recommend *not* sharing the details of the casual life I have described to you. We can keep those details to ourselves." I reassure her. We share tea and a few biscuits, swapping stories and laughter before Lady Calderwood and Lady Riley return.

"We could hear the laughter down the hall. What could be so funny?" Lady Riley inquires. Although she seems a little hesitant, she may not like the answer.

Being the expert in lying to my own mother, I jump in to answer. "We were just discussing the colors of the dresses this season. We much prefer the traditional colors, and we are remarking how dreadful some of the color combinations look together. Could you imagine a dress with both bright orange and a dull green?"

I nudge Evey, and she responds, "Oh yes, Mother. How awful those colors would look together! Do you not agree...?"

"Why yes, Evelyn, I suppose you are right. Have you decided which dress you'll be wearing to tonight's ball? Oh, and can we expect to see the two of you there?" Lady Riley looks between Lady Calderwood and myself.

Lady Calderwood answers, "Yes, we will be there. In fact, it will be the last for us before we travel back to the country tomorrow." She turns to me with a smile. "Miss Eton, I have, on your behalf, extended the invitation for Miss Riley to join us in the country at the end of the month."

Lady Riley addresses her daughter, "We will need to discuss this with your father, but I do not believe there would be any objections if you would like to visit." In my head, I can only hope her grumpy brother will not be included in the discussion.

Evey's face lights up, "Of course I would like to go. Thank you."

Lady Riley stands, "We should be going, Evelyn, to prepare for tonight." I also rise to stand next to Lady Calderwood. "Thank you again for hosting us this afternoon, Lady Calderwood and Miss Eton. We shall see you later."

I thank Lady Calderwood excessively the moment they leave. Aside from random visits from Mr. Berry, I have never had a guest in the country. When he came to visit, he always stayed with Lady Calderwood. This time, I will have a guest staying with me. I plan to start the preparations the moment I return.

THE FOLLOWING DAY, I am more than thankful for an uneventful ball the night before to close out my trip to London. While I was left without my favorite partner, Mr. Berry, I was able to find five suitors willing to dance with me who were each as unmemorable as the last. More importantly, I was able to let my guard down once I realized Mr. Riley would not be attending either.

Before I saw her, Evey came up behind me to let me know her father approved her trip. I inform her I will write to her and share the address and details of her journey. Instructing her to pack lighter summer dresses as we will be walking to Lady Calderwood's home regularly, and not to pack too much formal wear as she will not be needing it. I remind myself to send for the seamstress to make some country dresses and clothes for her to wear while visiting. The night went by quickly as Lady Calderwood and I spent most of the time discussing preparations for our return to the country and Evey's visit.

I have already packed most of my things before this morning and am now double-checking. A knock sounds at the door, alerting me the carriage is waiting.

Lady Calderwood is a great travel partner. She always thinks of topics of discussion to help the time pass. We speak about the eligible bachelors we have encountered and if we think they might be able to find a match with any of the young ladies in town. I always struggle to suggest any of the young ladies end up with such a boring partner. We discuss Mr. Berry's trip and how jealous I am that he is traveling internationally. An option I will only have after I am a married woman. What a scandal I would cause if I traveled throughout Europe as an unwed woman.

My heart beats faster as my country home comes into view. I exhale, finally able to relax since I left weeks ago. This relief is much more than the removal of the annoying London social scene; but the feeling that I can finally be myself again.

My family—Mr. Thomas Landon and Mrs. Emma Landon—will be waiting for me with open arms. It is difficult for me to describe what they mean to me...like parents, but that is simply not enough. The Landons raised me. Unable to have children of their own, they treated me as their own, which included providing an education beyond that which most women of society received. Always encouraging me to play with my hands and ask questions when I encountered something I did not understand. My education was not purely academic— I learned how to cook and clean for myself. Mrs. Landon did typically insist on handling the cleaning, but she regularly encouraged me to cook meals for the three of us.

Eton Cottage, my country home, is not as extravagant as Lady Calderwood's estate. I always assumed that was because my parents had no desire to spend much money on a residence that they never planned to visit. That is not to say Eton Cottage is small by any means. We have multiple sitting rooms, extra bedrooms for guests—that we never had—and even a library—my favorite room.

Just the sight of my home sparks many memories of my childhood. My earliest memories are with Mr. and Mrs. Landon, who were hired as the estate's caretakers while my parents permanently resided in London.

Once, I asked if they were upset that they never had their own children. Their response still brings a smile to my face. Mrs. Landon said, "At first, it was a great disappointment."

Mr. Landon carried on, "Then we met you. We were lacking a child, and you lacked parents...involved parents," Mrs. Landon continued, "it was in the stars for the three of us to find each other."

When I was younger there were far more staff here. I had a nurse in my younger years and then my governess through adolescence. My governess and Mrs. Landon were constantly at odds. While Mrs. Landon never saw a problem with the education provided by my governess, she felt there was more to teach me to be considered an "accomplished lady." Which my governess tried endlessly to put an end to while claiming "ladies" did not require any additional education.

I am thankful to be raised by the Landons, who are of a different social standing than my parents. They value things like art, but not from a distance at a museum, but as a part of life that I should actively participate in. They painted, danced, and sang with me. My favorite memories include all three.

One rainy day, I was feeling particularly energetic. Mrs. Landon brought out every color of paint we had, let me dip my feet in each color, and encouraged me to dance on an old white blanket she found in the back of the closet. A rainbow of small footprints filled each corner and every space in between. When it was covered, Mr. Landon picked me up in his arms and hoisted me over his shoulders straight to the basin in the kitchen and washed my feet before I could paint any other surfaces in our home. It was Mrs. Landon who laid the blanket in a spare bedroom to dry. It is now one of my most cherished possessions. That experience was far more fulfilling than staring at paintings on the wall.

There was no shame in my country home when trying new things, with the exception of my governess, but she was dismissed earlier than most girls, by my request.

Mrs. Landon taught me to swim, and Mr. Landon taught me to ride a horse, both side-saddle and not. This is where my love for wearing britches began. Now, I have a special tailor who makes them for me to wear around Eton Cottage during the colder months. They are far more comfortable than a formal dress, but no one but the Landons see me. I have attempted to convince Lily to wear them, but that is one thing she absolutely refuses. She enjoys formality more than I do.

Lord and Lady Eton also insisted on having more housekeeping staff, cooks, and footmen present. Over the years, the staff numbers faded, though we do not make that fact well known. We still have some staff, but only the Landons and I live at the house. The footman is called upon when needed. There are stable hands who come by once a day from a nearby town.

As for the cooks, Mr. and Mrs. Landon insisted I learn to cook for myself. I was excited to learn. I have a few meals I excel at, but I am still learning. Mr. Landon is superior with meats, and Mrs. Landon makes my favorite breakfast—fried eggs, toasted bread, and roasted potatoes with onions and peppers.

Aside from Albert Berry, Lily Calderwood is the only other person in London who knows the intimate details of Eton Cottage. She truly has been my closest friend for years. While she is a little more than ten years my senior, we still make great companions.

I remember when she and her late husband took residence at the Calderwood Estate. I was not yet ten years old at the time and on a walk with Mrs. Landon. We always enjoyed the view of the quiet estate on our walks, but this time, it was filled with movement. It was Lord Calderwood who spotted us and gave a friendly wave on approach. His young bride followed behind.

Lord Calderwood was a very handsome gentleman, at least that is what Mrs. Landon repeatedly said while he was approaching us and again on our walk home. He was not exceptionally tall but stood straight with his broad chest. His features were all light—neat blond hair, fair skin, and blue eyes. His wife behind him, also petite, had similar features. She had beautiful blonde hair tied at the back of her neck, green eyes, and a friendly smile.

"Hello there. Let me introduce myself. I'm Lord

Calderwood, and this is my beautiful new bride, Lady Calderwood," he says with a bow.

Mrs. Landon and I bow back with our manners. "My Lord, I am Mrs. Landon, a caretaker for the estate at the bottom of the road, and this is Miss Eton, the daughter of the owners of the estate, Lord and Lady Eton."

"Mrs. Landon, what a pleasure to meet you, and you as well, Miss Eton. Do you have any siblings, Miss Eton?" Lady Calderwood asks.

"No, Lady Calderwood," I answer.

"I understand. I do not have any siblings myself. Maybe we can be friends," Lady Calderwood says with a sweet smile.

Lord Calderwood slips his arm around his wife's waist and squeezes her into his side. He is clearly enamored with her. Returning his attention to Mrs. Landon, he says, "We will certainly be inviting you over once we are accepting callers." He winks at that last part. Mrs. Landon lets out a small laugh, but I do not understand the joke between them.

"Of course, My Lord. We look forward to seeing you both again," Mrs. Landon answers, gives her parting bow, and holds a hand out for me. The rest of us say goodbye, and we go on our way.

Once we are far enough down the path back to our home, Mrs. Landon leans down and says, "You may have some children to play with very soon!"

"Because they are married?"

"Yes, my dear. And they seem very much in love."

Similar to the Landons, the Calderwoods were unable to conceive a child. Lily wishes she had a piece of her husband with her, but she now looks back at that time with a fond smile on her face and says, "It was not for a lack of trying."

A couple years after that first meeting, Lord Calderwood died suddenly. Lady Calderwood was distraught. I recall the day that the tragic news arrived at Eton Cottage. The Landons and I went immediately to her. I had visited with her a week prior, but her appearance was completely altered when we arrived. I was younger at the time and struggled to reconcile what was different about her appearance. She just seemed broken to me. Her hair was down and had lost its shine, her eyes puffy and red, her skin pale. It was as if all the light she had was taken from her. Mrs. Landon explained it to me as a physical reaction to an emotional loss. I had never before known anyone who experienced such loss, nor had I experienced anything like it myself.

She was so lonely that I asked to stay with her, and she agreed immediately. I did not leave her side for weeks after the funeral. We were close friends before the death of Lord Calderwood, but after, we became family.

As for the estate, Lord Calderwood's family loved Lady Calderwood greatly and decided the estate would be given to Lord Calderwood's youngest nephew, who had been born only a few years prior. They asked Lady Calderwood to remain as the lady of the house at both her city and country homes until the Lord's nephew was old enough to take over the estate, and even at that time, she would be provided for the remainder of her days.

Lady Calderwood spent many days at our home. It was then that I insisted to my parents that my governess be dismissed. Between the Landons and now Lady

Calderwood acting as my guidance in society, they finally agreed. Lady Calderwood was happy to help me prepare for my first season, and she also agreed with the Landons by insisting when I marry that it is a love match.

In the city, we are proper ladies of the London society, Lady Calderwood and Miss Eton. In the country, we are Lily and Margo. Especially at my home, with no staff members, all formality is removed, and we are able to just enjoy ourselves. Now that we have finally returned, we will spend our summer days lying in the grass, reading our favorite books. Lily found a new romance author who published a book about two sisters looking for love. She received word another book from the same author would be published this summer and already ordered copies to be sent to us. I eagerly await their arrival.

As we pull up outside my door, the Landons are waiting for me. Mr. Landon is a large man in both height and width. He is responsible for most of the labor at the house, and it shows. He has dark red hair covering his head and face. A beard like that would never be acceptable in London, but in the country, he is considered very handsome in a masculine way. At least, that's what Mrs. Landon always tells him. She is a shorter lady with a fuller figure. Her hair is brown mixed with some gray and is usually in a braid that hangs in front of her left shoulder.

Both Lily and I exit the carriage, and before I can take a step, Mrs. Landon has her arms around me in a tight hug. "I have missed you so much, Margo!"

I laugh, still in her embrace. "As I have missed you too." When she lets me go, I am immediately swept into

Mr. Landon's strong arms. "Good to have you back home. I hope the London men did not give you too much trouble?"

I smile back, "Oh, on the contrary."

His smile drops immediately, the ever-protective father figure. I cannot keep him in torture much longer. "I did not mean I enjoyed them. I meant I was the one giving them trouble."

"My strong girl, give them hell. Only a man that can handle your sharp mouth will be worthy of you."

The Landons speak with Lily for a moment and then she gives me a quick hug. "Enjoy your guest Margo. You should enjoy your time together, but I will call on you about a week or two after her arrival. I look forward to spending time with you both."

"Thank you, Lily, for staying by my side in the city. I could not manage without you."

"My dear, as an old widow, you are the light in my life. Now, go share your light with the Landons. I have had you to myself for weeks. It is their turn." She climbs into the carriage and off to her home.

Walking back to the door, I am bombarded with questions from the Landons about my time in London. I write to them every few days, so they know most of everything I tell them, but they insist they want me to tell them again, in person.

There is fresh fruit on the table, and we are all eating while discussing my time in London. A proper lady would use utensils to select the few berries she wanted and place them on her individual plate, but in my home, we do not see the need to dirty additional plates. The bowl of raspberries, cherries, and strawberries sits in the center of the table, and we pick our berries and pop them directly into our mouths. Even more scandalous is the second smaller bowl that is left for our discarded stems and the hull of the strawberries.

"Tell me about this friend who is coming to visit. This is the first guest you have invited since Mr. Berry. Who is this young lady?" Mrs. Landon asks with excitement shining on her face.

"Thank you for reminding me of how few friends I have, Mrs. Landon..." I dryly respond.

"Oh, Margo, you know quality is far more important than quantity. We are just happy for you."

I spend the remainder of the afternoon telling them about Evey and her family. They are shocked to learn she is the younger sister of my enemy, Mr. Riley, but let that information drop quickly. We then start discussing preparation around the house for her arrival.

With Evey arriving in five days, the Landons and I spend all five days preparing. Mr. Landon plans activities, meals, and shopping for the meats he wants to prepare. Mrs. Landon does the remaining shopping, including picking up the britches I ordered for Evey. She might feel the same as Lily does about them, but I am hopeful she will like them. I am tasked with picking a room for her to stay in, cleaning it, preparing the bed, and anything else she may need in her room. Even though most of the rooms have gone untouched, I make sure to clean the bedding and blankets and leave them to dry in the sun. I must admit, I spent far too much time in the library picking out the perfect books to leave by her bedside. I find books of adventure and discovery, and I make sure to leave one of my favorite romance books on top.

8

Today is the day... I can barely contain my excitement for Evey's arrival. I keep myself busy by going through every room in the house to make sure they are ready for her. It helps to keep my nerves in check. Evey will be the first guest beyond those individuals whom I knew well enough that they would not be surprised by our lifestyle.

Lily Calderwood never flinched at how our home is run. Mr. Berry was beyond elated by the casualness when he first visited, insisting he would make his home the same once he settled. Evey is younger—she should be able to adjust. The night we met, she seemed desperate to be free of the formalities of London society.

I hear the carriage and run to the window to check— *she's here*! I take the steps two at a time down to the foyer. Shouting for Mr. and Mrs. Landon the entire way down, who meet me at the bottom of the steps. They have been very kind for enduring my obsessiveness this past week.

We enter the courtyard to meet Evey. She exits with

her lady's maid. I introduce the Landons and myself. There's a short pause, and then Evey introduces us to the two people who have accompanied her—Theo, her footman, and Marie, her lady's maid.

Mr. Landon is the first to speak up, insisting they stay for a meal and rest the horses. They both exchange a look of surprise at that offer, which is immediately followed by matching shoulder slumps, politely accepting the offer. Marie joins the women in the house while Mr. Landon directs Theo toward the stable. Mrs. Landon quickly strikes up a conversation with Marie about her journey, and I pull Evey to the side and greet her with an informal hug. She does not hesitate to hug me right back as she sighs in relief. That one sound, the release of her tension, bolsters my confidence. I did the right thing by inviting her.

"It is so good to finally be here, Margo. I am still surprised my parents actually allowed it."

I am taken aback by her confession. "Why would they not allow it?"

She hesitates for only a moment. "I have never traveled anywhere by myself." She turns to her lady's maid, "Well, without another family member with me. I feel like there are so many possibilities. I have time to myself, without lessons, balls, or an overbearing family dictating my every move."

"I am so delighted to hear you say that. That is exactly what I want my home to be for you. I hope it lives up to your expectations. First up, you must be starving. Mrs. Landon made my favorite sandwiches for us and your company." My mouth waters at the thought of the cucumber sandwiches.

After we eat, I insist on showing Evey her room. Mr. Landon had already shown Theo the room and he had left her bags placed neatly inside the door. She looks pleased as she takes in the room.

Walking straight to the window she stands silently, gazing at the view. "I wish my bedroom view was as beautiful as this, Margo! You are so lucky to have this outside your window." I join her, admiring the estate. This time of year, the grass is at its brightest, the trees are so full providing infinite amounts of shade, and the pond in the back with wildflowers all around. I must find a vase for her to fill with her choice of blooms each day during her stay.

"I am forever grateful for this home. The view outside a London window is so loud and busy. Here, I cannot help but feel at peace."

Evey turns back to her bed and notices the large boxes with bows. "I did not bring these," she says with a puzzled look on her face.

"Think of them as a welcome to the country gift." Evey remains still. "Well, open them," I insist.

"Thank you, Margo. This is too kind."

"Wait to thank me until you see what is in them. Please, do not feel like you must like them. I promise not to be offended."

As she opens the two larger boxes, her eyes light up at the sight of the pretty summer dresses I had ordered for her. "Margo, they are beautiful and so light."

"The sun gets very warm out here, and being it is only

us, we no longer need to dress formally when walking around the house or in the fields."

"My mother would die if she saw these. But I love them. I will wear one tomorrow." She sweeps one out of its box, clutching the soft cotton to her chest. As the skirt flutters around her, I feel a sense of pride noticing the color perfectly complements her eyes.

My gaze turns to the smaller box, and she follows my eyes. "Another dress?" she asks.

"Not exactly. Again, if you do not care for them, you do not have to wear them. I have come to enjoy wearing them here on colder days and nights. Lady Calderwood hates them, but I really enjoy them." Confusion streaks across her face. "Just open the box."

"Britches?"

"I had them made in your size. I have multiple pairs myself, but you do not have to wear them if you feel uncomfortable."

A smile grows across her face. "You really meant it when you said society rules do not apply here, Margo."

I shrug in response.

"I look forward to wearing them on the first cold night. Thank you." She closes the distance and pulls me into a hug.

Evey helps me prepare our dinner, and then we both offer to clean up so that the Landons can have some time to socialize with someone other than the two of us, who will be their only company for the next few weeks.

I hear Theo asking Mr. Landon several questions about the lack of formality in our home. Newcomers are always shocked to learn how our house is run, but we swear them to secrecy. Marie and Theo stand to take their leave, politely declining our offer to stay the night and deciding to return to town.

Evey and I find ourselves lounging in the sitting room, enjoying each other's conversation and company. She leans forward, warmth in her tone as she says, "I am growing concerned those two will be calling you soon, asking for employment. They have never spent time with my family in such a setting."

"We would be happy to have them." I nudge her elbow with a grin. "It is awfully quiet around this place most of the time with only the three of us."

"Has it always been the three of you?" she asks.

"Not always, but as I got older, the numbers quickly diminished. I like it better, just us. Lady Calderwood and Mr. Berry come to visit on occasion, but aside from that, it's just us."

There's a wistful, almost envious look in Evey's eyes, and I feel it again, that blooming of happiness in my chest telling me inviting her here was the right thing to do.

THE NEXT MORNING, the sun shines into my room, waking me with its golden light. Usually, if this had been any other morning, I would still be asleep or lazing in bed with a good book. But this is not any other morning. I have a guest!

Excitement tingles through me, and I immediately get up to start preparing breakfast for her. My attire today is much less formal than yesterday. Even though we informally entertained Marie and Theo, I was still dressed as is proper to receive guests. Today, I am wearing one of my favorite summer dresses. Lighter material than my formal dresses. The low neckline resembles the ones on my formal gowns. It is a pretty light blue color that fits tighter at the top and grows wider as it flows down my legs to my feet. I love the soft feel of the lightweight material swirling against my skin.

As I turn into the hallway, I hear laughter.

Could it be true? Could Evey be a morning person?

Maybe we are not as alike as I guessed.

9

The day after my dance with Margo, I awoke with a purpose and a plan. This was not the first time I found myself under her control by a dance, a simple conversation, or prolonged eye contact.

Margaret Eton has power over me like no other woman, and each time I am exposed to her, I feel like a different person. It is easier to pick one emotion to feel for her to maintain my sanity. Anger provides me with a shield against her. I focus on that emotion, using it as the reason for my outrage at Margo for attempting to persuade my young and impressionable sister into a friendship. In addition to being angry with her, I also know it is helpful to put distance between us.

I decide to decline any social invitations for the next month, not knowing how much longer she plans to stay in the city. When my father requests I travel out of town on business on his behalf at the end of this week, I am more than glad to oblige his offer.

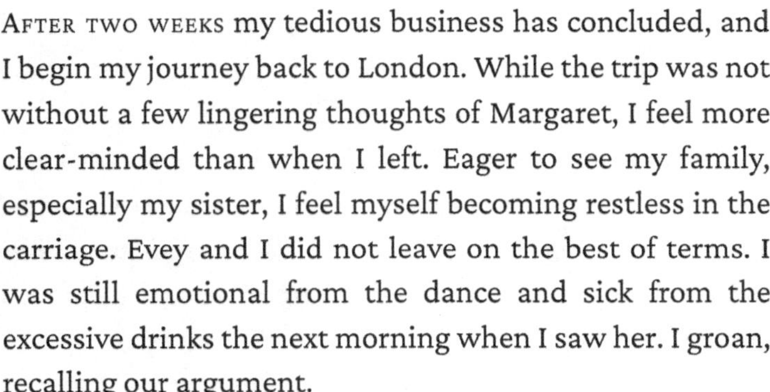

After two weeks my tedious business has concluded, and I begin my journey back to London. While the trip was not without a few lingering thoughts of Margaret, I feel more clear-minded than when I left. Eager to see my family, especially my sister, I feel myself becoming restless in the carriage. Evey and I did not leave on the best of terms. I was still emotional from the dance and sick from the excessive drinks the next morning when I saw her. I groan, recalling our argument.

"Evelyn!" I shout as she walks past me. My head feels as though my brain is bouncing from side to side in my skull. I would have preferred to keep sleeping, but this matter needed to be addressed as soon as possible, certainly before I left on business for two weeks.

"Yes, brother? No need to shout," she says calmly and, with a slight sense of irritation, turns back to face me. "Are you unwell?"

It is obvious I am, but she clearly feels the need to rub it in. "That is not important. We need to speak about last night."

"Have you been speaking with Mother? I thought you were on my side!" Her anger is coming out at a faster rate than my pounding head can process. "You said I would not have to do anything I did not want. Then you abandoned me, and I was forced to dance with Mr. Richmond."

I have not considered she would be mad with me. Another reason to dislike Miss Eton. She distracted me from my duty to be by my sister's side the entire evening. "I apologize for that, Evelyn, but I would not have been dancing if I were not looking out for you. A single dance with Mr. Richmond would not cause a fraction of a problem as much as Miss Eton speaking to you. I needed to make sure she stayed away from you in the future." Clearly, my sister will see my side and understand I was acting in her best interest.

"Pardon me, Eddy?" Her eyes narrow, her mouth parts, and she continues, "You believe Margaret Eton was someone I needed to be protected against? Not the man almost twenty years my senior asking me what type of martal qualities I possess during our dance?"

"Charles Richmond is harmless. While it may have been an unfortunate occurrence, I know Margaret Eton can do far worse damage," I correct her. "Your incorrect assessment of the two events is evidence that you are not old enough to make the proper decision of who to share your company with yet."

"You are being ridiculous, Eddy, but I see you are unmoving on this subject. I need to return to my room." And with that, she walks away. Quarreling is not uncommon between us, but her cool dismissal is new. While I would like to think it is acceptance of my directive, I have a feeling it is the opposite. Perhaps it is better not to dwell on this matter. She knows where I stand, and even if she is upset by it, I know she will not go against her own brother's wishes.

The next two days pass without as much as a word between us. I pack for my travels, and she mostly keeps her head down in a book.

It is the day of my departure, and I am walking past my father's office when I overhear my mother mention Eton Cottage. I freeze and continue to listen. Not long after, I hear Evelyn's voice enthusiastically say, "Please, papa. I would love the chance to visit with Miss Eton in the country."

Not waiting to hear my father's response, I throw open the door to the office and demand to know what is being discussed. My father explains with little interest, "Your sister has requested a holiday with a friend in the country."

I turn to Evelyn, "Miss Eton's cottage?"

My mother answers before my sister can, "Yes, Edward. We visited Lady Calderwood's this morning, and they invited Evelyn to visit with them in a week's time."

I turn to Evelyn who looks a little smug as it seems our parents do not see a problem with her trip. Bristling, I cannot keep the anger from my usually controlled tone. "You are not to speak with Miss Eton ever again, let alone holiday with that woman. Decline the invitation at once." My father looks confused, and my mother looks exasperated, as she typically does when I step over her when making decisions regarding Evelyn.

"Eddy! You cannot," Evelyn screams. As I make my leave toward the door.

I turn back to her, "My decision is final." I walk straight out of the house to the carriage that will take me out for two weeks.

Now that I'm back in town, I make a quick stop at the local florist to purchase a bouquet of flowers for Evelyn. I imagine she is still angry with me for denying her a trip to the country, but much time has passed for her to feel settled with the idea.

With the flowers in hand, I approach my family's townhouse and decide I will offer to take her on holiday. She can experience the countryside under my watchful eye without anyone's interference.

After being greeted at the door by two staff members, I

make haste to my sister's room. It is later in the day, so I imagine she will be upstairs reading by the window.

I knock on her door, but she does not answer. She must know it is me and is deciding to ignore me. It is time to apologize for my temper, not the decision. "Evelyn, as your loving and caring brother, I beg you, please open the door. I have a gift for you."

Still, no answer. I knock again louder. No response. I turn the doorknob and enter the room to discover it is empty. I turn and begin to search the house when I come upon my mother.

"Edward, you have returned," she says, slightly surprised. "How was your business? Did you have clear weather for your journey back?"

"Yes, Mother. Nice to see you." I place a kiss on her cheek. I'm overwhelmed by the familiar and all too sweet smell of her perfume. If she did not wear it in such an excess, it might be a complementary scent, but at this quantity, it makes it hard to breathe when I find myself in such close proximity to her. "Business went well, the weather was adequate. Where is Evelyn? I brought her flowers, but she is not in her room."

It is clear in my mother's eyes she is hesitant to answer. "Is she unwell? Is something wrong?" Raising my voice louder and louder as the panic rises in my chest.

Has something happened while I was gone?

Surely, they would have notified me had she taken ill.

My father comes down the hall, clearly concerned about the loud questioning of my mother. "Son, it's good to see you back. What is the matter?"

"Where is Evelyn?" Still, my voice is raised louder than it should be at my parents.

"She is at Eton Cottage, visiting with a friend. She left a few days ago," my father states with a matter-of-fact tone. A very brief sense of relief comes at the knowledge that Evelyn is in good health, but it is quickly replaced with the fury building within me that my orders were contradicted.

"I made it very clear that she was not to have contact with Margaret Eton ever again, and yet here you stand, telling me she's visiting the woman at her country estate," I say with a steady voice as I address my father. He is the head of the Riley household, but since Evelyn was born, I have accepted responsibility for her. My father takes notice of my tone but decides to dismiss me with little effort.

"Edward, one day, you will have a family, and you will learn you must pick your battles. Your mother and sister reassured me that their interactions with the Eton girl have been nothing but pleasant, and her family has a very good reputation. Lord Eton is one of the most respected men in London." I almost roll my eyes.

What he means is Lord Eton is rich. *Very rich.* My father goes on, "I have never heard a negative word mentioned about him or his family. You had not presented any evidence to the contrary. You simply seemed to be overreacting. As the father of a young woman, I simply could not deny her request when she asks so little of us. I was happy to learn she made a new friend. It's the first step in socializing."

"Father." I need him to take me seriously, but it is

becoming clear I was overruled, and my sister is sitting with Margo at this very moment at Eton Cottage. He meets my eyes with a clear lack of understanding. My mother remains silent during this interaction.

With a sigh, I hand my mother the flowers and remove myself from their company. I need space to decide how I feel about this and what I can do moving forward.

TWO DAYS. It has been two days since learning my sister is in the country at Eton Cottage. Two days of going back and forth in my mind, trying to restrain myself from going there to drag her back to London. I made lists, trying to find a resolution to my uncertain mind.

It is possible that Evelyn will not come to any harm while under Margo's care. Albert considers her a close friend and has never said anything bad about Miss Eton. Maybe she is not as much of a menace as I have convinced myself she is. I know that Evey will not come under any physical harm. But on the other hand, Margo may be whispering in her ear, planting unrealistic ideas in my sister's head, convincing Evelyn to refuse marriage as she has all these years. We do not have plans to arrange a marriage for Evelyn. I just want her to find a man who would love and support her. I cannot have Margo poisoning Evey against my best intentions for her.

If I go to Eton Cottage and demand she return to London with me immediately, it will drive the current wedge further between us. And, if I go to her, I will have to see Margo again, which is not something I want to put myself through. It would reverse any progress I have made since our dance.

A headache is brewing, and I try to roll some of my anxiety out of my neck. The inability to make a decision is crippling me. How I wish Albert were in town. I could use his counsel now more than ever.

10

The sun is bright and warm on my skin. This is where I belong. Lying side-by-side, drying off after what has become our daily afternoon swim. I did not know what to expect from Evey's visit, but we quickly fell into a routine as if she had always been here.

The first week of Evey's stay was filled with an enjoyment that I had never experienced before. I imagine it would be similar to having a younger sister. In my life, I am only surrounded by people older than me, but this is the first time I have been able to share my knowledge and interests with someone younger. We have found ourselves equally speaking for hours and being able to enjoy moments like this with a comfortable silence between us.

THE NEXT DAY is not as warm, but no one would consider it a cold day either. The sun makes rare appearances in the sky but, for the most part, remains covered by clouds. Yet, it does not appear like it will rain either. Looking over the breakfast table to Evey, I ask, "I think a swim might not be a wise choice today. What would you like to do instead?"

"I would still enjoy being outside. Do you think a walk around the property would be suitable?"

"Sure, we may just want to dress a little warmer, but I think the exercise will warm us up."

We take my usual walking route and are nearing where I would turn to visit Lady Calderwood. I am reminded of my excitement for the new book she purchased and wonder if it has arrived yet. I noticed Evey has been reading the book I left in her room but did not mention it before now, afraid I would accidentally spoil the ending.

"How did you enjoy the book I left out for you?" I ask.

"I did, and I must say, I'm surprised you enjoyed it, Margo."

"Why is that?" I absolutely loved the book, I would never have recommended it to her if I did not.

"This book is a love story. I was not aware that you had any interest in love or marriage…"

I turn to look at her, at first with disappointment that my London reputation has colored her opinion of me. "Evey, I will confess a secret, but you must promise it will not be shared with anyone."

"Of course."

"I am a romantic. I would give anything for a love story like the ones in those books." Evey's mouth drops open. I giggle and nudge her with my elbow. "As you are well aware, a love match is not common in London society. Even those matches that claim love, I believe only a small percentage are actually in love. These books are fiction, especially the gentlemen in them."

A minute passes between us in silence for Evey to absorb my confession. She finally responds, "I would never share your secret, Margo. Yet, even if you announced that at the next ball, I am afraid no one would believe you. You have done well to build a reputation that is the complete opposite."

"Yes, I'm well aware of my reputation. I sometimes want to share this with everyone, hoping it will cease the constant foul looks I receive when entering a room. But you are correct—they would never believe me. Also, I do not feel like they deserve an explanation or the privilege to know me, the real me."

"If you found love, would you marry? Willingly?"

"I think I will eventually need to marry regardless. If I found love...real love, I would run to the church. Yet, I know I'll never be able to find that type of love. My fortune makes it tough to trust any man who shows interest in me. I worry that the man who would provide a romantic courtship would turn me out as soon as we are wed."

Evey stops walking and faces me, "How extremely sad."

"It may be unlikely for me to find love, but I hope those books and your time away from London will help you figure out the type of husband you are looking for. Evey, you deserve nothing but the grandest love this world has to offer. Do not ever forget that."

"Of course, Margo. But, like you said, it is rare for people to find love as such."

"You are right. I think it is rare, but I know two couples who were able to find it. Even in the days since your arrival, you cannot deny the love the Landons have for each other." I try to reassure her.

"They are a perfect pair, but I feel they were able to find each other because of their social situation. Neither was under the pressure we are."

"Fair point, but I have another example, much closer to our situation...Lady Calderwood." I hate to think of Evey not being open to finding love.

"I know she is a widow, but I do not know much else about her marriage."

"I will not share their story with you since it's not mine to tell, but I know she would be happy to relive all of the details of her romantic courtship and marriage. We can visit her now if you'd like." Surely, no one could feel pessimistic after hearing their love story.

"That would be lovely."

Lady Calderwood's estate comes slowly into view as we approach her home.

"That is a magnificent home," Evey says with admiration. "So large for just one person."

"Yes, I try to visit her often, but I cannot imagine how lonely she must get."

A rustling sound begins, and we turn to see a carriage driving down the lane in the direction of Lady Calderwood's home. We both stop. It is too far away to make out the occupants of the carriage.

"Perhaps we should visit another day. It seems she

already has guests today to entertain her." We turn to walk in the direction we came. Lady Calderwood hardly has visitors. It may be some of Lord Calderwood's family. I hope everything is well.

WHEN WE RETURN to the house, I decide to write to Lily Calderwood.

> Dear Lily,
> It has been almost a month since I have enjoyed your company, and I'm missing you terribly! I grew so used to seeing you daily in London that this time apart is becoming unbearable! I hope you are enjoying the country sunsets and fresh air.
> I'm very much enjoying being home again.
> My guest arrived over a week ago, and she has been a pleasure to have around. We spend almost every afternoon swimming in the lake and then drying in the sun with a good book. Please know, you are always more than welcome to join us!
> We look forward to visiting with you at your earliest convenience!
> Your friend,
> Margo

It seems the clouds from yesterday were preparing for

the excessive rainstorm that would come today. At breakfast, Evey and I make plans for the day that keep us inside and dry. We include a stop in the library to select a few new books to read. Before we know it, the day has passed, and Mrs. Landon is calling us down to start preparing dinner.

"Evey, you can add the carrots now. Do not forget to stir them throughout the soup before you cover it again." I could not have asked for a nicer evening. We have been blessed with so many sunny days since Evey's arrival. I was glad to see the rain today. After spending so much of our time outside, I was longing for a night of reading by the fire. It also provides the opportunity to show Evey how to make my favorite soup.

"It smells delicious," she says, standing over the large pot. "Are you sure we cannot start eating now?"

"It will need another hour before it is ready," Mrs. Landon says as she walks into the kitchen.

A loud banging comes from the front of the house. Mr. Landon gets up from his seat at the table. "Are we expecting guests, Margo?

"No, not that I know of," I answer quickly as the four of us look around.

"I'll go check it. Girls, you stay here." He makes his way out of the room, and Mrs. Landon follows after him. It is a rare occurrence for us to receive unannounced guests, but it happens from time to time. I am not too worried, and I certainly do not let any concern show on my face. No need to startle Evey.

In a matter of minutes, we hear shouting with Evey's

name called out. I turn toward her, expecting her to be frightened or surprised, but she almost looks frustrated. We make eye contact, and she murmurs under her breath, "Eddy..."

11

"What is your brother doing here, and why is he shouting?" This is all happening so quickly that I cannot be sure it is real.

"He did not approve of me coming here...and my parents let me go after he left home on business," she confesses, and we both are out of the kitchen, walking toward the door.

"He did not approve." It is not a question but a statement of shock. Obviously, he is not the head of his household and was overruled, so why come here to cause a problem?

We turn the corner to the foyer, and there stands Edward Riley, drenched from the rain. I know I need to be angry. Evey said he voiced his disapproval of her coming, but the anger is suddenly quieted by the view in front of me. His dark hair is dripping wet and flattened by the weight of the rain. I follow a drop that spreads down his forehead to finally land on his long lashes before it is blinked away. He is not looking in my direction, and I feel a brief sense of disappointment. I continue my appraisal of the visibly angry man, I feel a bit of excitement.

What has come over me?

As I return to my senses, I notice he is speaking with Mrs. Landon in a hushed voice. Mr. Landon calls out to the footman, Theo, to follow him to the barn to take care of the horse and get out of the rain. It must be Theo who brought Eddy. He was already familiar with the journey. I wonder if Eddy knew how familiar Theo is with my family.

When he turns and notices us, he sends me a look of resentment and then quickly moves to his sister. "I need to speak with my sister," he informs Mrs. Landon.

It is becoming clear that I will not be acknowledged any further. Mrs. Landon nods and pulls on my arm to guide me out of the foyer. I resist. Evey meets my gaze, "It's fine, Margo. We will be right behind you," she says with such confidence that I cannot help but be proud. Eddy looks even more surprised.

Mrs. Landon and I return to the kitchen where we find Mr. Landon and Theo. Theo is a man of middle age, not very tall, with short light brown hair and a smile too bright for someone who is subjected to Eddy on a regular basis. I notice that he has now changed into dry clothes. How frustrating that Eddy would drag this poor man out in the rain for something as silly as this.

We quickly insist that Theo stay through the night and even longer if the rain persists. He politely accepts on the condition that Mr. Riley is planning to stay as well. After we exchange pleasantries, I return to oversee the soup.

Ten minutes pass before Evey enters the kitchen with

her brother behind her. She makes her way to me. Mr. Landon stands before Eddy. "Mr. Riley, I assume you will be staying for dinner at the very least. Can I offer you some dry clothes?"

"I have some in my trunk," Eddy answers while he eyes Theo with surprise. I am not sure which startles him more, the new dry clothes Theo is wearing or that he is seated at the table with Mr. Landon.

Theo jumps up quickly, "Your trunk is in the foyer, Mr. Riley. When I brought it in from the stable, I was unsure if you were staying, and if so, I did not know which room you would be occupying."

Eddy, still looking at Theo surprised, quickly turns to Evey, who has her feet planted and chin high as she stands next to me. He sighs, and Mr. Landon interjects, "You are both more than welcome to stay as long as you would like. Can I show you to your rooms?"

"I would like to stay here with my sister a little longer. Thank you for your hospitality, Mr. and Mrs. Landon," Eddy answers with a strained expression on his face. He has not so much as looked at me since he re-entered the room. I would enjoy nothing more than to revoke that hospitality, but Mr. and Mrs. Landon would not be happy with me.

I need to speak with Evey to find out why he feels it is necessary to stay with her. He can clearly see she is in perfect health, and does he really worry I would harm her in some way? I knew we did not like each other, but could his opinion of me really be this low?

The men all take their leave, and I can only hope Mr. Landon gives them the extra rooms on the opposite side of the house. This is the first time I have ever wished that this cottage were bigger. But honestly, Buckingham Palace would never have been big enough to give enough distance between us.

I pull Evey to the stove. "What was that about? Why is he staying here?"

"You know Eddy, you may not like him, but you know him. He is stubborn and has certain ideas of you that just are not true," Evey says with frustration in her voice.

"I do not care what he thinks of me," I state as if it was not clear enough already.

Evey looks at me, exasperated. "Well, for me, you should. I want to visit you again after this, but it will be a nightmare for me to do so if you two cannot come to an understanding. You do not have an overbearing older brother, so I know this is difficult for you to see from my perspective, but I'm asking you to try, Margo."

"What does this have to do with him staying?" I question her.

"He was concerned that you brought me here to fill my head with ideas against marriage and whatnot. I told him to stay and see for himself. He is so proud. He cannot possibly imagine you for the kind and creative person you are. He agreed to stay and see for himself." Evey seems proud of her solution.

"So now what, he is to be included in all of our plans? For how long?" I cannot have this man in my house for a prolonged amount of time—I will go mad.

"I do not know how long he will stay. I guess long enough for him to see the real you and what we are doing here. No, he does not have to be included in our plans but let him see what your life is like here and what I'm being exposed to. And maybe you can try to be civil toward him during his stay?" She says that last part with an accusing tone I do not care for.

"I do not claim innocence, but may I remind you, your brother has not said one word to me since entering *my* home. I only received one glance filled with disdain. How can I trust him to not use what he sees here against me when I return to London?"

"I spoke with him and told him that he is to be on his best behavior and not to embarrass me while he is here. I think, at this point, the only way he was able to do that was by not speaking to you at all." She turns to face me and places her hand on her hip. "Margo, what happened between you? Why is it that you seem to have such strong opinions against one another? I was not aware that you two were acquainted until we met at the ball."

I must think before I answer. It is not that I do not want to be honest with Evelyn, but I must be mindful of what I share—he is her brother.

"We are of similar age and had some pleasant interactions as children. Then, after we both entered London society, we each had certain expectations on our shoulders. Some people find my decision to not marry immediately, or at all until this point, a rebellion against those expectations and traditions. We started to grow apart at first, then gradually, your brother made his negative view of me well-known over the years, and I have felt the need to defend my choices, especially toward him."

"You were friends?" she asks quietly.

I do not like admitting that.

I do not even like thinking about Eddy as my friend. It makes me too soft, and my disappointment in the man he has become hurts too much.

I shrug and allow for a few moments of silence before changing the subject. "He did seem quite put off by the sight of Theo at the table," I say with a smile on my face. As much as I hate the idea of Eddy Riley in my home, this could be fun watching him try to acclimate to our way of life.

Could he really survive here without servants waiting on him?

"Yes, I am sure he had many questions for Mr. Landon on the walk to his room."

"Do you think he would not allow Theo to be treated as a guest too?" Surely, he cannot be that rotten, I hope.

"Eddy would never go against Mr. Landon or the expectations set in a home he was visiting," her response comes as a relief. "Eddy is not always the way he is around you. He actually can be polite and charming, Margo. Perhaps he will be unable to hold on to his anger throughout the visit and you will be able to see another side to him as well?"

My eyes cannot roll any further back if I tried. Thankfully, Theo is the first to emerge from his room and return to the dining room before I can make another comment about Eddy. He looks unsure of how to act, but then Mr. Landon gives him a pat on the back. "Theo, you can relax. You are our guest."

"Thank you again, Mr. and Mrs. Landon and Margaret, for having me. This is truly an unexpected treat." While

Theo is just as courteous as he was when he brought Evey, he does seem quite on edge. I imagine Eddy is the source. We spend the next hour getting to know Theo more intimately, learning where he grew up, how many siblings he has, and about a very special lady who also works for the Riley family.

After several glances toward the stove, Evey asks if I can check the soup, and I confirm it is ready. She looks at me apologetically. "I should go get my brother. Where is his room, Mr. Landon?"

Theo jumps up. "I can go fetch him, Miss Riley."

Evey smiles at him. "How about you show me where his room is, Theo? I will need to eventually know where to find him." Theo nods, and they both leave for the stairs. I should probably know where he is so I can avoid it at all costs, but I do not ask. That would make it too real that he will be spending the night, and probably more, here.

Turning to Mr. Landon, I ask, "How was he? When you showed him to his room?"

"I hate to disappoint you, Margo, but he was very kind and even apologized for coming without any notice."

I slouch with disappointment. Mrs. Landon lets out a laugh under her breath. "You will have to remind me why you dislike him again, Margo. As children, I recall you both getting along splendidly. What happened?"

I sometimes forget that Mr. and Mrs. Landon do not participate in London society and are not present to witness the countless hours of deadly glares and snide comments that Eddy and I shoot back and forth at each other. "It's very simple. He has taken my decision not to marry as a personal attack on all men and the tradition of marriage. He is only here because he is worried I am filling Evey's mind with the same sentiments."

Mrs. Landon lets out a burst of laughter. "That could not be farther from the truth, Margo. Have you not explained this to him?"

"And why does he deserve an explanation?"

"Stubborn as always, Margo," she says with an exasperated sigh.

"You believe me to be stubborn, Mrs. Landon? I think you will change your mind when you realize just how stubborn a person can be once you spend time with our new house guest."

"Keep your voice down, Margo," Mrs. Landon scolds me.

"Edward Riley would not be surprised to hear any of it, I promise you."

"What would not I be surprised to hear, Miss Eton?" Eddy says, coming into the room behind Evey and Theo.

I cannot help myself. I know better, but I just cannot keep the words from coming out of my mouth. "Well, Mr. Riley, Mrs. Landon has taught me the utmost of manners, and you did ask what we were saying about you—let me inform you. I was simply relaying to my family that you and I do not get along. And you have supported my claim by refusing to acknowledge me in my own house until this very moment. How very rude of you, considering that you have been here for well over an hour." I pause.

I know I will hear about this later. I can see the disappointment on Mrs. Landon's face. I am a grown woman, but you never outgrow dealing with a disappointed parent. I cannot even enjoy the deep shade of red that is consuming Eddy's face at the moment. Trying to regain some manners, I paint a faint smile on my face and say to him, "Welcome to my home, Mr. Riley, please sit. Would you like some soup?"

He does not respond, not because he is speechless. No, I can tell from the way he is pressing his lips together that he has much to say in response but is using every bit of self-control to stop himself from letting the words escape his mouth.

Evey's body moves in a way that I believe is the result of her kicking her brother under the table. Eddy jolts and faces her. She says to her brother in a firm voice, "Eddy, would you like some soup?"

"Yes, please," he answers and then pushes his lips back together as if fearful more words might slip out.

I bring a bowl to him and Theo. Eddy's fury is evident on his face, but I do not care. He started this by coming to my home, insinuating that his sister was not safe, and then ignoring me. He deserves how I am treating him.

Dinner is a little more civilized. We each ignore each other for the remainder of the meal, speaking to everyone at the table but each other. Mrs. and Mr. Landon insist on cleaning the dishes because Evey and I cooked. They also insist we give our guests a tour. Reluctantly, I comply. I exclusively speak to Theo, who is a more than willing guest. He is polite and thanks me more than he should for letting him stay through the storm. He informs Evey and me that he will be heading back to the Riley's London home as soon as the storm ends.

After the tour, Mrs. Landon joins us, offering options

to our guests for the evening's entertainment. Eddy asks Evey, "What are your plans?"

She looks at me. "I was planning on reading by the fire if you are interested."

"That sounds lovely," I say to her.

Mrs. Landon says next, "Evey, why do not you take Theo and your brother to the library to find a book that may interest them?"

She nods politely, and they leave the room.

The remainder of my night is spent in my chair with a book by the fire. Theo is in a seat toward the back of the room. I assume he wanted to distance himself from the obvious tension in the room. Evey is in the chair next to mine. The Landons are in and out throughout the evening. Eddy occupies the chair directly across from mine. I doubt he is comprehending his book as he keeps looking up at Evey and me. Almost like we are children, he needs to keep watching to make sure we are not up to something we should not be. And his constant gaze is distracting. Frustratingly so. I barely get any reading done. I cannot concentrate on the words in my book because my anger and frustration are producing a constant mental shouting in my head. It's not long before Theo excuses himself to his room. Finally, when an appropriate time has passed, I stand and begin to excuse myself to retire for the night. I have a better chance of reading in my room than here, with Eddy Riley staring at me all night.

Speaking directly to Evey. "Please excuse me. I think I will retire for the evening. Please feel free to stay up as long as you would like. I shall see you in the morning."

"I think I am ready to retire as well." She must be as

frustrated with her brother's presence as I am. "The events of the day turned out to be exhausting."

"I will escort you to your chambers, sister," Eddy says, standing and walking over to his sister. Like a repelling magnet, the closer he gets to us, the further I step back. Refusing to look toward him, I continue on to my room. I was hoping for a moment to speak with Evey in private, but that is clearly not happening tonight under his watchful eye.

We arrive at the entrance to Evey's room first. I give her a quick smile and say goodnight. I keep walking, hearing her brother offer her a goodnight and her door close behind her. Expecting to hear his footsteps, there is only silence.

Why has he not turned to go to his room?

I open my door and cannot help but look back at him as I enter my room. He is looking at me—his strikingly handsome face is covered with pure hatred. Returning my own version of the look back at him, I slam my bedroom door as hard as I can. I know it will not get him out of my home any sooner, but it felt good to do it.

12

As the hours go by, it is evident sleep will not find me tonight. Hours have been spent tossing and turning in a bed that is located under the roof of Eton Cottage.

In London, stories were told about this country home over the years, but I was vastly unprepared for what I have experienced since arriving this evening. Still reeling from the evening's events, Theo, my footman, seemed to make himself right at home here. I was aware he was the person to bring Evelyn, but he failed to mention that he spent any time inside the home, let alone with its occupants.

If I thought he would still be awake at such a late hour, I might seek him out for more information. Now, hours after we have retired, I'm sure he is asleep. There is nothing to keep him up all night with worry. No foolish, stubborn woman parading through his mind. A bewitching pair of golden brown eyes are not haunting him.

How foolish of me to think earlier today that I would

be able to prepare myself for seeing her while on my travels to Eton Cottage. Aside from reciting what I would say to my sister, the remainder of the ride was spent thinking of Margo. At first, I rebelled against her image, but then it occurred to me that maybe I should take the time to prepare for when we would eventually meet. It is her home and I knew she was far from a gentle lady who would hide at my arrival. By the time the rain began, I was certain I would be able to see Margo without being affected. My irritation from the rain did not help my mood.

I was absolutely irate as I stood at the door, slamming my fists instead of knocking while I screamed my sister's name.

"EVELYN!"

"EVELYN RILEY!"

"EVELYN!!!"

Like a fool, I do not anticipate who will be greeting me at the door. Yet, there is no way for me to predict this man. It is as if the door opens and is replaced with another door. A man's large build takes up most of the space in the doorway as if to block my view of the inside of the house. Fumbling slightly on my feet as I take a step back, I notice more of this man's features. He is older, perhaps a little younger than my father. He is not dressed as a servant but wearing a white shirt and dark brown trousers. His face is unmoving as he crosses his arms over his chest. He does not speak, and neither do I. We both stand in silence as the rain falls on us. At this moment, I do not regret coming to see my sister, but I do regret not sending word of my arrival and perhaps requesting permission.

"Good evening, Mr. Landon!" Theo yells in greeting from

behind me. I quickly turn with a look of shock at Theo. Is he trying to anger this man more than he already is?

By the time I turn back to face the large man, who I now assume to be "Mr. Landon," it is as if a different man is standing in his place. Gone is the intimidating muscle of man; his scowl is now replaced with a smile that meets his eyes as he looks past me to wave at Theo.

"Good Evening, Theo. Nice to see you again." He then turns his attention back to me. "Given you are accompanied by Theo and shouting Miss Riley's name, I can assume you are related to her?"

I must remember to thank Theo later. I do not know what position this man holds in this house, but it is clear that I would not have gained access without Theo's assistance.

With hopes to remain on this man's good side, I put forth my best manners. "Yes, sir. I greatly apologize for the intrusion. Please allow me to introduce myself. I am Edward Riley. Evelyn is my younger sister."

"Mr. Riley. Welcome to our home." A female voice I do not recognize comes from behind Mr. Landon. He turns his head back with an affectionate grin. "Let him in. It's raining," she continues. When the woman is finally in view, I am introduced, "It is nice to meet you, Mr. Riley. I am Mr. Thomas Landon, and this is my wife, Mrs. Emma Landon."

Mr. Landon moves out of the doorway to allow me to pass and then returns to speak with Theo. I take this opportunity to win over Mrs. Landon. She is far more agreeable than her husband. I am pleasantly surprised by her greeting. "Welcome to our home, Mr. Riley. I'm sure the girls will be along soon. I hope it was not dire news that brought you here. Is your family well?"

After thanking Mrs. Landon for her welcome and concerns, I explain that our parents are well. A moment later, my sister enters the room accompanied by Margaret Eton. She looks different, not the image I have prepared for in my head, but even more beautiful and relaxed than I thought possible. How dare she continue to catch me off guard like this?

I stare at the ceiling in frustration. The bed is comfortable, but I know that woman is somewhere in this house...

When Evey saw me standing in the foyer of Margo's home, I realized before my sister spoke a single word that I had overstepped.

I took the first option that she gave me to resolve this matter. She shared valid arguments and appears to have gained confidence since I last saw her. Yet, that might not be confidence but Margo's influence on her. As a result, I now find myself in this bed, unable to sleep and unsure of how to move forward with my time at Eton Cottage. Evelyn admitted she understood that I was here out of concern, but she insisted I stay to see that my concern is ill-placed.

My sister has a way of only seeing the good in people and due to my mother sheltering her as much as possible, she does not have experience with deceit. I will stay and be witness to when Evelyn discovers Margo's true nature.

I sit and contemplate how long it would take for Evelyn to realize how rebellious Margo truly can be. My limits for being in Margo's presence for an extended amount of time have never been tested to this length.

How long will I be able to hold my composure here?

As I replay the events of this evening in my head, I

realize that it is a welcoming environment aside from the anger radiating from Margo. The Landons have been more than generous upon my arrival and seem pleased to have additional guests in their home.

I wonder if this is their doing or Margo's?

In recent years, I have only witnessed her interactions with Lady Calderwood in public, who she does not hide her affection for. But anyone would be shocked to see the familiarity and affection she shows the Landons.

With my head beginning to ache, I assume it is from the combination of sleep deprivation and the puzzle of Eton Cottage that will not be solved tonight.

At an appropriate time, I dress for the day and leave my room looking to speak with my sister and attempt to convince her to leave with Theo today.

13

"Margo, wake up." I hear Evey whispering, and the bed shifts as she sits next to me.

Even before opening my eyes, I can tell the sun is shining brightly in my room. It must be late morning. "Is something wrong?" I ask her. This morning is the first time that she has come to wake me up.

Something must be wrong.

"You mean other than my overbearing brother staying in your home and intruding on my holiday? No, I think that's it. Or did you forget?"

I did forget. Hopeful thinking.

"He has not had a change of mind and decided to return to town with Theo?"

"We are not that fortunate, Margo," she says as I sit up against my headboard.

"Good point. I'm glad you came to see me. He was trying to prevent a chance for a private conversation between the two of us last night. Well, how should we move forward? What would you like to do today?" I ask.

"I think we should pick up with our daily schedule. We will have breakfast, then head down to the lake."

"The water might be too cold from the rain for a swim, but can we take a book?"

Before she can answer, we hear Mrs. Landon's voice in the hallway. She's obviously trying to be loud enough to warn us. "Good morning, Mr. Riley! I hope you slept well."

We both move from the bed to the door as quietly as we can and push our ears against the door. Eddy replies, "Yes, Mrs. Landon, thank you. I was just coming up to check on my sister." I can excuse it because they just met, but he truly underestimates Mrs. Landon if he thinks he can sweet-talk her.

"I was coming to check on the girls myself. I will be happy to check in on your sister. These ladies have a habit of sleeping later than I imagine they do in the city. I think it must be the country air. Speaking of such, Mr. Landon and Theo are outside getting the carriage ready for its return to London. I'm sure they would appreciate an extra hand if you would not mind," she says in her sweetest tone.

"Certainly, Mrs. Landon," he says before we hear his footsteps grow further away.

Lighter footsteps approach the door as we back up for Mrs. Landon to enter. "Well, ladies, you almost had another for your secret morning meeting." She places a tray of fruit on my bed.

"Thank you, Mrs. Landon. We were just discussing what we should do for the day. We are planning to head down to the lake to read outside after we eat," I answer.

"Evey, how are you doing with your brother's arrival?" she asks.

Evey stares at her hands in her lap as she answers. "I never expected him to make the journey, but I cannot say that I was necessarily surprised when he arrived. As I'm sure you understand, Mrs. Landon, we all have stubborn family members whose actions, while they may be intrusive, are done with the best intentions."

Mrs. Landon chuckles with a pointed look in my direction.

"I take offense to that, Miss Riley!" I act thoroughly offended.

"I meant it in the best way, Miss Eton." Evey mocks back.

They both exit my room, Evey taking the plate of fruit with her.

I'm doing this for Evelyn. I can be nice for a few days, just enough to get rid of him then I can go back to my guest and holiday. I repeat this to myself the entire time I am dressing for the day.

I stop at Evey's door and knock, but there is no answer. She must be downstairs already. I find her in the sitting area, dressed extremely formally.

"Are you going somewhere?" I ask. Before she can answer, Eddy walks into the room and answers for her.

"Evelyn said we are going down to the lake," he says before actually looking at me. When he does, his eyes turn wide, "What are you wearing? Are you not dressed yet? Do you often wear your night dress around your cottage when you have company?"

Deep breath, Margo.

"Mr. Riley, this is a country dress. It has been designed by my tailor for life in the country, taking long walks on warm days and lying by the lake to allow for better movement and prevent heat exhaustion."

"It is inappropriate," he snaps back at me. He should have thought his words through before answering. This was getting too easy.

"Well then, Mr. Riley, if you find my dress inappropriate, you can decline our invitation to accompany us to the lake. Better, if you are so offended, you can always go back to London." I pause to give him a moment for a response, but he doesn't speak and continues to stare at me. I walk closer to him. "For someone so offended, it is interesting that you haven't looked away yet. Also, I can guarantee this is not a nightdress. You would know if it were—they are far more revealing," I say with a smile, grab my book with one hand and extend my other in Evey's direction. Eddy walks to the lake behind us without another word.

"You can guess why I decided against wearing one of the dresses you bought for me this afternoon?" Evey whispers quietly into my ear on our walk.

I nod with an apologetic smile. I hate that he is here ruining her time in the country. While I was glad to have left him speechless, arguing with Eddy is not helping Evey very much. I can see it on her face. I will not allow this to continue for the entirety of her stay. If I need to appease Eddy for him to leave, that is what I will try to do.

The sun is bright and warm by the lake. There is very little conversation as each of us is invested in our books.

"How is your book, Eddy?" Evey asks her brother.

"Almost as good as the scenery," he responds.

"I knew you would like it here. You always enjoyed traveling to the country when we were younger. Surprisingly, you have not yet found yourself a home like this."

Keeping my eyes on the pages of my book, I stop reading to listen in on their conversation.

"Maybe one day, I will need to ask Miss Eton for advice when selecting a place," Eddy says in my direction.

I peek my eyes up over my book at him.

Eddy continues, "Any neighbors looking to leave the area? I'm sure my sister would enjoy a place close to you."

Did I hear him correctly?

"Margo?" Evey grabs my attention back.

"Sorry, I am not sure, Mr. Riley, but I will let you know if something becomes available." I answer quickly, but then the question pops into my head, "Is the Riley Estate not up to your approval, sir?"

"The Riley Estate is vast and apt, yet it belongs to my family. It might be nice to invest in a smaller place that is just for myself. Something similar to Eton Cottage, perhaps."

He gives a self-satisfied look and returns to his book. Evey and I exchange a surprised look and follow his lead.

I had hoped the walk home from the lake would be just as quiet as the walk there. I was wrong.

"So, Miss Eton, should I prepare to cook for you this evening? I noticed last night you had my sister making dinner. Is that why you invite guests because you no longer have cooks? Did your glowing personality scare them away like the rest of your staff?" His smirk grows with each word that comes out of his mouth.

"*Eddy!*" Evey scolds her brother.

Deep breath, Margo. You need to behave for Evey. He is trying to bait you. "Mr. Riley, I must ask, did it take you all afternoon to think of that insult?"

His smile fades just a little. "You did not answer my questions, Miss Eton."

I try to look unaffected, but a sigh slips out under my breath. "You are more than welcome to help with dinner preparations this evening, Mr. Riley, but please know it is not expected of you. I believe Mr. Landon is preparing one of his favorite beef dishes. He would be more than happy to teach you, as he has done for me." I pause to look over and am surprised to see Eddy is actually listening to my explanation. "We did not force Evey to cook for us last night. She is always included but free to make her own choices without worry of judgment. As for my staff, I am sure you have been through this with Mr. Landon, but over the years, we found it unnecessary to have any staff. The three of us are more than capable and happy to care for the estate and our needs."

I look at Evey, who gives me a pleased smile. With hopes my explanation will be enough, I do not look back at Eddy again and continue my walk to the house.

After a quiet lunch with the Landons, Evey excuses herself to her room to write a few letters.

"If either of you have anything to go out, I will be going into town tomorrow and would be happy to send them," Mr. Landon offers to Eddy and me.

"That is a wonderful idea. I need to write to Lady Calderwood about the recent exciting events," I answer.

"I think I will do the same. Mr. and Mrs. Landon, thank you for the lunch," Eddy replies as he cleans his place setting. Mrs. Landon takes it from him on her way to the kitchen.

I wait until we are out of the Landons' view before I let my panic get the best of me. I rush to Eddy's side.

"Writing letters?" I inquire

"Yes, Miss Eton, I have quite a few letters that I will need to get out. Why do you ask?" Eddy answers as he continues walking away from the dining room.

Before I realize what I am doing, my hand reaches out and grabs his arm. I do not use force, but the gesture is successful because he turns back to face me. His eyes focus directly on the point of contact, but he does not pull back. His look lingers a bit longer, then slowly meets my eyes.

"Mr. Riley, I understand you are not pleased with the lack of formality in my home. It would not only ruin my life but the lives of the Landons as well if you were to share what you have witnessed here. They are good people, you can't deny that. They do not deserve that fate just because you dislike me."

Eddy's face shows more expressions than I have witnessed in a long time. Recently, anger and disapproval were the only expressions I was shown by him. At this moment, I notice surprise and possibly relief. I cannot be sure. I am so unfamiliar with any emotion but his anger.

One side of his mouth starts to curl upward, but before an actual smile develops, his gaze returns to the grip I have on his arm. I am not letting him go until I have an answer. At this moment, I can only hope for the best, but the least he can offer is a warning so I can prepare the Landons.

Eddy lifts his other hand and places it over mine. It is a gentle gesture, one I was not expecting. Meeting his gaze, I realize it is unlike any I have seen on him recently. If I did not know better, I would say it was kind. When he finally speaks, he does not move his arm or his hand away from mine. If anything, I feel a brief tug as if to pull me closer to him.

"Miss Eton, most of my letters are strictly business matters. The Landons have been the most gracious hosts I have ever encountered on my travels. I have nothing to report to anyone outside these walls but the generosity they have shown while I am staying here."

Relief floods through me, and without bothering to disguise it, I release the breath that I have been holding while waiting for his answer. "Thank you, sir. Your discretion is greatly appreciated." I need to leave before he changes his mind.

I start to pull my hand away, but he holds it in place. This time, he dips his head down closer to mine and lowers his voice.

So much for feeling like I can breathe again.

He parts his lips, and suddenly, I forget that his face has any other features aside from those lips. "I was planning to write to our mutual friend, Mr. Berry, with a very scandalous bit of information." He waits for my reaction for only a second or two, then continues, "I planned to tell him that I am actually starting to enjoy your company...but I know it is not worth writing. He would never believe it," Eddy says with a wink and finally releases my hand and makes his way toward the stairs.

My hands moved over my dress. It seems tighter as I struggle to get more air in my lungs. As my body regains composure from the infuriating reaction to Mr. Riley, I attempt to process his words. Perhaps he was trying to be cordial on Evey's behalf. I saw them talking earlier while outside. I'm sure she gave him the same lecture I received yesterday. Yes, that must be it. We are both adults and can act civilly for Evey's sake. I need to just be grateful he is not planning to expose my family situation to the London Society.

Hastily, I run up to my room and sit down to write to Lily.

Dearest Lily,

If you are not already seated, please sit down before you read the remainder of my letter.

I know you dislike rainstorms, and I must admit, I have found a new dislike for them as well. The storm last night, in particular, delivered an absolute nightmare to my doorstep. Mr. Edward Riley journeyed from London the moment he discovered his sister was visiting with me in the country.

Yes, you read that correctly. Edward Riley is here...in my home. He is insisting on staying with his sister until he is "satisfied" that I am not holding her hostage and encouraging her to denounce the marriage market.

You will not be surprised to learn that Mrs. Landon has found the need to scold me multiple times for my sharp tongue and "lack of manners" since his arrival. As much as I would like to insist he leave my home and never return, it is clear if I did that, he would take Evey with him.

She has insisted that he is acting out of concern, which is wrongly placed, and in a matter of days, he will see reason and leave. Yet, Evey has also pointed out that the more confrontational I am, the less likely he will feel comfortable leaving. I am trying very, very hard to be on my best behavior for her so he will leave and she can get back to enjoying her holiday.

How I wish Albert wasn't in Greece and I could invite him here to distract Mr. Riley. I have yet to receive any letters from him yet. Have you? I hope he is simply enjoying himself too much to write.

Please feel free to visit us. As always, an invitation is not required. Also, I would love an excuse to visit you with Evey. It would give me a break from her brother's constant company.

I look forward to seeing you soon!

Your friend,
Margo

I see no reason to include Eddy's brief reprieve from his usual unappealing personality. It is possible I was dreaming, and it never happened in the first place.

14

Evelyn is my concern. She is my entire world and the reason I find myself at Eton Cottage. I wish for her to take the marriage prospect seriously by actively searching for a man she can love and who will provide for her. The last thing I want to see is her finding herself at Margo's age, unmarried and without any concern for marrying.

Another point of unease has become clear since my arrival at Eton Cottage—my relationship with Evey is strained, possibly now more than before I arrived. She believes it is a matter of trusting her. She refuses to acknowledge that it is Miss Eton who I do not trust. I need to put in the effort to rebuild our relationship while we are here since my actions have only pushed her away from me lately.

While it is only my first full day here, there has been no mention of marriage or London society from Margo or Evey. That is with the exception of Margo suggesting I return to London if I was too offended by her dress...that dress. Here, I thought the gown she wore when we danced together would be the death of me. This was far worse.

Sure, she always looked beautiful while in London, but she looked exceptional, breathtaking, and enticing in the country. Her curly hair hung with little effort down past her shoulders, her skin was tan from the hours spent in the sun, and her face seemed more relaxed, similar to how she looked as a child.

My mind quickly goes back to her dress and how I pray that it is the only one of its kind. My stay at Eton Cottage will prove to be much more difficult than I anticipate if she continues to wear such clothing. It curved her body in the perfect places and then flowed with excess fabric down to her ankles. That dress will haunt my dreams for the rest of eternity. If the men in London could see her like this, they would be lined up to secure her hand and forget her family's fortune entirely. They would finally realize she alone would be enough of a prize as I know her to be.

Even with the change of her looks, that did nothing to change Margo's disposition. She is as fierce a woman as ever and seems to have some influence on my sister. I suppose I never really considered Evey's upbringing as lacking due to being an only daughter. While our relationship has always been close, I suppose there are some things she may not feel comfortable sharing with me knowing I will truly never understand. If I knew Margo's intentions were purely good, I might find myself thankful my sister has found someone to confide in, knowing our mother has never taken that role with her.

I left my hosts with the declaration of writing letters. I cannot spend the next few hours lying on this bed thinking of Margo's dress and then return without a single letter. It was my intention to follow up with my father on some business matters, but I do not have much else to write. I move myself to the desk in the corner of the room and quickly write a few letters, allowing my mind a quick break from its constant thoughts of Margo.

With three letters signed and sealed, I sit back in the chair, and my attention pulls to my left forearm. I raise it for further inspection. It does not appear any different since Margo's touch, but somehow, I can still feel her warmth. The vulnerability in her eyes was an emotion that I cannot recall experiencing from her in many years. She looked frightened at the thought of their exposure and the consequences that would follow. She is right to be worried. I would be just as protective of a life like this with such extraordinary caretakers. As quickly as I wanted to reassure her that their secret would be safe with me, I attempted to prevent Margo from pulling her hand away too soon. As she looked at me with pleading eyes, her touch felt as though she was anchoring herself to me. At that moment, it is imperative that she understands she can trust me in this matter. Closing my hand above hers was my way of expressing more than my words were sharing.

In the short time that I have been here, my guard is falling at an alarming rate, accelerating each time I am in Margo's presence. Evey seems content here at Eton Cottage, but I must stay vigilant to be sure she is not being swayed against the idea of marriage.

If anything, Margo could use someone who would encourage her to start seriously considering settling down before it is too late.

Am I concerned about Margo finding a husband?

A more reasonable explanation is that I am growing in affection for Eton Cottage and the Landons and worry her future husband might jeopardize it.

It would be helpful to have Albert here—she seems to listen to him. Knowing he is traveling, I find myself unable to request his presence, but I write him a letter he will receive on his return.

Albert,

I understand you are probably at sea at the moment, and cannot offer any immediate guidance, but I'm sending you my current dilemma regardless. You may have noticed this letter has been sent from Eton Cottage. That is no mistake. My parents allowed Evelyn to visit with Miss Eton against my wishes, and I found myself with no choice but to come here at once.

I must confess that each moment since my arrival has been quite surprising. I will not go into certain detail as the Landons have mentioned that you have visited many times and are familiar with the estate. My discoveries are not at all what I expected to find. The Landons are superb hosts, yet I cannot say Miss Eton has been as welcoming as they are. My sister was also not pleased by my arrival, but with any hope, I will be able to repair our relationship sooner than later.

The interactions with Miss Eton have varied. You will be surprised to learn that between our verbal sparring matches, there have been moments of civility. Yes, I am just as surprised. In fact, on my way to write to you, I told her I may confess to you that I am starting to enjoy her company, but you would surely never believe it.

I will continue to write to you to document this journey I am on, as I hope you will do with yours. Although, I fear I will face far rougher waters here.

How I wish you were in town; I could use your guidance now more than ever.

Safe travels, my friend.

-Edward Riley

A quick knock fills the room, and I freeze in place. My sister's patience dries up quickly, "Eddy, it's your sister"—followed by much louder knocking—"open the door."

"Hello, sister." I tread lightly with her, as I am well aware of how easily this can take a negative turn. Opening the door wide, I motion her to enter. She walks past me and sits on the bed. Out of self-preservation, I grab the chair from my desk, sit across from her, and try to sit in a relaxed manner.

"Well…" she says with an accusatory look, her arms crossed and her posture so straight it must be painful.

"Well, what?"

She leans in my direction, narrows her eyes, and tightens her jaw. "I'm just surprised you are here, in good health and a shockingly good mood this morning. So much so that you are asking about purchasing land nearby. Yet, when I asked to visit this very cottage, you were so very against it that you forbid me to come." Her arms fall to her sides as she continues, "And yet, I have not received an apology from you yet."

Explaining that I am not actually interested in living anywhere close to Eton Cottage is out of the question, especially since I simply said it to antagonize Miss Eton. It is most likely not going to guide this conversation in the direction that I would like so I decide to refrain from doing so. "Before I apologize, I need to know the truth, sister. How are you finding Eton Cottage and its occupants?"

Evelyn's back returns to a rigid posture. "I have not lied to you, Eddy. I am enjoying myself."

"I'm not accusing you of lying, and I am sure you are

having a grand time, but I do feel as though you are purposefully neglecting to tell me things as to avoid the need to lie to me."

Evey rolls her eyes, "What is it you think I am keeping from you? Perhaps you believe she has shared with me secret maps over each ballroom in London with all their exits marked for easy escape?" She's standing now, pacing around the room, her mocking tone increasing in volume with each suggestion. "Or did you find the foul-smelling perfume she gifted me for when I was to dance with undesirable men?" She throws both hands in the air. "No, I know. You must have overheard her telling me the best ways to poison suitors without their notice."

Honestly, I do not disagree with the idea of perfume if there are undesirable men trying to attract my sister's attention, but I will not share that with her. "I am not in the mood for mocking, Evelyn." With a scowl on my face, "Are you content here?"

Evelyn stops at the door, pausing her exit as she turns to me. "Of course, I'm content. I'm more than content here, Edward. I have been shown nothing but love since entering this cottage. It is the first time in a year that I have not been expected to dress, act, and think like a prospective bride. Here, I can just be me. I have been reading, swimming, laughing, and taking comfort in knowing that nothing else is expected of me under this roof. Believe me or not, it is your choice, but Margo has not spent a moment since my arrival trying to discourage me from marriage."

Her shoulders slump, "I love you, brother, but this

holiday has not been about you; it is something I have done for myself, and I do not regret a moment of it."

With that, she walks out of my room and closes the door. I suppose I should be happy she does not slam it, although that is mostly not a courtesy to me but to our hosts. With a sigh, I realize I never actually apologized.

15

As we finish dinner that evening, the Landons excuse themselves early, and Mrs. Landon suggests that I offer for Eddy to join Evey and me by the fire for the evening to play cards.

As Eddy and Evey are moving the table closer to the fire, I fetch three glasses and my favorite bottle of wine. Before I know it, a heated debate begins. It is a matter of perspective who is responsible. The topic of discussion is whether Evey should be allowed to drink wine openly and socially. This is something that is typically only acceptable of married women in society. Unbeknownst to him, she had already partaken prior to his arrival.

"Let me see if I have this correct, Mr. Riley. It is fine for Evey to be out in society and enter the marriage market but not have some wine after dinner? While on holiday, miles away from London?" Evey's glass is already full, and she is a very bright girl. I walk to the opposite side of the room, and as planned, Eddy's complete attention turns toward me.

Evey takes a long sip.

"She is old enough to marry, yet I did not make that decision. Do I personally want to see her married this year…no. But that decision is not mine to make. Yet, I do not want her destroying her reputation in the marriage market either." When speaking of his sister, Eddy uses a different tone than when discussing other topics. He is a confident man in all conversations, but when he speaks of Evelyn, his true love for her is behind every word.

Evey takes another sip and places the glass quietly back on the table before calling her brother's attention. "You do not wish to see me married now?"

Eddy looks defeated at his sister. "Very few girls get married in their first season, and any serious suitors would have to get approval from our father, and I would also be present in the room."

"It would have been helpful to know that before I attended my first ball, I might not have been as terrified as I was. However, if I had not been so upset, I would have never met Margo, and we would not be sitting here. You are forgiven, brother." Evey picks up her glass, raises it to him, and takes a sip.

She makes me so proud.

Eddy gives his sister a disappointed look. "You will not tell Mother what has been said here, sister."

"Not a word," she replies. "I shall expect the same of you." She tips her glass and once again takes another sip.

"We shall see…" Eddy looks back at me. "And you, Miss Eton… I would ask that you not encourage such behavior from my sister. It is not acceptable in society for a young lady to enjoy liquor before marriage."

"Ha! Well, it is a good thing that we are not currently in society and there are no eligible gentlemen around who would be considering marriage with Miss Riley, is it not."

"Although, Margo, the same cannot be said for you!" Evey says while standing from her seat with her now empty glass.

"What do you mean, and what are you looking for?" I ask

"Well, my dear friend. You may not be in London, but technically, you are in the presence of an eligible gentleman." She nods her head in Eddy's direction.

Perhaps Evelyn should not be allowed such drinks if it is already impairing her memory. She is more than aware of her brother's utter disdain for me. "Evey, your brother has long since removed himself from the list of my possible suitors, and I'm quite sure he has also petitioned others to avoid my hand as well…"

"I did not realize you were interested in suitors, Miss Eton. Your actions in town demonstrate otherwise," Eddy responds with a smirk.

Evey lets out a mocking laugh. I know she is recalling our discussion about marrying for love. She best not mention this in front of her brother. Trying to change the subject, I ask her, "What are you looking for?"

"The bottle," Evey answers, raising her empty glass at me.

I clear my throat and raise the bottle that is on the floor by my side. She comes toward me, glass first. I refill her glass, then mine. Eddy holds his hand out for the bottle, and I pass it, thinking he is looking to refill his glass, but he just sets it down next to his chair.

"I suggest you make that glass last, sister. It will be your final drink of the evening."

"I am on holiday, brother. I can have some wine." He does not bother to respond. "Margo! Are you going to let him do this?"

Turning to face Eddy, I respond to Evey. "He may have a nearly empty bottle. We have other full bottles in the kitchen."

And so begins the argument.

"You may think you know everything, Miss Eton. But she is my sister, and I actually care about her health."

"Excuse me, sir! What are you insinuating?" He is drawing a line and making assumptions about my character. In my home, which he was *not* invited to. I was feeling my forced kindness beginning to wear toward him.

"From where I am sitting, it appears you will put no restraints on my younger sister and let her drink herself ill. Then who will care for her when she makes herself sick."

I may have a glass of wine running through my system, but that is not the cause of my outburst. He is hurting my feelings. I stand before speaking and look at him with a glare that I hope displays my murderous feelings toward him. Surprisingly, he rises from his seat and locks eyes with me. He is looking for a fight as if he is excited. I immediately change course; he must know his statement went too far.

I walk closer to him, barely an inch between us. He is not much taller than me. *Time to crush him.* "Is that what you really think of me, Eddy?" It works. With each word, I watch the amusement fall from his face. Using a nickname

I have not used in years, not since we were both much younger and much kinder toward each other.

Evey stays silent on the couch, looking between her brother and me.

"I know you disliked me for my choice not to marry yet. I know you think I am disrespecting the tradition of marriage. But this... I care for your sister. Even if we were not friends, I would not allow someone to make themselves ill or leave them while sick." The words come out more passionately than I want.

I certainly do not plan for my next words to crack as they leave my mouth. "I now understand why you rushed here from London when you found out she was staying with me. It was more than concern for my influence over her, but clearly, you thought I was such a monster; you worried her life was in danger."

His mouth opens, and the struggle for him to find the words is apparent on his face. It's not his turn to talk yet—I have more to say.

"I thought with your time here we were growing an understanding, but given your comment tonight, I see I have made no progress to show you that I am a decent person."

He remains silent.

"It is obvious the niceties you have displayed are only on behalf of the Landons. I will still thank you for your kindness to them. I'm sure you will waste no time returning to London to tell everyone how correct you were about me. But, just know, you will not make a difference. All of those men in London want nothing to do with me. Even the men who think they can stomach the idea of marrying me for my fortune. You will just be telling them what they have already decided about me is true." Unsure of why I am taking this so far, but I blame the wine and certainly not my bruised ego.

His look becomes confused with a hint of what I can only guess is embarrassment. As if to dismiss him, I walk over to Evey. Leaning over, I kiss her head. "Goodnight, darling. You know where to find me, especially if you feel sick at night."

She nods with a kind smile. Straightening my stance, I face him one more time. "Goodnight."

Averting his eyes, he returns a swift and silent nod.

Evey's whispers are not as quiet as she thinks they are as I can still hear her as I am walking up the stairs. As I approach my bedroom door, I hear hurried footsteps behind me. I do not look back—if it is Evey, she will follow me into my room, but I have a feeling they do not belong to her. The footsteps are too heavy. I grab the door handle as I feel his presence behind me.

"Miss Eton..." His tone is strong but quiet.

I turn to face him and notice Evey's door closing. She must have followed him but decided to listen from behind her bedroom door.

"The night is over, Mr. Riley. I think you have made your point." I'm not letting him off easily.

"Now I'm Mr. Riley; when moments ago you had no problem using my name again?" He is trying to bait me.

Not tonight.

I roll my eyes and turn away from him. His arm shoots out and blocks my door. I turn back to him with a huff and stare in silence.

"You were correct in what you said downstairs. About some things, but very wrong about others." As he speaks, his voice gets deeper and stronger with each word.

He clearly is still interested in arguing with me tonight, and I will be damned if I am going to give Edward Riley his way in my home. "Well, you can make a list for me, and I will review it in the morning. I am finished talking to you this evening."

"Just when I think I have witnessed a human side to you, Margo, you let your stubborn attitude get the best of you."

My name. This is the first time he has said it in years. It would mean something if he was not trying to use my own trick against me. "Maybe it is my stubborn attitude that keeps men like you at a distance, a very far distance, and if that is the case, I do not see any problem with it." I am raising my voice. I cannot help it. I just hope I do not alert the Landons.

"It may not be a problem today, but I promise it will catch up to you, Margo. You think this life is going to last forever. You will have to marry, and when you wait until the last possible moment, you will have to choose from a very small selection. Then what? What happens when you cannot find a decent man to marry because you waited too long?" He is right. It is something I have thought about many times, but he is wrong to assume there were good men available now.

"First, I find it interesting that you are so concerned with my marriage prospects. What do you care if I end up in an awful marriage, alone or on the streets? Second, you assume there are decent men interested in me now. Well,

I'm sure you will be happy to know. It is already too late for me to find a decent gentleman. Congratulations on your victory. Surely, that will help you sleep tonight." I hate being this honest with him.

"There is that very uncharming attitude of yours. You cannot claim to know the men of London because you never give any of them a chance to know you. You are living on borrowed time, and you need to realize this." Again, he is right. I will not win this argument, and I hate him for getting the best of me. I feel my inner child pushing through to stomp my foot at him as I let out a growl of frustration, but he will only use that against me later.

But one last parting comment slips from my lips. "Is marriage all I'm good for? Is being a wife fated to be my only desire? I come to the country to drop all the pretenses of formal city life. I come here to enjoy simple friendships and to just be me. Why is that not enough?"

His eyes hold a hint of sadness, but as his lips part to respond, I turn on my heels and sweep into my room, slamming the door. It is childish, but it feels good. I can hear Eddy let out a loud huff and I can picture his head shake that always accompanies the huff.

"Mr. Riley, may I have a word?" Mr. Landon's tone is one he rarely uses. I have heard it on occasion growing up when I stepped out of line a time or two. Thankfully, it has been years since he has used it with me. Not to mention, this is the first time Mr. Landon used Eddy's surname since he arrived.

Eddy's footsteps shuffle, Mr. Landon must have startled him from behind. "Mr. Landon, I did not see you there." His comment is met with silence, which is even worse than the tone. Eddy takes the hint. "Of course, sir. What did you want to discuss?"

Footsteps walk further away from my door. I take a seat on the other side of my door, getting as close to the gap on the floor as possible. I want to hear this. "I can respect your reason for being here, Mr. Riley. Wanting to protect your sister is an honorable act. You have been here for a full day and have not removed your sister from our home, so I imagine you deem it a suitable place. Just as you are being protective of your sister, I want to make it known that I am protective of my daughter. If you continue to push Margo to arguments, I will have to step in."

My heart swells, I love Mr. and Mrs. Landon as my parents, and I knew they felt the same. But it was another step for them to discuss it with an outsider. My own father never cared enough to be in my presence, let alone protect me from another. I was a business plan to my father. But to Mr. Landon, my papa. I was his daughter who he taught to stand up for herself, but still just as happy to come to my defense when needed.

"You're daughter? Margo is *your daughter*?" Oh no, Eddy, do not take this the wrong way. The last thing I need is for a rumor to spread that I am not the actual heir to the Eton estate.

"She is the blood of Lord and Lady Eton; you can be sure of that, Mr. Riley. Yet, she is mine in every other sense of the word. I held her hand when she took her first steps, and I was there when she lost her first tooth. She is my daughter, and I will not allow the home my wife and I worked so hard to make a place of comfort for Margo to be infected with the negative attitude you hold. You are more than welcome to stay and enjoy yourself and our company, or you can take your leave, Mr. Riley."

"I understand, sir. My sister is happier here than I have seen her in a long time. I appreciate you letting her visit. My concerns were unfounded."

"Evey is more than welcome to stay as long as she likes. She is a beautiful and charming young lady, Mr. Riley. I hope you do not find yourself so preoccupied with your own agenda that you miss the opportunity to really get to know her."

"Thank you, you are very kind. I am sorry for the disruption I have caused to your family. I can take my leave tonight if you would prefer. Please send Margo my apologies." I can hear Eddy's feet start to move.

Why do I have a pit in my stomach?

It would be much more peaceful if he left. But, our interactions have improved slightly, not that Mr. Landon saw those.

"I did not say that you need to leave. You are welcome to stay if you can act as a gentleman. And I will not relay your apologies to my daughter for you. If you are truly sorry, you will tell her yourself." I hear Mr. Landon's loud feet walking away. I can only hope Eddy takes Mr. Landon's advice and stays a little longer.

The hallway goes quiet. I move away from the door and into my bed.

As soon as the door to my room closes, I move directly for my bags and begin to pack. How could I let my emotions get the best of me? I should know better than to allow my guard down around Margaret Eton. My sole reason for being here is my sister. Why do I care what happens to Margo? I do not. I just need to make sure she does not convince Evey to make the same mistakes.

A soft knock came at the door.

Could it be Margo? Why is my chest tightening at the thought of her being on the other side of this door? Am I afraid to face her? Am I hopeful it is her so I can apologize for being so blunt?

Another soft knock, then a whisper I recognize, "Eddy, it's Evey. Let me in."

Disappointment floods me, but I refuse to think about why it does. I rush to open the door, and my sister closes it behind her. "I heard the argument," she states without a hint of emotion behind her voice. "And I heard Mr. Landon speak with you." She waits for me to say something, and when I remain quiet, she continues, "You were wrong to talk to her like that." Again little emotion behind her words.

"I understand, and I apologized to him. I'm glad you came by. If you would return to your room to pack, we will be on our way in the morning," I instruct her.

"You are welcome to pack, brother. I will not be leaving in the morning. I have no reason to leave. I did not offend our hosts, and neither did our hosts offend you. You are the only one in the wrong here, and if you choose to run from your poor actions, you will do it alone." I sit down on my bed. When did my sister grow into such a mature woman? I look at her in awe. "Eddy, I need you to be honest. Why did you say those things to Margo?"

At the mention of Miss Eton, my frustration returns. "You will have to be more specific. There were many things discussed this evening," I say, still not willing to take the blame completely.

"Outside her bedroom door. You were cruel and oddly specific. The argument downstairs was far more spontaneous and typical of the two of you. When you were in the hallway, it was detailed. So much so that I cannot help but think that it has crossed your mind prior to this evening." She holds her stance a few feet away from my bed. Her arms crossed in front of her and her gaze staring through me.

"Margaret's decisions have crossed my mind, all in terms of you and the impact her decisions can have on younger girls." It is a lie—not a complete lie, but not the complete truth either.

Evey remains quiet as she steps closer to me and eventually sits down next to me, but not turning to face me when she speaks. "The night I met Margo, she told me only those that really know her call her by that nickname." She meets my gaze now, "You have called her Margo twice, and before that, she called you Eddy." She pauses for an explanation. I remain silent. "You knew each other before I met her."

Aside from our father, no one in my family is aware of my connection to Miss Eton, and he does not know much beyond that we were friendly as children. I never spoke about her to anyone, including Albert, except for the few occasions she would get under my skin. "Yes, we knew each other as children. Her father had business with our father, and as the only Eton heir, Margaret was included in many business dealings."

Evelyn looks at me in only the way she can. She sees through me, sees feelings I am not even ready to admit to myself. Unsure of how my face looks to her, I only see empathy staring back at me. "Something must have happened between you that would cause this much hatred in you for her. Yet, I do not know if it is hatred, but maybe another emotion that you are not expressing clearly?"

Leaning forward with my elbows on my knees, I rest my face in my hands. How can my sister understand what is happening here better than I could? Staying like this for a while, Evey rubs my back in silence. I am not deserving of such an amazing sister.

After some time has passed, Evey says, "As I said before, I will be staying, and I hope you do the same. I think you need to spend some more time at Eton Cottage to resolve these feelings. While you are here, try to be a little nicer to our host."

I pick up my head and turn to hug her. "Sister, I will stay and promise to improve in the coming days." I pull back and hold her hands. "I truly came with only your best interest at heart."

She rubs my knuckles with her thumbs. "I know, Eddy. But I think you have witnessed enough to know I am not in any danger. Unexpectedly, I believe it is you who may be changed during this holiday." She kisses my forehead and walks to the door only stopping to say goodnight before she leaves.

After unpacking my bags and returning them to their original place in the corner of my room, I find myself in bed wondering what tomorrow could look like for me at Eton Cottage. Mr. Landon was clear he was not going to tolerate any more arguments between Margo and me. I did not plan to upset her. Our discussions tend to accelerate to an argument. Though, this is the first one that truly seemed to upset Margo. I am not an angry man —I cannot recall speaking with anyone the way I did with her. The trouble is, she is just as argumentative as I am.

Tonight, we—no, I—crossed the line. I should not have pushed the subject of her marriage so much. I should have stopped when she tried to end the conversation outside her bedroom, but I blocked her. Now, I need to decide how to make it up to her. Showing concern is not wrong but using it against her is something I need to apologize to her in the morning.

As soon as I wake the next morning until I am ready to leave my room, I repeat my apology to myself, so I do not forget it. Every muscle in my body is tight, and I must remind myself to breathe as I plan to speak with Margo before either of us can sit down to eat.

Upon my approach to the dining area, I hear voices, all but the one I am looking for. Perhaps she is in the kitchen cooking breakfast. I head in that direction but only find Mrs. Landon alone. I greet her good morning and proceed to the table once again, only to be disappointed that Margo is not seated there. After greeting Mr. Landon and Evey with a good morning, my sister notices who I am looking for. "She has not yet come down."

"Thank you, sister. Would you mind going to fetch her? I would like to apologize before sitting down to eat," I ask, noticing Mr. Landons smile at my words.

After a few moments in silence, my sister returns as Mrs. Landon delivers the morning's breakfast. "She is not in her room," Evey speaks in the direction of the Landons. They exchange a look, and Mrs. Landon responds, "Eddy, Evey, please sit down before the eggs get cold. I will go look for her." She does not appear to be worried, but I am. I barely touch my food until she returns.

Mrs. Landon speaks to Evelyn, "Margo is fine. I think she is just taking some time to herself this morning. I'm sure she will be around later."

Clearly, Margo wants to be alone, and Mrs. Landon is not going to give up her location in the house. If it would not be considered impolite, I would have gone through every room in the house until I found her.

Eddy's words repeated endlessly in my head until the sun began to rise the next morning. My worry is not his fault—he spoke only the truth, but hearing it aloud made it more real than ever before. I have known for years that it was a mistake to refuse the idea of marriage during my early years in society.

Once my father announced that his title and land would be given to my husband, it was immediately apparent that any hope for a love match was no longer an option. My suitors were more aggressive in their perusal of me, getting short with me when I would attempt to get to know them. It did not take long for me to dismiss each one of them.

Now, I risk this life I have built with the Landons by refusing to acknowledge our inevitable future.

Without any sleep, I know I won't be able to restrain my emotions around anyone especially not around him. Looking back out the window, I am certain I am the only one in the house awake at this hour. It is too early to run off to Lily's home, but I want to be alone. I change into a day dress and head to the library. I leave a book on my pillow; the Landons will understand it means I am in the library. I cannot imagine Mr. Landon withheld his exchange with Eddy last night from Mrs. Landon. Evey might come looking for me, but Mrs. Landon will cover for me.

The library provides a sense of comfort. It is a place that offers me a chance to live many different lives and guarantee happy endings. It is not lost on me that I most often seek books with happy endings because it is not likely that I will have my own. I select a book I have not read in years. I cannot remember all of the details, but I remember very much enjoying it. This will provide enough distraction to settle my mind.

"Margo, dear," comes from a soft voice accompanied by a gentle nudge. Mrs. Landon is standing above me with a bowl of fruit in her hand. The book falls to the floor as I begin to sit up from the odd position I moved into while sleeping in the oversized chair.

"Darling, you've been up here all day. I checked on you this morning and wanted to let you sleep, but I was getting worried that you have not ate yet today."

Rubbing my eyes, I notice the curtains which were open when I came into the library are now closed. I can assume that was Mrs. Landon's doing this morning. "Thank you, Mrs. Landon. I was unable to sleep last night and came to the library to settle my mind."

"Clearly, you were able to settle enough to sleep most of the day."

"I'm sorry, I did not realize. Is Evey offended?" In all my self-pity, I hope I have not offended my guest.

"I cannot imagine anything that would offend that sweet girl. I think she was just concerned...after last night..." Mrs. Landon is so easy to read. I know she wants to talk about the argument with Eddy. I am not sure where to start, but I do want to talk to her about this. Eddy let the cat out of the bag, and I do not believe I could ever put it back. It's time to face the facts.

"He did not say anything that is not true." I do not look at her at first. "While in London, I have been attending balls and social events, but I never take them seriously. I spend most nights just waiting for the moment I can leave." I finally look at her. "I never give any gentlemen a chance to get to know me. I just assume they are hunting for my fortune and will destroy my life and everything I love about it. How can I trust any of them not to lie to me until the vows are exchanged and then turn into another person completely?" The words are coming out quicker as I continue to speak. The panic begins taking over during my admission.

Mrs. Landon pulls me into her arms. "Oh, my sweet Margo, I understand your concern, but that does not mean you should not try to find love."

"What if I spend the next season looking for someone and cannot find anyone?" There it is. Confessing my true fear out loud did not feel as good as I had hoped it would.

"I do not think you know what you are looking for, Margo. It is not fair for you to make assumptions that these men aren't what you want when you do not even know what you are looking for. Did you ever really stop to think about that?"

"I want someone who truly loves me. Like you and Mr. Landon or Lily and Lord Calderwood."

"Yes, well, before you can know if someone loves you, you have to spend time with them. Have conversations, shared interests, and values. Something that cannot be achieved with just one dance." I sigh. She is right. I need to get serious about marriage. She continues, "Margo, I'm not saying you need to pick a husband tomorrow, you do still have time, years most likely, but it is better to start now and take your time."

I wrap my arms around her neck and whisper in her ear, "I am so thankful for you. I promise, when I pick someone, I will guarantee they will be just as good to you. I won't let anything happen to you."

"My sweet Margo, all we want is for you to be happy, and we will be too. I am certain we will always be together." She pulls back and pushes my hair back. "Now, about our guests..."

"They are not leaving, are they?"

"I do not believe Evey has any intention of leaving. She has been asking about you all day. I believe she feels some responsibility for the argument last night, as it was her brother's behavior that caused you to go into hiding today."

"Of course, I do not blame her. It has been a pleasure having her here."

"That is what I told her. I think she will feel better when she sees that you are all right."

"Mr. Riley told Mr. Landon that he would leave

immediately last night after their discussion…" I look at her, waiting for confirmation of Eddy's departure.

"Mr. Riley has been in an interesting state since the morning, but he is still here, and I have yet to see his bags packed."

"Interesting state?"

"You will see…" she says with a smile and then continues, "Now, my girl. You have spent more than enough time with your self-pity in this library and catching up on your lost sleep. You have a plan for going forward, and it's time to continue with your life. You are not allowed back in this library for at least two days. Do you understand?"

Most people think I get my tough attitude from Mr. Landon. He is tougher on the outside but soft on the inside. His wife is the exact opposite. If he were to come up and sit with me this morning, he would let me lie here, cry, and bring me all my meals for the next week.

Mrs. Landon is a very sweet lady on the outside but extremely tough on the inside. Again, I find myself being extremely thankful to be raised by such a strong woman. "Yes, I understand," I say as she rises from the chair and holds out her hand for me to follow.

"Now, wash up, get dressed, and take on this day like any other. This is your world, little one; go and take it! Think of it this way—you can get any man you want. You are not every other young lady who hopes for the best. You get to pick the best for you."

I give her another long hug that ends with my "Yes, Mama," and out the door I go, down to my room to get dressed for what is left of the day.

When I enter the sitting room, I find only Mr. Landon. "How's my girl this...evening?" he says to me with a joking smile.

"I did not realize the time lost in a good book, I suppose," I respond, walking over to where he is sitting. As soon as I am close enough, I throw my arms around him and thank him for last night.

"That is what fathers do, Margo."

"I am the luckiest girl in the world to have a proactive parent like you, Papa." I stand back up, listening to hear Evey and Eddy, only to be met by silence. "Am I to assume that you have fed Mr. Riley to the horses this morning? Is that why he is missing?"

"Yes," Mr. Landon replies with a wide smile. "His sister is headed home to inform the family of his tragic passing." I laugh. I guess you can say I received Mr. Landon's sense of humor, too.

"Who's tragic passing are we discussing today?" *It couldn't be.* A voice I so longed to hear... "I attempt to leave the country on holiday, and within a month's time, you two have already committed a murder?" Mr. Berry shouts with a large smile across his face.

I am not sure who runs to greet him quicker, Mr. Landon or myself. I manage to jump into Albert's arms, then allow Mr. Landon to give him a warm handshake.

Mrs. Landon pushes us both out of the way. "Albert!" Her voice sings, "Margo said you would be in Greece for months. What a pleasant surprise! I would much rather you be here than countries away." She quickly wraps her arms around him.

My family loves Albert just as they love Lily. In truth, they both are considered a part of our family. Before Mrs. Landon decides where to seat him, she starts with questions about when he last ate. "I am quite all right at the moment, Mrs. Landon, thank you."

"Are you here to stay, Albert? I do not see any bags, and I must insist you do not make your way back to the city this evening," Mrs. Landon asks.

"Actually, I stopped to see Lady Calderwood before coming here. She has graciously agreed to host me while I'm visiting you both in the country and informed me that you already have a guest. Is Miss Riley still staying with you?" He begins looking around.

If he stopped at Lily's first, he must know that Eddy is here too, but he has yet to mention his friend. Has she received my letter? I forgot to ask Mr. Landon if he dropped them off. Before I can ponder this any further, Albert pulls a letter out of his pocket and hands it to me. "This is from Lily. She asked me to give it to you when I saw you. I believe she is hoping you and Miss Riley will visit her tomorrow afternoon for tea."

"Thank you. Yes, Miss Riley is here. I'm not sure where she is at the moment." I answer, and Mrs. Landon continues, "She is out on a walk to the lake."

"She went for a walk alone?" Albert asks, with a hint of sarcasm in his tone. "Well, Margo, your independence has certainly rubbed off on the young Riley girl quite quickly."

Mrs. Landon interjects, "She is not alone, Albert. Not

long after Miss Riley arrived, her older brother, Mr. Riley, came to stay with us as well."

Albert lets out a loud laugh and turns to Mr. Landon. "Well, that explains the murder you were referencing when I walked in, Mr. Landon."

"Yes, the very same, Albert," Mr. Landon confirms, returning Albert's smile.

"Although, I'm surprised Margo let him live long enough for you to get your hands on him." Albert mocks me, "I'm thoroughly disappointed that I missed your reaction when he entered the house, Margo." I roll my eyes and shake my head. Today is not the day to concentrate on my anger toward Eddy. "I would love the chance to stretch my legs. Margo, what do you say to walking down to the lake with me to meet with your guests?" Albert stands and extends his arm to me. I stand and slip my hand around his arm.

Both the Landons give me a nod of encouragement before I exit the door with Albert. As tough as I feel, I am more than grateful that I will not have to face Eddy alone when I see him for the first time after last night. This will break the awkwardness between us, and I can act like it never happened.

Once we leave the house, Albert insists that I share everything that has happened since Eddy's arrival. I never get a chance to ask why he is not in Greece. I suppose that conversation can wait until we are with everyone.

As soon as he is caught up in the events of last night and how I hid in the library all morning, he stops walking. Up until this point, he has kept a straight face, but now he stops dead, turns to me, and places his hands on my shoulders. He takes a deep breath and looks at me as if he is going to be able to see the pain Eddy caused me on my body. When he is done, he pulls me into him. Holding me in a hug, breathing heavily. I can feel how tense his body is, and he lets out a soft "I'm sorry."

Tears water in my eyes; Albert truly cares about me. "Albert, you have nothing to be sorry for."

I start to pull away, and he lets me, but he keeps his hold on my shoulders and looks into my eyes. "I'm sorry I wasn't here sooner. I know you have the Landons, and I know you are one of the strongest women I know, but he is my friend, and if I had any idea he would have done this, I would have stopped it before he could have come." Albert, always my protector, both in London and now the country. I give him another quick hug and pull away to place my hand in his arm again. I want to keep walking before I allow myself to get upset again.

"You know, you cannot protect me from everything in this world, Albert." He starts to speak, but I cut him off. "But I greatly appreciate it when you try to," I say with a smile. "What he said was the truth, and I cannot expect any communication between us to be amicable, so it sounded harsher than it needed to be. I spoke with Mrs. Landon this morning, she pointed out that his words only bothered me so much because they were fears I already had but would not acknowledge. I need to start taking the idea of marriage more seriously and be open to finding someone to fall in love with before it is too late."

"She is a wise woman, and so are you, Margo."

Before our conversation can continue, we approach the lake as Evey and Eddy come into view. They do not notice us at first, so I look over at Albert. With a silent exchange, I ask if he wants to surprise them first or not. He takes the invite and loudly yells in their direction.

"Edward Riley, enjoying a sunny day by the lake at the estate of a Miss Margaret Eton... A scandal if I have ever seen one!" Albert is perfect in so many ways. He is aware of my nerves after seeing Eddy today and he is able to completely break the tension with a joke. I am able to smile on his arm, completely unphased by Eddy's surprise.

"Margo!" Evey yells as she jumps up from the grass. Albert and I let go of each other to go to each of the Riley siblings. I grab onto Evey, and motion for her to sit back down and begin asking about the book she was reading.

"Albert! Why aren't you in Greece?" Eddy asks as he and Albert meet for a handshake, and then he looks in my direction. We make eye contact, but I keep my face completely indifferent. He opens his mouth as if to address me, but Albert cuts him off.

"Eddy, I'm happy to tell you about my lack of adventure, but I think your current destination is a far more interesting story... Walk with me." The last three words are said with a stern voice. All three of us take note when Albert says them.

Eddy addresses us, "We will meet you at the house later." Evey just nods, and I keep still.

As soon as the gentlemen are far enough away, Evey grabs my hands in her own. "Margo, please accept my apologies for last night... I cannot believe..." I hold her hands up and look her in the eye.

"Evey, stop right there. You have nothing to apologize

for. Eddy's actions are not yours, and you should never feel responsible for another's bad behavior. I'm so glad you are here. Your company is worth more than any annoying argument with your brother."

"Oh, Margo. I was so worried when I could not find you this morning. I thought you would never want to see me again. I know you do not, but please do not give what Eddy said any second thought. He is just turning his frustrations onto you. Our parents have been insisting he needs to marry before his thirtieth birthday. He does not have any interest in the young, eligible ladies my mother brings to the house. Anything he says to you about marriage, just tell him he needs to worry about himself first."

This information does not come as a shock to me. "Evey, that is a good thing your parents are focusing on his marriage prospects. It might give you a break for the next few seasons."

"I would love a break from never-ending social occasions and men who are far too old for me! I think I will promise to help my mother find Eddy the perfect girl when I return to town. I think she would like that."

Mrs. Riley might see through Evey's attempts to distract her, but now that her daughter has entered society, she could be a valuable asset in connecting her brother to the eligible young ladies of London. Although, I struggle to imagine Eddy would be interested in marrying a girl of Evey's age. I stop myself before I put too much thought into Eddy's preferences for a wife—something just doesn't feel right about it. "Please share your pursuits.

I will need to send my sympathies to the girl he eventually marries."

We both laugh and then return to enjoying each other's company as we did before Mr. Riley arrived.

I could not be more grateful to Albert for staying for dinner. His presence in the room keeps Mr. Riley and me on our best behavior. We are able to participate in shared conversations but never address each other directly. As Albert is leaving, he confirms that Evey and I will be by the following afternoon to visit with Lily. He nods at Eddy but does not mention any plans. Edward excuses himself shortly after, and Evey and I spend the remainder of the night playing cards with the Landons.

18

Margo did not emerge from her hiding spot until late in the afternoon, and I was unsuccessful in delivering my offer of apology. My sister and I both felt the guilt of Margo secluding herself from our company. Upon Mrs. Landon's suggestion, we spent most of the day at the lake reading.

It is growing later in the day when Margo finally joins us, to my surprise, accompanied by my best friend, who I thought was in Greece. After the shock of seeing him subsides, I turn to face Margo and plan to accept the wrath of the previous night's argument she surely has planned for me. She holds her face as if meeting a stranger. She never speaks to me but turns all of her attention to my sister. When I attempt to engage her, eager to apologize, Albert interrupts and insists we take a walk together.

"Eddy, you are like a brother to me, but you better have a good reason for coming out here and treating Margo like this." Once we are far enough away from the girls, Albert turns on me. As he should for how I have behaved. "And do not give me some bullshit that this is for your sister. Evelyn has nothing to do with you treating Margo as you have."

He is getting closer to me. This may be the first argument between Albert and me, but it is clear he is ready to defend Margo in any form needed. "Explain yourself immediately."

Letting out a deep breath, the only way I am going to save this friendship is by being honest with him. "I'm sorry, I acted poorly, Albert, and I have no excuse for it. Just know, I am sorry...more sorry than you can understand."

He stares at me, still not looking satisfied. "Well, that is a good start, my boy, but I am going to need more detail than that." He is right; I am able to think more clearly in Margo's absence, and he is the person I want to confide in. Over the next hour, I tell him everything.

We walk in silence for more time than I can bear. Finally, I ask, "How do you recommend I proceed here, Albert?" I genuinely need his advice.

"You've got yourself into quite the predicament. I have known Margo for years. She's a tough but stubborn girl. You hit a nerve with her. I recommend following her lead; I doubt she will admit how much she was affected."

"You think I should stay?" I ask the questions I am terrified that he will affirm.

"If that is what you want. If you want to resolve this matter with Margo, even if you are just doing it for your sister. I cannot see this resolving itself if you were to leave.

But do not push her if she does not want to acknowledge it. Just move forward if she allows it."

Albert explains that his travels are rescheduled, and he found himself at Lady Calderwood's when Margo's letter about my visit to Eton Cottage arrived. He agrees to join the Landons for dinner that evening, acting as a distraction from the previous night's events.

While Margo never speaks to me, she does carry on a conversation with everyone else at the table as though nothing has happened to offend her. I speak with the rest of our party as well, not pressing her to talk to me. It is then I notice how pleasant she can be in a room full of people she cares about. I cannot help but feel jealous that her smiles and laughter are never directed at me.

Not wanting to upset her further, I take the opportunity to retire early in the evening. Settling myself with a good book, reading with one candle and the moonlight. Tomorrow, Lady Calderwood has invited Margo and Evey over for tea, and Albert extended the invitation for me to visit with him as well. I told him I would consider it and decide if I should give the girls some more space.

A soft knock comes at my door, very familiar to the one that came last night. "Evey?" I ask before opening it.

"Yes, brother. Let me in," she answers.

"How was the rest of your evening, Sister?" I ask her.

"It was pleasant, but your company was missed." I look at her with surprise, and she continues, "By me..." and gives a mischievous smile.

"I am glad you enjoyed it. To what do I owe for tonight's visit? I must say, my behavior today has been much improved since your visit last night."

"It is sad that your improved behavior is simply because you have not spoken with Miss Eton the entire day," she answers in a mocking tone, and I shrug in response. "We are planning to visit Lady Calderwood's tomorrow. Are you planning to join us to see Albert?"

"I have yet to decide. I will sleep on it," I answer honestly.

"Are you planning to avoid Margo for the remainder of your stay? If that is the case, you might as well leave," she asks, sounding slightly frustrated.

"I truly am still undecided on how to approach Miss Eton, Evelyn, but I am hoping for suggestions, and you seem to have an opinion."

"I am so glad you asked, Brother. I think you should spend time with Margo. Alone. You need to decide what you are feeling toward her and then move forward." Evelyn makes it sound like such an easy task. It is clear she has never been in love before. I roll my eyes with a sigh as she continues, "Don't huff at me!"

"Huff? I never huff. I am breathing," I answer in defense.

"You huff when you do not get your way. Even Margo has noticed your huff. You do it quite often." Margo noticed? And she mentioned it to my sister. What else did they say about me?

Evelyn stands. "I think I will be too tired to make the journey tomorrow and you should accompany Margo to the Calderwood's. Keep the huffing to a minimum." She quickly turns to leave but says over her shoulder, "You are welcome." The door closes behind her.

Tossing and turning, thinking of tomorrow, has left me unable to find sleep. My sister is devious in her plan to decline tomorrow's invitation. Perhaps she can see more than I can. Does she notice evidence of a friendship that was dissolved long ago? Or she may just be trying to distract my attention away from her.

We have been known to do that throughout the years when entertaining less-than-desirable relatives during the holidays. That is not likely. It could be that my actions toward Margo, both negative and positive, have been more emotional than any interaction I have shared with acquaintances in London. Outside of my family, I am known for being aloof to those around me. This may be the first time Evelyn has witnessed me give such attention to a young lady. Margo is different. She is not just some young lady—she is my friend...

Could we be friends again?

I know better than to trust her with more than my friendship, but I cannot go down that road. I must prepare myself for tomorrow, spending time alone with Margo on our journey to Lady Calderwood's estate. For Evelyn and the possibility of a renewed friendship, I will be kind and polite during our journey.

19

I sleep in most of the morning hours which forces me to rush in getting dressed for my visit with Lily this afternoon. When I find my way to the kitchen, it is empty. Assuming Evey was up earlier, I quickly eat a bowl of fruit before heading to the stables.

"Good morning, Mr. Landon," I call as soon as he comes into view. We discussed last night that I would travel to Lily's on horseback to increase the time I can spend with her rather than traveling by foot.

"Good morning, Margo," he calls in return while hitching the saddle to my favorite horse, Lady. She is beautiful, mostly brown, with small spots of white fur throughout her body. Her mane is as dark as my hair. "She is just about ready for your journey."

I approach Lady and begin petting her nose. "Hello, my beautiful Lady." Looking around for Jack, the horse Evey is riding during her stay, I notice he is ready with his saddle already in place. Though, Evey is not here yet. Mr. Landon notices my confusion and answers the question I do not need to speak aloud. "She is not coming. Did Mrs. Landon not tell you?"

"No, I have not seen anyone since I left my room."

"Mrs. Landon checked on you both this morning. She said you were still sleeping. When she checked in on Evey, she was awake and unsure about joining you for today's journey."

"Is she unwell? Should I go be with her? Lily will surely understand."

"No, that is not necessary. Mrs. Landon must be with her now. From what she said, it was more exhaustion than illness. I think that she just needs a day to rest."

The house has been full of stress since Eddy arrived, and I promised her a peaceful and relaxing vacation. Jack neighs, and before I can question why he is saddled, the answer walks up behind me.

"Morning, Mr. Landon," Eddy's voice rings throughout the stables.

"Morning, Edward. I have Jack saddled and ready for you."

"Thank you, sir." Eddy walks past me toward Jack. "Morning, Margo," he says with a cautious smile.

"Good morning, Mr. Riley." I politely smile but decide to use his formal name to let him know I am still a little upset with him. "May I ask why you will be riding Jack today? Are you going into town?" *Or leaving*, I think to myself with equal hope and disappointment.

"I have plans to meet with Mr. Berry at Lady Calderwood's estate this afternoon," he answers with a hint of excitement in his statement.

Mr. Landon interjects, "Looks like you will have a

riding partner after all, Margo." I scowl toward him and see the smile across his face as he finishes with Lady's saddle. "You are all set."

"Thank you, Mr. Landon. I plan to be back before nightfall."

"Be mindful of the weather, Margo. If it is storming, wait until tomorrow to return," he says with his firm and parental tone.

"Yes, of course," I say as I move to mount Lady. "With so few clouds in the sky, I do not believe we will need to worry about the rain. Mr. Landon."

Eddy is already on Jack with the reins in his hand as he waits for me. I give Mr. Landon a wink over my shoulder, then meet Eddy's gaze as I mount my horse. Eddy's face contorts as his brain tries to process what he is seeing. It starts with confusion, then surprise, and then his face finally settles on anger.

"Miss Eton," he says with a clear indication that I have achieved my purpose of upsetting him yet again. "Do you not know how to ride sidesaddle?"

"I am very well trained in riding sidesaddle, Mr. Riley. I am simply choosing not to this afternoon."

"What if you are hurt?" He knows precisely what to say to upset me. "Or seen."

"As we have discussed, being seen in the country is not a concern for me. I can also promise that Mr. Landon spent numerous hours teaching me how to properly ride a horse. You are welcome to quiz him before we leave if you'd like." I know taunting Eddy with Mr. Landon is childish, but I still enjoy it.

"I can promise you, Eddy, she can handle her own on a

horse. Now, before you two waste the entire day bickering in the stables, I think it is time for you to begin your trip. Be safe," Mr. Landon says with a smile in my direction, and then he gives Eddy a nod.

"Try not to spend the entire time arguing. I will see you both upon your return." I know he means we are to travel back together. I am grateful that he does not stress this in front of Eddy, who might twist it into that, as a Lady, I cannot handle the trip alone. This is not his intention, but Mr. Landon did have a strict rule about traveling in pairs. I could respect his concern and follow his wishes.

The ride begins quietly. While we ride close enough for conversation, it is quite some time before we can think of anything to say to each other. My thoughts travel to Evey and how much we would have to talk about if she were my companion today. I wonder what she would think of Eddy and I traveling together. She would probably be telling us both to be nice. While this silence does not include arguing, it is not exactly a friendly conversation either. She is our shared interest, so maybe we can keep a conversation on the topic of his sister to pass the time until we arrive at Lily's estate.

"Were you able to check in on your sister this morning? I did not have the chance before we left, but Mr. Landon said she was staying back to rest," I ask.

He responds, "Yes, I saw her this morning with Mrs. Landon. She does not appear to be in ill health but more in need of a restful day."

"The country can be tiring. She is in good hands with the Landons. They are the very best at spoiling someone."

He looks back and, with a genuine smile, answers, "I am not sure it was the country she was tired of, but the Landons are impeccable people. There are few I would trust as much with my sister."

"What do you think is the cause of her exhaustion? Did she mention something?"

"She did not mention any specifics, but I can imagine she wanted a day of rest away from our bickering. While we are capable of war between each other, I think we are both guilty of forgetting her feelings of being caught in the middle."

I feel my entire body sink at his confession. I have been feeling the same about Evey's situation, but that it caused her to want to remove herself from my company breaks my heart.

"I'm so sorry, Eddy. I—" He cuts me off before I can finish.

"I cannot blame you, Margo. I am just as much at fault if not more. I feel no one in this world can love my sister as I do, but I am just as guilty of causing her such distress."

"I suppose we can try to be a little more mindful of our actions around her," I suggest.

"Yes." I can see he is not going to give more away than needed.

"I understand what we have between us will not change, but we must respect your sister's company." Pleading with him, hoping we can come to a truce.

"Perhaps at the end of the day, we could retire, write down all of the thoughts we had in her presence, and then just slip them under each other's doors to be read in private." His face appears like that of a great philosopher who just discovered gravity.

I laugh—I cannot help it. But I genuinely laugh. "Mr. Riley, I think that is a marvelous idea. I shall be sure to keep a list in my head of the many insults I think of for you during the day."

"Yes, I would be disappointed if the list was not comprehensive, Miss Eton."

"You have my word, sir." With that oddly positive exchange, we remain peacefully quiet until we arrive outside of Lily's estate.

Albert and Lily greet us upon our arrival and welcome us into the foyer of the large estate. A round table sits at the center, displaying vases filled with the most beautiful roses. There must be dozens. I gravitate toward the flower arrangement, leaving my friends to follow behind me.

"Is this how you repay Lady Calderwood for your stay, Albert?" Eddy asks behind me. They all chuckle.

Albert replies, "While I wish I could claim responsibility for the young ladies' delight at the flowers, I did not send them. They come from an admirer of Miss Eton."

My shoulders slump and I back away, turning to Lily for confirmation. She nods with an apologetic look on her face. It is not her fault; it is not even the roses' fault, but then their color dims just the slightest with this information.

"Who sent these flowers?" Eddy's voice is lower, and

all humor has disappeared. "Why were they sent here and not to Eton Cottage?"

"Someone of so little importance that I do not share information about Eton Cottage with him. It's better if he believes I spend my time here at the Calderwood Estate when I am in the country." Harold Granger has not crossed my mind since I last saw him in the city, as it should be, but then he likes to send gifts to remind me.

Albert and Eddy share a look while Lily interjects, "It is better...at least for the majority of the time. He typically sends flowers, sometimes gifts, always with letters."

"That I have directed her to place into the nearest fire," I add with a wicked smile.

"Yes, with the exception of the few times he has shown up unannounced looking for an audience with you." She laughs and rolls her eyes.

"He has come here uninvited to see you?" Eddy is addressing me now.

"Yes, and I'm thankful I was only here once. The other times, Lady Calderwood simply said I was feeling ill in bed." I shrug.

Agitation spreads across Eddy's face. He attempts to ask more, but Albert interrupts, "Shall we get started with our days?"

We quickly separate into pairs. Albert and Eddy go off for a hunt on the property, and Lily has tea and sandwiches for us on the terrace.

We take a seat, and she excuses her staff before she sits back in her chair. "You two seemed cordial enough this afternoon. Have you finally made peace?"

I laugh while shaking my head. "Only a peaceful agreement."

"Explain," she says with a knowing look.

"We have decided to be civil for his sister's sake. I'm afraid she declined today's invitation to get a break from the bickering."

"I cannot say I'm surprised the young lady would seek a quiet day. Mr. Riley and you are both fierce warriors and tend to declare war on any enjoyment that may be had during your battles."

"Is it that disruptive?" When I do not think I could feel worse, Lily is making things even more clear for me.

"Margo, I have known you for more years than I have not. I have been present to your distaste for others, but none compare to when you and Mr. Riley share the same room."

"Well, now we have a common interest—his sister. We both decided to be much improved...more mannered around her." It does seem unlikely that we will be able to agree on something, but I hope my words hold true.

"Well, aside from your letters and what Albert connected to me last night, has anything else of note happened between you?"

"Other than our planned truce for Evey on the journey here, no." There is certainly nothing to tell about how he looked when he arrived drenched from the rainstorm or how it felt when I grabbed his arm and he placed his hand on mine. "Enough about Mr. Riley. It has been weeks since we have parted. How has your rest and relaxation been? And your unexpected guest showed up days ago. Tell me all about it!"

Lily shares her days are mostly filled with reading and painting since she returned from London and how happy she is that Albert decided to join her for some time. She shares that she was growing lonely in her large home before his arrival and missed my company. She and Albert are great friends. While I do not believe they knew each other very well before I joined society, over the years, they have developed their own friendship. They share many personal hobbies between the two of them. Lily smiles brightly as she discusses the new paints and brushes Albert bought for her.

It is not long until the conversation turns to future plans of returning to London. She confesses Albert had shared with her the argument between Eddy and me regarding my need to find a husband.

"I cannot be too cross with him, Lily. He spoke only the truth. I believe when we return to London, I need to start taking my potential suitors seriously. Perhaps Albert may be of assistance? I would also like to request your assistance. I can imagine you can also recommend some men who have honorable reputations."

"Are you sure that this is what you want, Margo? It worries me that you are making too hasty a decision because Mr. Riley got in your head."

"I'm not pronouncing that I will be taking a husband immediately, Lily. I just want to start taking the marriage market seriously. I still hope to marry for love, but I cannot fall in love with someone if I do not even speak to them outside of a brief conversation during a dance. The only man I have meaningful and pleasant conversations with outside of my family is Albert."

Lily looks up at me, "Do you plan to pursue Albert?" She has an uneasy tone. I'm not sure why she seems slightly upset.

"I did not plan to court Albert. I believe if those were his intentions, he would have made them clear years ago. Yet, I was so clear at the time that I did not desire a husband, maybe that is why he did not declare intentions. What do you think, Lily?"

Lily has always been a poised woman. She speaks her words so eloquently it is as if she rehearses each of them. This is the first time I have witnessed her stumble on her speech. "I do not... Margo, I'm not...quite sure. He has not expressed any such intentions for you to me"—she pauses with a confused look—"but that does not mean that he has not felt them." Lily, who lost her love so many years ago, now only had her friendships to keep her company. This conversation might be upsetting her with the thought it may change our circle of friendship the three of us took too long to build. I suppose if one of us found we were not romantically interested, but the other was, it would be difficult to remain friends.

"If it is a love match you seek, Margo, do you consider yourself in love with Albert?" she says the question quieter than her previous comments. As if she is whispering so no one else can hear.

"I care for him immensely." The truth comes out of my mouth without a second to think.

"But is that care romantic? You've never mentioned any romantic feelings toward him to me."

"You are correct. I do not believe they were ever of the romantic type. And even now, thinking of him, I do not feel the way you would describe how you felt about Lord Calderwood or how Mrs. Landon describes her feelings for Mr. Landon. I suppose my love for Albert is that of a friend, or I imagine a brother."

Lily nods while taking a sip of her tea, her shoulders still raised high as she sits forward.

"Yet, I worry that the day may come when I am not able to find love. What then? Would friendship be enough to warrant a marriage?"

Lily leans forward, taking my hand. "Let us not worry about that now. You deserve a grand love, Margo. I wish to help you find nothing less. I am sure Albert will be more than happy to help as well."

"Would you speak with him about this?"

"Of course. I will discuss it with him while he is staying with me. We will take care of you on this next step in your journey, Margo."

Hours pass catching up with Lily and I am so happy to be back in her company. I almost forget that we are not alone in our party. I am quickly reminded as "Hello ladies" rings out in Albert's smooth voice behind me. "Mr. Riley and I are famished from our day of hunting. Any sandwiches left from your tea?" he asks as he approaches the table and reaches over me for the last sandwich on the tray.

"Albert, it must be close to dinner. I am sure you would both like to freshen up. Please, Mr. Riley, let me show you to one of the guest rooms." She stands and then turns back to me. "Margo, will you please go check with the cook on the time for dinner, and I will meet you in the library?"

"Of course." I rise and take my leave as the three of them turn in the opposite direction.

Dinner will be served in one hour's time and I enjoy the library while waiting for Lily. She never comes as the hour almost draws to a close, and I make my way to the dining room. No one else has arrived and I take my seat. I continue reading the book I started in the library.

The door opens, and it is Mr. Riley who walks in alone. He gives me a polite nod and then sits across from my seat to the left. I assume to leave the seat directly across from me for Albert and the head of the table for Lily, our hostess. As per my manners, I note the page number and set the book down. And then we sit in silence.

21

My efforts to prolong my arrival to the dining room in hopes of avoiding being alone with Margo prove worthless. As I enter, she is seated next to the head of the table. I notice her looking at the book she just put down next to her, clearly I have interrupted her reading. In an attempt to continue the cordial day we are having, I address her. "How was your afternoon tea, Miss Eton?"

She answers in her polite tone, "Wonderful, thank you, sir. How was your afternoon with Mr. Berry?"

"Very well, thank you," I respond just as flatly. Noticing the empty chair next to Margo, clearly set for my sister, I forge forward with our conversation. "I must say, I forgot how much I enjoy country life. I can see why your suitor, Mr. Grange, is so interested in visiting you here." My frustrations with that sorry excuse for a gentleman are not Margo's fault. I should not be taking them out on her. It was clear from our conversation earlier that she is displeased with his advances, but I need to hear it from her.

As expected, my statement is enough to spark Margo back into her true personality, which I have come to believe is mostly made up of her antipathy for me. So why is it that I enjoy the fire in her so much? Best not to look too deeply into that right now.

"Is that so, Mr. Riley? I must say, I am shocked but pleased to hear that. Considering you rushed here so quickly just a few days ago, afraid of the impression the country life might have on your sister," she speaks to wound me.

It is clear that the country's exposure is never my true concern for Evelyn but her exposure to Margo. I am disappointed that she will not acknowledge my comment about Mr. Grange. That could be proof of her dismissal of him or that she is far more concerned with defending her friendship with my sister, or perhaps both. I would have preferred this discussion to continue in private, but there was no putting it off now. Looking back, Evelyn was correct. She is not in half as much danger as I am in Margo's presence.

"My haste to join her was not out of concern for the influence of the country life over my sister. It was your influence that was of primary concern." This is becoming a sick obsession of mine, but I love watching Margo flush in the face with anger. Weeks ago, I would have meant those words, but it's less about that now. There is not a single woman in London who would so fiercely defend themselves as Margo does. While I am sure that I am not the only man who invokes these reactions from her, I selfishly do not want anyone else to experience her intensity.

I am glad she is so dismissive toward Harold Grange. The physical reactions of her cheeks blushing, her chest rising, her eyes growing wide, and her unsteady breaths are enough to bring a man to his knees. Yet, her passion is what ties me to her, and with each frustrating argument, I feel that pull getting stronger each time.

"Mr. Riley, as we have been over this." She answers with an exasperated sigh, "I have not tried to influence your sister in any way. I have simply been trying to provide her with some freedom from your overbearing personality and insistence on pushing her into the marriage market before she is ready."

"Do not accuse me of forcing my sister into a marriage. I simply wish her to present herself as a Lady in society like all other girls of her age. One who is open to marriage when she finds the right suitor. Unlike you, who has refused to even acknowledge the suitable men who have shown you attention because you believed you are above the marriage tradition for so long."

Does she truly believe that her current way of living will sustain much longer?

She both enchants me and annoys me with equal measure when she acts this obtuse. Without intention, we both rise from our chairs and lean toward each other over the table. Arms and hands waving in the air as we speak with raised voices.

"You know nothing of my thoughts on marriage and love. Do not speak as if you ever have taken the time to ask me." My thoughts cry *You never gave me the chance*, she then continues, "The same can be said for you, Mr. Riley. It is widely known that you have yet to proclaim your intentions of settling down. So I ask, why are you so opposed?"

Fair point in her favor, but I will not concede so quickly. "As a gentleman, I have no need to explain myself. I will choose a bride when I find her."

"But as a gentleman, you believe you have the right to demand a choice from me? I have the right to decline anyone whom I do not love." In the past few years, she has shown nothing but evidence to her point. I should not be surprised by this...confession if that is what it is. Has she decided to decline love for the rest of her life?

"You may have that right today and even tomorrow, Miss Eton, but if you do not act, the choice may one day be taken from you." How can she forget so quickly that there is a deadline to her freedom as a woman beholden to her father's estate?

She seems silenced at the moment, so I go on, "Love? Interesting how little you mention that word when speaking of marriage. It's almost as if you never see them connected, Miss Eton." Pleading in my voice, hoping she does not want to be without love. There are different types of love, but surely, growing up in the company of the Landons, she must have been witness to the love shared between them.

"I know more about love and the importance of its presence in a marriage than you can ever imagine, Mr. Riley," Margo speaks as if it were the truth, but still she rejects that it had anything to do with her life.

The door opens, and Albert rushes in with Lily close

behind. "Can you two not be left together for more than a moment without arguing." Albert looks exasperated, like a father scolding his children. Lily is equally displeased. "As the hostess, I must ask, can you two contain yourselves enough for the four of us to have an enjoyable meal, or must I separate you?"

Albert's words cut through me. Turning to Margo, she seems to feel equal embarrassment. "I'm so sorry, Lily. I swear to sit and not say a word during dinner. I am truly sorry," Margo says.

I include, "Please excuse my behavior, Lady Calderwood, Albert."

Albert and Lily exchange a look as if they are having a conversation we can not hear. Lady Calderwood turns back to us, "You both may sit, and I would wish neither of you to be silent. I would prefer the four of us to have a delightful conversation over dinner."

Albert continues, "I will separate you if needed, but you two must learn to control yourselves around each other."

"Yes." Margo nods.

And I continue, "Of course."

As our food is being served, Margo and I do our best to make small talk with Albert, and as Lady Calderwood insists I refer to her as Lily. Albert clears his throat and asks, "What is it you two were arguing about when we came in?"

"Albert!" Lily yells at him.

"Maybe the way to end this is to get everything out on the table, Lily." The way they speak to each other is something I have witnessed before my arrival at the

Calderwood Estate. The understanding and respect that is shared between the two of them is something I envy. Only in my dreams would I be able to carry a friendship with Margo like that.

"Do you really think that is the best topic during dinner?" she asks Albert.

"Yes, love. I think it is. They are adults. We are wiser adults." He enjoys acting as the wiser older brother, and Lily must fit the same role for Margo. "If they can discuss their issues without raising their voices, we may be able to help them come to some understanding before they return to Eton Cottage and subject poor Miss Evelyn Riley from enduring their incessant arguing." Lily sighs but does not argue.

Albert then turns to the only other woman in the room. "You can do this, Margo. Be open and honest in your discussion." She throws her hand toward my direction and opens her mouth, ready to accuse me of the same, but Albert gets to it first. "Same for you, Eddy. Can you be honest? Can you both be honest?"

We both look at each other across the table. Margo says, "For Evey."

I respond, "For Evey."

Then we turn to Albert and answer "Yes" at the same time.

"While this is going on, please continue to eat so your dinner does not go cold," Lily begs. Margo gives her a smile, and she returns with a look of encouragement. As if Margaret Eton needs encouragement to discuss her resentment of me. If anything, she will need help not coming over the table to strangle me.

Albert clears his throat. "Margo, you shall start. Lily has shared with me your plans for when you return to London. Mr. Riley may be of some assistance. I think you should share your plans with him." Plans? I am under the impression she is regulated by her father to visit London and attend balls, but is she now going to refuse that, too?

She takes a deep breath and turns to face me. "As you have reminded me, Mr. Riley. I have ignored the marriage market for far too long, and my father is not getting any younger. I will need to marry sooner than later. When I return to London, I plan on using my time wisely. I hope to meet with the eligible gentlemen and be more open to their acquaintances." My mind is silent for a moment, only to be overwhelmed with confusion.

"You are planning to get married this year?" I say, with a mixture of shock while trying to contain the anger building behind my eyes.

"It is unclear if it will be this year, but if I fall in love, it may be. If not, perhaps the next." Where is this coming from? Did she truly misinterpret our argument so much that she has decided to just marry the next man who asks her to dance? "My apologies, Mr. Riley, but is this not the reason for your displeasure with me? That I am not married?" The reason for my displeasure...

Albert jumps into the conversation while I am searching for my answer. "Eddy, maybe you should explain to Margo why you feel the way you do about her not being open to the marriage market."

I shake my head as if to clear out the countless thoughts racing through my mind. I take a deep breath and try to stay calm while I address Margo. "I told you my concerns, Miss Eton. Should you wait too long to find a suitable match, then you could be forced to select someone who does not care for you at all. You have built a life here in the country, and the wrong husband can take it all away from you as soon as the vows are said. You could still end up with a miserable life." Wait, that came out wrong. She needs to marry to secure her life, but am I now trying to convince her otherwise...

Hurt flashes across Margo's eyes, and she instantly becomes defensive. "And I am to believe you care if my life is miserable, Mr. Riley?"

Albert looks at me for my response. I shift in my seat. How am I to answer when I no longer know my own feelings on the matter? Thankfully, Lily interjects, "Margo..."

"I'm sorry, Lily." Margo sits back relaxed in her chair. "Mr. Riley, can the same not be said about you finding a wife? What if you missed the woman who was created to love you during these years you have been ignoring the young ladies on the marriage market?" This question helps settle my mind. The answer is upsetting but simple.

"It is not the same for me, Margo. I will take a wife when I must, and even if I have absolutely no love for her, I can maintain my lifestyle. I can choose to keep my home in London and buy a country cottage if I like. I have the freedom as a man to marry the wrong woman but still be in control of my life. As a woman, you do not have that freedom. That is why I worry for you, as I worry for my sister. I want her to find a true love match, and I do not care if she finds him this year or in three. I just do not want her to miss out on it because she was ignoring the men right in front of her, as you have."

Something shifts in Margo's disposition when she answers, "That is all I want for Evey too, Eddy. I can promise you she does not see the marriage market as I do. It is different. She has the luxury of being open to love and having a true chance at finding it."

Albert and Lily return to their meals, eating quietly and whispering to each other during our conversation.

The honesty rang out in her answer, but it comes back to this idea of her being against a love of her own. It makes no sense to me. "And what of you, Margo? Why is it that you cannot look at it that same way?"

"As I told you two nights ago, Eddy. It is too late for me. Since Lord Eton announced to all of London that my husband was to inherit his entire estate, every gentleman in town lost sight of me and only saw the money that is to be theirs if they can secure me in marriage. Not to mention, I am no longer Evey's age. I would be long considered an old maid if it were not for my fortune. Gentlemen want a young, beautiful, and cooperative bride, not me." With each word Margo speaks, her passion slips from her speech until her last few words sound deflated.

"Is that what you believe?" My brain goes silent except for this question. I need her answer.

"It is what I know, Mr. Riley. You have made your disdain for me and my decisions more than known throughout London. I believe the only people who reside in London and do not judge my actions are in this room."

She quickly looks toward Albert and Lily, then back to me, "…with the exception of your sister."

I remain quiet for some time while my world comes crashing down around me. I am a monster who is guilty of this accusation. No one speaks until I clear my throat and respond with my eyes unable to meet hers. "I see."

She gives a nod and goes back to eating her dinner.

"Do you, Eddy?" Albert says firmly. "Do you really?"

"Yes!" I exclaim at Albert. How can he not see I am in a great struggle? I stand quickly. "Lady Calderwood, thank you for your hospitality and this exquisite meal. Please excuse me. I must get some air."

"Yes, of course, Mr. Riley. Take as long as you need," Lily responds kindly.

I quickly rise to my feet. Without looking at her, I speak in Margo's direction. "Miss Eton, please enjoy the rest of your dinner and the company. I will be back prior to your departure to accompany you on your return to Eton Cottage as I promised Mr. Landon I would." Before she can answer, I bow and leave the room.

22

Dinner continues with little conversation, none of which pertains to Mr. Riley or what was just discussed. Once we finish, it is time for me to return to Eton Cottage. Albert approaches me first. "Are you all right, darling? Would you rather I escort you back?"

"Thank you, Albert. I can handle Mr. Riley as my escort." I give him a reassuring smile as Lily approaches us. "You were right. It did feel better to explain myself and to hear his view of my actions and his concern."

"I think you two are well matched in your stubborn attitudes but have similar values underneath it all. I hope you two can find peace for the remainder of Miss Riley's visit with you. I shall be sure to call on you before I leave." He hugs me. "I will fetch Mr. Riley for your departure and meet you ladies by the horses."

I thank him and then turn my attention to Lily. "I'm so sorry for the disruptive dinner party, Lily."

"Margo, you certainly know how to make an evening

memorable." She shakes her head and laces her arm through mine as we walk toward the front of the house. "Are you truly all right after all that was discussed at dinner? Is there anything I can do for you before you leave?"

"I will be fine, I was honest with Albert. It did help. I just hope Mr. Riley feels the same. After his sudden departure. I can only hope our journey back will be quiet enough for me to enjoy the sunset and the sounds of nature around us."

"I am sure Albert is with him now, instructing him to be on his best behavior this evening."

We exit through the front doors to find Eddy already on Jack and Albert holding Lady's reins in his hand. I hug Lily, and she pulls back to say, "Write soon, and safe travels this evening. I hope the rest of your time with the Rileys is more pleasant than it has been, but you can always come here for seclusion if you need."

"Thank you, Lily, for your unending friendship."

I take Lady's reins from Albert and get myself in place on her saddle. Eddy stays close to my side while bidding farewell to Albert and our host. "Thank you again, Lady Calderwood, for your invitation. I hope you and Albert have a pleasant evening. And Albert, thank you for everything, friend. I will see you soon." Then, turning to me, Eddy simply asks, "Ready?"

I stay equal with my own response, "Yes" and we both wave then are on our way back to Eton Cottage.

The ride back is almost completely silent. It is not until we are able to see the stables in the distance that Eddy breaks the silence. "I will help you, Margo."

"What are you offering to help with?" I keep my eyes forward—no need to look at his handsome face.

"When we all get back to London. I shall keep my eye open for a suitable gentleman for you to marry."

It takes everything in me to stop myself from telling him that I do not need or want him thinking he can pick who my husband should be. I take a deep breath and answer, "I would never ask that of you, sir. Really, I'm sure Lily and Albert's assistance will be more than enough."

"It will be no trouble. I am not actively meeting with the eligible men of London for my sister, but if I encounter someone I think she may find admirable, I will share that with her. It would be nothing to inform you of the same."

Against my better judgment, I turn to address him. "And you feel you are the right person to determine who I would be compatible with, Mr. Riley?" Why must he look so handsome on his horse? With the sun setting behind him, this looks like a scene from one of my romance books. He speaks, and I imagine hearing the hero declaring his undying love for the woman he must have for the rest of his days.

"Margo?" Eddy asks, looking over at me. Oh, yes, he was speaking, but I did not hear any of it.

"Sorry, what did you say?" Whatever it was, it was not romantic. He is not the hero, and I am not the woman he wants to spend another day with, let alone the rest of his days.

"You could be sure I would only send the most upstanding and honorable gentlemen I know, Miss Eton," he says with a frigid tone.

"I believe you would recommend a great number of

honorable men, but I am interested in the other qualities that you deem to be compatible with me?"

Eddy seems taken aback by this question. Of course, he never considered this before offering his assistance. "I suppose someone who enjoys spending the majority of their time in the country would be compatible."

"Yes, I would prefer that in a man, among other qualities. You are also forgetting that you will not only need to find a man appealing to me, but you would need to make me seem appealing to these gentlemen." I point out as we enter the stables.

"I know it would take very little convincing once they knew it was you that I was looking for. You are known by every household in London," he states with a matter-of-fact tone.

"Of course, what man would not be eager to gain a chance of being recommended to me as a potential suitor and their chance at being the heir to the Eton fortune?" Silly me for thinking that any man would need convincing.

Eddy is silent as he dismounts his horse. I hope he is beginning to absorb my words. Maybe after our conversation, he has started to understand my concerns about falling for a fortune hunter.

I release the reins and gather my skirts to dismount. When I am halfway down, I feel strong hands around my waist, realizing Eddy is helping me. As my feet touch the ground, his hands are unmoving as I turn to face him, staying on the opposite hips he originally placed them on. I naturally place my hands on his arms to steady myself. I look up at him to thank him for the assistance, but he speaks first.

"No, Margo. It would not take much convincing because of your beauty and passionate disposition. Fortune or not, any man in London would jump at that chance to wake up next to a woman as beautiful and intelligent as you for the rest of his life."

"Eddy..." Words escape me, and my heart races. He has never paid me such a compliment or spoken with what sounded like honesty in his voice. Never feeling the need to hear Eddy's opinion before, I now find myself longing for him to continue. "Thank you." I am not sure if I am thanking him for the assistance in dismounting the horse or the kind words he just spoke.

We stand here in silence, unmoving for more than a few breaths. It seems as if he has more to say, as do I. I want to tell him that I truly cannot believe any man has seen past my wealth and sees me as a beauty. And that his kind words give me hope to actually find love in my future husband. But neither of us is able to let the words escape our lips. It seems at that very moment, we wake up from a trance, both dropping our hands and taking a step back.

"You're welcome, Miss Eton." Eddy lets out in a quick breath.

I need to gain some space and I quickly move to grab Lady's reigns. "I can put the horses back into their stalls. You are welcome to make your way to the house, Mr. Riley."

Eddy insists, "I can help. Just point me to which stall belongs to Jack." I smile and point while waiting for Lady to get entirely in her stall and lock it behind her.

23

As night falls, we begin walking back to the house.

"Shall we get back to our conversation about your potential suitors, Miss Eton? What qualities must a man possess to win your heart? As you surprisingly mentioned, love is very important to you." I start to get the feeling that he will revert back to mocking me now that we are returning home.

"I understand you must have a difficult time with the idea of love and being romantic. As you have made clear, you have no desire for love with your future bride." I flash my most mischievous smile.

"Well, Miss Eton, we cannot all be Romeo looking for our Juliet. Besides, what are the benefits of love? I believe a marriage should be looked at as a contract from both parties with equal goals."

I laugh, "You sound like my father, Mr. Riley. You two would get along perfectly well." It would be foolish to think most men of London's society have similar views as my father and Mr. Riley. Perhaps it is only women who hold out the hope for a love match.

"And what is wrong with being compared to Lord Eton? One of the smartest businessmen in London? From what I hear, your mother is perfectly happy with her life, is she not?"

"I am confident she is very happy with most aspects of her life, but I can guarantee you none of that happiness is provided by my father's company. They live completely separate lives."

"Separate but still happy. I believe, if you are not able to find your one true love, Miss Eton, you should be content to live a separate but happy life as well."

He truly acts as though he knows everything, and it is becoming absolutely infuriating. In an attempt to maintain my composure, I calmly explain my feelings on the matter. "What about love, Mr. Riley? I do not mean flowers and courting. I mean two individuals with a shared interest in each other's minds and bodies. Real passion that cannot be denied. The idea that you cannot live without another."

"You speak like a child, Margo. You should know that true love is rare and becoming more and more unrealistic in the world we live in." Hints of anger are returning to his tone, but I cannot understand why he would feel that way.

"Maybe it is just that in your infinite experience, you have not experienced love on such a level, sir. That is a sad life for you, to be destined to live your entire life with the outlook you have." I mean to say it as a cautionary sentiment that I would be sad to see him without ever loving another. That is not how it was perceived. The warning signs returning to his face, we are back on the battlefield.

We are still outside the house with only the moonlight to guide the insults that we are throwing at one another.

I know that I have hurt his feelings with my last statement, but rather than be the better person and apologize, I stand my ground and brace for his next offensive remarks. "The many years you have remained unattached are a gift to whoever the poor fool who ends up as your husband. It is at least allowing him a chance to experience warm and kind women...unlike you."

The battle has begun yet again, and Evey is nowhere in sight. I bared my heart to him earlier and that moment in the stables was a moment of weakness. My response to him comes far too easy. "I can almost guarantee that any woman who has found herself in the unfortunate position of lying beneath you has been turned off from intimacy for the rest of their days."

His face falls with such haste that his lips may fall straight off his chin. Pride swells through me. There is no greater prize than being able to hold my own in an argument with Mr. Riley.

"You speak of intimacy with such familiarity...I knew it." Eddy looks angry when he continues, "You speak of your want for love so clearly. It must be the reason that you never considered any man in London. You are in love with another. Who is he? Is he from the country? Have you been compromised?" He pauses and runs his hand through his hair before turning back to face me. "It is the only explanation as to why you act so desperate for love but in no way pursue it. You must already have it!"

My stance shifts at his words. How can he make such an accusation? I should ignore his false assumption that I am in love with another man. If there was, he must know that Albert and Lily would have known. They are my closest friends and would certainly not announce to the likes of him I was looking for a husband otherwise. "There is a difference between being compromised and being educated, sir."

"Call it whatever you like, Miss Eton. I'm sure the gentleman enticed you with many vague terms, all in the name of love. Although I cannot imagine you were too difficult to be convinced to be...*educated*, had you thought yourself in love." He spits the last words at me.

How could I have instilled such hatred in this man? As the years passed, we avoided each other's company as much as possible, but I would never slander his reputation in the way he did so freely with mine. Does he think this poorly of all women, or am I the only recipient of such hatred? I will not let this conversation continue beyond this evening. I must prove to him that I am not compromised. I have an idea...one with a semi-violent end. "Would you like to meet them?" I ask while I try to maintain a smooth disposition.

"Excuse me? The man who compromised you is here?" Eddy's gaze flies in the direction of the cottage as if he is expecting a man to jump out at him.

"Right this way, Mr. Riley." With my hand extended toward the front door. We walk in quickly and come upon The Landons and Evey in the sitting room by the fire.

24

This is the explanation that I have searched for years to understand. Since she entered London society, every eligible man has thrown themselves at her at one time or another. Harold Grange has not stopped since he learned about the Eton estate, but surely he does not deserve her, and she does not return his advances.

Here, I thought her heartless all these years, speaking so poorly of the men in London, myself included, for seeing her as a reward instead of a person. It is because she could never see herself with a gentleman of high society when she loves a man from the country. Perhaps a man like Mr. Landon, who has shown their small family love, affection, and support throughout her life. Unlike her father, who did the very opposite, barely giving his wife and daughter a fraction of his attention.

How long has she had this secret lover? Was this man on their household staff? Maybe the son of a staff member? Perhaps they grew up together. Margo was a remarkable young woman, and I could not blame this mysterious man for falling for her.

I did. But unlike me, this man was successful in winning her heart.

Am I angry or jealous that she has a lover here in the country?

Jealous...

No, I must focus on anger, it is the only thing to push the other feelings toward Margo away.

Has this man been living under the same roof as me for days? Sharing the residence with my sister without either of our knowledge? Or worse, did Evelyn know about this man? Was she keeping Margo's secret from me? If this is Margaret's plan, to convince my sister that love cannot be found in town but only in the country, it would destroy Evelyn's prospects.

We exchange quick pleasantries with the Landons and give a quick summary of our time spent with Lady Calderwood and Mr. Berry. Then both Margo and I check on Evey to see how she has been feeling since the morning. "Much rested, thank you both for your concern. The Landons were more than gracious to me throughout the day."

"As I knew they would be." Margo says in their direction, "Thank you both." They simply nod.

Evey looks between us. "Would you care to join us?"

Margo turns her look on me, prompting an answer. Does she think she will get out of this? "We cannot just yet," I blurt out.

"Why not?" she asks Margo, continuing her mocking look.

When I cannot think of anything, Margo replies to Evey. "It has been a long journey, I would think we would both like to freshen up before we join you all. Please excuse us, we won't be but a few moments." Evey seems satisfied with the answer, and she goes back to her book. I quickly walk Margo through the parlor to the staircase. Margo maintains her distance, staying a couple of paces ahead of me. Most likely to avoid any additional conversation until we arrive at our destination. My footsteps are not loud, but enough to let her know that I have not abandoned our excursion.

Within a few moments, we stop at the doorway of a room in the house that I have not yet visited during my stay. It was not included in Mr. Landon's brief tour upon my arrival. Margo slightly opens the door and slips inside. Night has already fallen. Even with the curtains open, there is barely enough moonlight to see much of anything. Before I can find Margo in the dark room, a very heavy object hits me in the head. I turn around in the direction it came, bracing myself for a fistfight with Margo's lover. That's when I notice a few candles lit on a table next to Margo, who is standing in front of a bookshelf. She has one arm behind her head, I lower my hands and try to make out what she is holding when she quickly throws another book in my direction. Luckily, I am able to duck that one.

"Bloody hell, woman. That hurt. Was this a ruse planned for you to attack me in your library? Is this your way of threatening me into keeping your secret?" I yell at her.

Margo moves closer to me and lights one of the

candles on the table to my left as she answers, "You asked who educated me about intimacy between a man and woman. I was introducing you." Her calm demeanor never wavers while moving to a different table to light more candles. How can she remain so composed during a time like this?

"Yes, do they live in the library?"

"Look at the books, Mr. Riley."

Leaning down, I straighten the books that lay on the floor around me. "Medical Journals...?"

"Educated, as I said, Mr. Riley." Her face finally shows emotion, a common one at that. It is a mix of anger and being insulted.

"You read these?" I ask, putting the puzzle together. Remorse washing over me for accusing her of such torrid affairs.

"I have read most of the books in this library, Mr. Riley. Try not to act too surprised. You are in the presence of an *actual,* well-read woman. A rare creature for someone in your social circles."

"I do not believe it is in good taste for a woman to have such knowledge of intimacy, but I must apologize for my previous statement. You clearly have not been compromised. If you had, you would probably be more fun to be around." I am in the wrong here, but she is still Margo, and I am still Eddy. I cannot let an apology out of my mouth without following it with an insult toward her. She huffs and leaves the room.

I grab the candle off the table and sit on the floor amongst the journals. I hadn't noticed my breathing had changed, but my chest loosens, and I take a deep, relaxing breath. She does not have a lover—she is educated, just as she said. I should have known. When we were children, she would come to each meeting having read multiple new books from her father's library. She would go through his ledgers and ask to help manage the household numerous times, always being met with rejection. Yet, I was beginning to see her as the selfish young woman that all of London saw her as, the awful lies I promoted about her. She was right; none of those people had any idea of the woman that Miss Eton has grown to be, and I believe none of them deserve that chance, *including me.*

As I read the pages about the "marital act" between a man and a woman, it is more print than photos and the pictures were not particularly enticing. In Margo's attack on my ability to make my own conquests pleasurable, she indicated more than is related in these journals. They only speak of the man's pleasure and that it is required in the act to produce offspring. I wonder if there are other books in this library that describe a woman's pleasure in the act. I close the journals and begin to walk around, reading the titles of books throughout the room. I am paying no attention to details as my mind is racing, creating ideas of the scandalous things Margo may have read. She spoke of passion in love, and this must have crossed her mind at that moment with me.

It does not matter what she has read in these books. She could never dream of the things I would do with her.

A wicked smile widens across my face. Her skin glowed in the low candlelight as she scolded me before she left. Looking around the library, I can picture pulling her in here on a dark evening, with nothing but the moonlight to guide us. Backing her up against a bookshelf to grab her legs, wrapping them around my waist while I nuzzle into her exposed neck from that revealing country dress she wears to tease me.

The book I was holding drops out of my hand and the noise it makes startles me out of my daydream.

What am I doing?

I run my hand through my hair to gather my thoughts and notice that I am sweating. I need to get out of this library; it is a dangerous place.

25

I stop by my room to change into a more comfortable dress and then join Evey and the Landons downstairs to read another romance book. Hoping I might also have the chance to throw it at Eddy before the night is over. Yet, the chance never comes. He does not join us in the sitting room. Evey asks if I know where he is. I lie and tell her the last I saw him, he was headed to the library. I assume that he has decided to stay there for the remainder of the evening.

The next morning, I find a folded piece of paper under my door. I quickly remember Eddy's promise from the trip to visit Lily's home. With a smile on my face, I open the letter.

You will certainly never gain a husband with a reputation for throwing books at eligible gentlemen suitors. A reputation I will be sure to spread upon my return to London. Everyone will know you are the one who is responsible for my newly acquired chronic headaches and the exceedingly large bump on the right side of my head. - Eddy

A mischievous laugh escapes my lips as I imagine Eddy standing in the low-lit library, rubbing his head. I fold the letter and leave it on my bed as I sit at my desk to draft my reply to Mr. Riley.

I will be more than happy to receive the burden of being known as the woman who threw multiple books at a man who falsely accused her of being compromised. It will help to quickly filter out any less than desirable gentlemen from my consideration. I hope your headaches continue long enough for you to learn your lesson. Please let me know if you are ever in need of a reminder.
I will be happy to oblige. - Margo

I fold the paper and continue to dress for the day. Quickly and quietly, I pass Evey's door and head to the hallway where Eddy's room is located. I kneel down and push the paper in between the floor and the bottom of his door. As I rise with a smile on my face, the door begins to open. He looks from me to the paper on the floor in front of his boots. Believing I have covered everything in my note, I simply nod and make haste down the hall to the kitchen.

With my wishes of good morning to the Landons, I continue on to the sitting room to find Evey with a book in her hand. She jumps up at my arrival and asks, "How does a day at the lake sound?"

"Marvelous," I answer. "Let me just run to grab myself a book, and then we may take our leave."

There is no discussion of Eddy joining us as we walk to the lake. We speak of my day at Lady Calderwood's estate, the company of Mr. Berry, and the dinner the four of us shared. I did manage to leave out all mention of the arguments between Eddy and me, but I said we enjoyed a pleasant conversation with our closest friends.

Our topic quickly changes to how Evey spent the day with the Landons. "After resting during the morning hours, the Landons invited me to accompany them into town." While I missed her presence yesterday, it was for the best that she spent time with the Landons.

"And what did you think of your journey into town?" I ask. It's clear she enjoyed herself more than I would have expected.

"Oh, Margo, it was wonderful. So many wonderful street shops and vendors." Her smile is shining extremely bright. "Mr. Landon introduced me to his brother, Mr. Richard Landon, and his family."

"What a kind family they are. I'm so glad you met them. They visit Eton Cottage from time to time. Those sons of his were a handful when they were younger. It was almost impossible to keep up with them." Thomas and

Arthur were always filled with endless amounts of energy when they stayed at Eton Cottage. It would take twice as long as their stay just to clean up the mess that they made.

"They visit here? To Eton Cottage?" Evey asks with a nervous tone to her voice. "Are they coming soon? Will I see them again before I return to the city?"

The last thing I want her to do is feel uncomfortable, "Please do not feel like they will be interfering in your holiday, Evey. I will ask Mr. Landon to be sure that they do not visit until your departure." I can see why she would not want young men trespassing on her seclusion while here.

"No," her response is so intense, that I jump at the volume in her voice. "Sorry, that is not what I meant. I quite enjoyed getting to know Mr. Landon's family. I would actually enjoy some additional company at Eton Cottage. Could you possibly request that they visit soon?"

"Yes, I can ask if that is what you want." Surprised by her request, I try to rationalize it. I suppose Eton Cottage has become a bit of an unpleasant place with Eddy and me, so having fresh guests may lighten the mood. Her smile grows at my response as her mind seems to wander. Could it be that she has taken a fancy to one of the Landon boys? I suppose we will have to wait and see.

We sit for what feels like more than an hour, enjoying the warm sun and our reading before we are joined by Mr. Riley. He approaches quietly and raises the book he brought as he walks closer. As if to declare he is only joining us to enjoy his book and not to disturb us. I nod and return to my reading.

The afternoon is peaceful. I assume that is thanks to

Mr. Riley not speaking a single word to me while we were by the lake or during our walk back to the house.

When we return to the house, he excuses himself to attend to some business letters in his room before dinner. Evey and I assist the Landons with the preparation of tonight's chicken meal for dinner. Eddy returns while we are setting the table, and he offers to assist Mr. Landon and Evey. We eat without any incident. Laughter is constant throughout the dinner, with everyone talking between each other and telling stories of the past, including comical tales about my childhood from the Landons. Then the Riley siblings are in a contest to see who could share the most embarrassing story about their sibling.

When Mr. Landon offers to clean the dishes, Eddy rises from his seat and insists on helping him. He turns back to us, "Ladies, please relax after this delicious meal you have prepared for us."

The evening continues just as pleasant as the day. I find myself afraid to question Eddy about his recent change in behavior and then decide it is best to just enjoy it while it lasts.

26

Sitting back in the chair, I place the quill down on the desk. A soft chuckle comes out of my mouth as I look over the note I just finished writing for Margo. It proves to be a difficult task as we are having a particularly pleasant day, but I enjoyed her letter this morning. I want to continue our game.

Surely, she will be asleep at this hour. I will just slip it under her door now so that she will find it when she wakes up tomorrow. Before I can open my door, the entire room is engulfed in a flash of light, shortly after accompanied by a loud bang. I go to my window to check it is closed before the storm gets stronger. That is when I notice a figure running away from the front of the house to the left. It is her very recognizable mane of black curly hair that identifies this ridiculous individual.

My feet move before my mind has a chance to catch up. I throw the letter back on the desk and race to find Margo before something happens to her. What is she thinking running outside in a storm? This woman continues to find new ways to drive me mad. As I exit the house, she is no longer in sight, so I follow the path I saw her on from my window. The rain has started, but it is not as heavy as I expect it will soon be. Another flash of lightning brightens the landscape, and I can see her destination. I follow the patch and the thunder finally rings out.

I enter the stables and look around. I do not see her, but I hear her. "It is just a rain storm, I promise you are safe." Her voice is so soft that I almost walk right past her. Standing next to Lady, she pets the large horse with gentle strokes. First, I notice her compassion for this animal. Then, I take note of her attire. It is late and very dark, with only a single candle to light the space. It must be the way she is standing that makes her dress look like britches. I shift my stance to confirm and give my presence away.

"Eddy? What are you doing here?" Before I can answer, her smile grows sarcastic "Are you also afraid of the storms?"

"No, darling." Why did I just call her that? I have never used any term of endearment with her aside from her nickname. "I noticed a young lady running into a storm instead of away from it. Call me curious."

"If you must know, I saw the lighting and could not remember if we locked the stable doors. Lady gets startled by the thunder and ran away once before." The sadness in her voice has cut through me. Another side to her, I was certain had been lost long ago.

"Will you stay out here until the storm passes?" I am fully prepared for either answer. If it is, yes, I shall stay with her. Even if this storm continues until sunrise.

Suddenly hope rises within me that we will be able to spend hours of uninterrupted time together.

"No, I usually only stay until she settles and then return to the house when there is a break in the rain." Disappointment runs through me as all hope for an evening together is dashed, but I remind myself that we are safer in the house.

"You continue to tend to Lady, and I shall monitor the storm until you are ready to depart." Her attention returns to the horse and for the first time since I saw her, I turn my attention away from her to check the rain. My mind drifts back to her, and I quickly recall that she is wearing britches. "Margo, why are you wearing a man's britches?"

"I was curious as to when you were going to comment on my attire, Mr. Riley." She laughs but does not turn to face me until she continues. "As you seem to be very concerned that I have a man hidden on this estate, let me put you at ease. These britches do not belong to a man. They are mine, made to my measurements." She lifts the hem of her top just enough to show me the fit. I must school my thoughts. I came out here with only her safety as my concern. Now, it is clear that it is my safety and sanity that is in far more severe danger.

"Clearly, a man would not have such a figure that would also fit me so precisely." She continues talking but I have a hard time comprehending what she is saying. I would like to think I am just a gentleman who is relieved to hear she does not have access to another man and his clothing, but that would be a lie. I thought the fit of her country dress would haunt me, but it has a rival in these pants that cling to her body. Every curve, every line, is perfectly visible to me. She lowers her shirt back into place, but the image of those britches around her waist and backside will never leave my mind.

"Eddy." Her loud tone grabs me back into the present.

"Yes?" She giggles at my clear break with reality.

"I think Lady is settled. Are we clear to return to the house?" she asks, and I quickly turn my attention back to the rain. It has slowed to a drizzle.

Things have shifted in my feelings toward Margo since last night. These are not new emotions—no matter how many years I have tried to extinguish this fire, it now burns hotter than ever. Where can I go from here? I will figure that out later when I can think more clearly. For now, I let my heart lead my next actions. With a gentle smile, I hold out my hand for her. Relief flows through my body as she takes it without hesitation.

The moment we step out from the stables, the rain begins to pick up. She giggles again at me but does not let go of my hand. "Shall we make a run for it?" I ask. She nods, and we are off running back to the house. Not long after our sprint begins, I feel her pull my arm back. Before I can turn to see the cause, my feet are kicked back from under me, and we both go crashing to the ground. As my back hits the grass, I hear her scream. Quickly getting to my hands and feet, I crawl over to inspect the source of her painful cry. With a mixture of ease and urgency, I cradle her head in my right hand and check for damage by caressing her hair and face with my left hand.

"My back...a rock...my back." The words are strained as they leave her lips. I cross my body over hers and roll her onto her right side to better inspect her back. We have never been this close, and it is certainly inappropriate, but the manners of society rules are not going to prevent me from seeking the source of her pain. The rock is larger and sharper than I expected. I throw it as far away from us as I can. I'll come back tomorrow to make sure it will never be in her path again.

Her cries have slowed and have been replaced with erratic breaths. I run my hand up her back. She is bleeding but not too badly. I rip the back of her shirt so I can gather as much as possible to apply pressure with my left hand. "Margo, you are bleeding, but I'm going to apply some pressure to slow it. Is that all right?" She nods and begins to curl her body closer to mine as if to prepare for the added pain. "I need to just check if there are any additional cuts." She answers again with a nod, and I feel helpless. This ferocious woman was reduced to this state by slippery wet grass and a sharp rock.

Using my left hand, I put pressure on her cut as I run my right hand up her back. By the time my hand reaches her shoulder, I have to remind myself why I have access to her smooth, delicate, bare skin. I take my time running my hand down to her back again. Margo's body is no longer shaking, but it does seem to be responding to my touch. Switching hands, my left hand makes its way down her lower back.

It is a struggle to remember we were lying in the grass during a rain storm as I caress down her backside, which is still hugged so tightly by this soft fabric. Her breath hitches as her body closes the distance from mine. Switching hands again one last time, I lean back and allow her to lay on her back.

Something changes. The air is thicker, the rain has slowed, and our eyes meet. Without a choice, my body leans forward, and my face is inches away from hers. I may never have a chance to be this close to her again. The only thing stopping me from claiming her in this instant is the cut on her back. Her chest rising to meet mine is evidence of her breath becoming erratic again. Her back settles onto my hand as she reaches to hold onto my arms. I cannot let this continue; with every last effort in my body, I break our eye contact, only to foolishly land my gaze on her mouth. My body responds against hers as she parts her lips. I look back into her eyes for confirmation that she wants this, that she actually, finally wants...me. A fight between my head and my heart breaks out in my mind.

Unfortunately, my head wins, and my heart accepts defeat, but is truly a sore loser based on my next action.

Accepting that this cannot go any further tonight, I linger above her and revel for a moment in the feeling of her beneath me. The right thing would be to stand and get her back to the house immediately, but I cannot move, not yet.

Like a magnet, this pull to her is so strong that I'm unsure if I will even be able to separate my body from Margo's. Her eyes are pleading for me to make my next move. All signs of pain and discomfort have faded, replaced with desire. If I do not break our eye contact soon, things will end very differently than the way they should.

In an attempt to cool this fire building inside me, I lower my head onto her left shoulder. It has the opposite outcome as her entire body responds. Beneath me, a shiver moves from her hips up to her shoulders. Her hands tighten around my arms, and she nuzzles her head up against mine. My resistance begins to waver. Lifting my mouth to her ear, I take a deep inhale, then allow only one word to escape on the exhale, "*Years.*" Her entire body shifts into me while a soft moan escapes her lips. Damn the consequences.

A thunderous boom that feels like it was strong enough to shake the ground we lie on crashes over our heads. We both startle and she winces in reaction to her back. The spell is broken. I come to my senses and quickly rise to my feet. I lean down to help her up. "We need to get you inside."

"Thank you." She does not let go of my hand after she is on her feet. Her right hand goes to her back, and when she pulls it forward, she looks up and says, "It still hurts, but it seems to barely be bleeding."

We continue our walk to the house, "Yes, it may be for a few days, but I do not think any permanent damage was done." I try to soothe her.

She gives me a weak smile, and I know she is trying to process what happened between us. Once in the house, I walk her to her room and bid her goodnight.

27

When I first wake, I find myself looking for him. I lie in bed reminiscing about the dreams that Edward Riley dominated last night—dancing in the library, laughing in the kitchen, and then there was the moment in the rain. I cannot deny the fact that he is a very handsome man, but I never let that surpass the anger and hurt that I have felt toward him, at least not until now. Our shared residence provides the opportunity for more intimate interactions. Perhaps it is the close proximity of Eton Cottage and Eddy's awareness that his behavior is being monitored by Mr. Landon. This side of Eddy is starting to grow on me. A smile comes to my face when I think of what he might say about me dreaming of him.

As I rise to sit up, I am startled by a pain in my back, primarily on the right side. I move my hand to investigate and notice dried blood on the sheets beneath me. Every part of my dream comes flooding back to memory,

Edward and I laying together in the grass during the rain storm after I slipped and fell on the rock. I look out the window and notice the rain is still falling.

It was not a dream. We lay together in the grass after I fell. My body starts to move as I remember my reaction to Eddy's touch, many touches. The way that it felt when he caressed my back with such a gentle touch. That look on his face, in his eyes, as if he wanted to kiss me—as if he wanted to do much more than kiss me. I must confess, at least to myself, that I believe at that moment I wanted his kiss. Thinking about when he dipped his lips to my neck, I place my hand where his warm breath heated my entire body. Pushing the thoughts from my memory, I refuse to be fooled by him. I cannot feel this way about Edward Riley. I manage to sit up and remove my hands from my body, shaking them as if it would shake these feelings out of me.

Before I can process what happened, there is a knock at the door, Evey pokes her head in. "Good morning, Margo!"

"Good morning, Evey." I typically enjoy Evey's early calls, but today, I feel embarrassed and confused by my thoughts and desires for her brother. If this were any other man, I would already be sharing every detail with her, but this is her brother. She already has expressed dislike of being put in the middle of things with us and last night's events make things even more complicated.

"Breakfast is almost ready. Mrs. Landon asked me to come get you."

"Thank you. I will get dressed and be right down." She

accepts my answers and turns, closing the door behind her. I let my face fall into my hands. With a deep breath, I pick my head up. I need to speak with Eddy before I talk to anyone else. It becomes apparent as I try to stand that my physical state is just as hopeless as my mind. Slowly, I dress in one of my country dresses. My mind remembers the way Edward looked at me the first time he saw me in it. I smile but quickly stop myself. No, do not do that. This cannot be considered until I speak with him. My plans are foiled when I find Eddy's room empty.

"Good morning, Margo. How is your back?" Mrs. Landon asks as she approaches me with open arms. Not for a hug but to turn me around as if she will be able to see through my dress.

"My back?" Is there more to this story than I do not remember? Did I also hit my head? How does she know about my back? At that moment, my answer comes through the kitchen door. Eddy's face lights up when we make eye contact, but he does not get a chance to greet me.

"Yes, dear." Mrs. Landon seems offended that I would question her knowledge of anything that occurs in her household. Did she see us last night? Did Mr. Landon see us? No, he could not have. I'm sure Eddy would not be standing here if Mr. Landon had seen us. She continues, "Edward let us know what happened last night when he came down a few minutes ago."

How could he? I should have known better than to act in such a way with Mr. Riley. An even bigger fool to think he would not use it against me. I turn toward Eddy, feeling the fury and betrayal rise through my body, and it must be clear on my face based on his reaction. He quickly realizes the source of my anger and scrambles to exonerate himself. "Yes, I told Mrs. Landon if it were not for the lightning of the storm, I would have never noticed you on the ground when I looked out my window. She explained that you often go to check on the horses during storms."

Mrs. Landon interjects, "I have warned you it's dangerous to do that, darling."

Eddy continues as if he could not get the words out quickly enough. "I explained that I went outside to help you and got you safely into the house. It was not until we were back inside that I noticed the blood on your shirt." He ends with a slightly sly smile spreading across his face. So this is the story we are sticking to. I suppose we couldn't conceal the entire event based on the blood on my clothing and sheets. I assess the reactions of my family and Evey. No one seems to be wiser. I look back at Eddy, and he winks when no one else is looking.

The day passes without a chance to speak with Eddy in private. In my room, waiting for dinner, I decide to write him a letter regarding his deceitful retelling of last night's events.

The ease in which your deceitful retellings of last night's events causes me great concern. While I appreciate you keeping the entirety of events to yourself, it only confirms that you are a master at deceit, and your words cannot be trusted.

The note is placed under Eddy's door, and I continue on to dinner. Eddy is not there. Good, he must be in his room and will receive the letter. It is not until I return to my room for the evening that I notice a note from him on the floor of my room.

No need to concern yourself with the serenity of my words, I believe my actions last night were more than enough to convey my true intentions.

In bed, I pull the covers over my head and unsuccessfully try to rid my mind of the endless thoughts of Eddy's *actions* last night.

~

THE FOLLOWING DAYS CONTINUE PEACEFULLY. Eddy remains present throughout the activities but avoids any situations where we would have a moment to speak in private. It does not take long for me to deduce that the moment we shared in the rain was a lapse in judgment. I am not angry at his rejection. I am not even sure if I want his affections. No, that is ridiculous. Why did I even consider him in that way? We are two individuals who were friends as children, grew to hate each other, and have now found a way to be civil acquaintances for the sake of his sister.

It is not until the evening of the fourth night that I leave everyone in the sitting room to gather their drinks when Eddy offers to help me. "You are a phenomenal card player," he says with his back toward me, placing the glasses on the serving tray.

"Thank you. I see your game has begun to improve with practice."

Eddy turns toward me, seemingly upset. "I have to ask you something, a question I asked before, but you never clearly answered."

"Which question was that?" I try to replay our many arguments in my head to remember the questions he asked.

"The other night when you clearly explained that you had not been compromised. You did not answer if you already found love. Possibly someone from the country? I cannot imagine it was someone from London, or I would have assumed you would be married by now." He continues to ramble after clarifying his questions. It was almost as if he was trying to work out the answer himself. Once he finally finishes, I give him my answer.

"Technically, yes, I found someone to love in the country." Proud of my answer. It is honest yet vague.

"Oh." Eddy's face falls and I notice his chest lets out a deep breath. Could he really be affected by my answer? Maybe he is simply worried that I would convince Evey to fall for a countryman as well and ruin her chances at a suitable future. For her sake, I must clarify before the ceasefire between us ends.

"Eddy, let me explain."

He turns back at me with a genuine look. "You do not need to explain your relationship to me, Margo. He is a lucky man to have won your affections."

"No, Eddy. You misunderstand." I pause to prepare my answer. "Being here in the country and being raised by the Landons has provided me freedoms most young girls of London society are not allowed. Having the privilege to stay unwed as long as I have has allowed me to discover myself." I pause, noticing he is hanging on my every word as he takes a step closer to me. "Most young girls are taught skills and interests that will gain the attention of possible suitors. Never getting a chance to discover what they might prefer. At such a young age, these girls are too impressionable and only motivated by their desire to please those around them. And if they are successful, they are married and mothers before they have a chance to discover the world for themselves."

I feel myself getting upset. Not at Eddy but at society. Too many of my peers with glowing personalities as children are turning into nothing but wives and mothers without an interest or opinion of their own once they come of age. "Eddy, you may hate me for this confession." This is most likely a mistake, but I need to share it with him.

"I have been presented with every hobby imaginable and allowed to pursue what interests me. That is one of the reasons I am so particular about the idea of marriage. I do not want someone who expects me to lose myself and become nothing more than a figure to act as wife and mother." I am the opposite of his qualifications in a wife, but I do not allow it to come out with anger. He is entitled to want that in a wife, and I am entitled to want the opposite. "I am in love with the person I have become. I need someone who loves me for my mind and my values and interests." He stays still, now only a foot away from me.

I step closer, grab his hands, and meet his gaze. "Eddy, I care for your sister more than you will ever understand. You must trust me. I do want her to find a happy marriage, I want that for her more than anything. But you must know I want her to find herself now so that when she marries, she can be happy with herself and share that happiness with the family she will create. Please know you may rest easy when she is here with me. I am only trying to provide her with the peace and quiet to allow her to make decisions for herself, not what a suitor may find desirable."

He is quiet for a moment but does not seem upset or angry. He opens his mouth to speak, and the kitchen door begins to creak as it opens. At the moment we both realize how closely we are standing, I drop our hands, and immediately take a step back from each other as Evey enters the kitchen.

"You were taking so long, I was beginning to worry." She looks between us. "Is everything all right? Have you been arguing again? I'm not a child. You do not have to hide in the kitchen to have words with each other."

"Not at all, sister. I was simply thanking Margo for her warm hospitality toward us, particularly you. As an older brother, it is hard for me to understand what you are experiencing as you have come of age. We are both lucky to have someone like Margo, who is experienced in London society and so wise to the needs of young women." Eddy continues looking at his sister while he speaks and then meets my gaze when he finishes. "And thank you, Margo, for answering my question. It provided great clarity...and relief."

"How wonderful, brother. It is about time you recognized the truth about Margo, which I shared with you the day you arrived. Can we please get back to our card game now?"

I smile at Evey's frustrations and look at Eddy. He says, "You ladies go ahead. I will be right behind you with the drinks."

Evey grabs my arm and walks out of the kitchen. "Be honest, Margo. Were you both arguing? You seemed flushed when I entered."

I laugh at her observation. How can I explain to her the growing complexity of my relationship with her brother? "No, I believe I was flushed from the sun today. I should have ignored his questioning and focused on a refreshing drink."

"What question?" she asks

I could tell her, but that would take a day to explain the context and every discussion between us. I lie, which I do not want to do with Evey, but it is for the best. Now that her brother and I are getting along, there is no point in bringing up days-old arguments. "He asked what I wanted for your future."

"My future? In what way? I thought he was more distracted with your future these days. What did you say?"

"I simply said that I wanted the greatest of love matches for you. I said while you are not actively hunting for a husband while you are here, you are still preparing yourself for adulthood." She looks at me questionably. "Being in the country away from your mother and all of society who expects you to be nothing more than a gentleman's desire for a wife. Here, you get to discover who you are and what you want in a husband. To find a husband, you must know yourself, what you like, dislike, and, then, what you would want in a partner."

"Now I understand why Eddy had that look on his face when I entered." She shakes her head.

"His surprise that my motives are not purely evil?" I ask.

"No, his expression wasn't that of surprise. It was more like you turned his world upside down. Yet, in a good way. So, I should thank you for that."

"Well, do not thank me yet. Not until he agrees to let you come visit again. Or, at the very least not attempt to arrange a marriage for you."

"Oh, do not speak those words, Margo. You will give him ideas." Evey says as we enter the sitting room and take our seats at the table to resume our card game while we wait for Eddy to return with the drinks.

"Is everything all right in the kitchen?" Mr. Landon asks.

"Yes. All is well," I answer.

"I see you have returned without Mr. Riley. You have not harmed him, have you? Many sharp knives in the kitchen, Margo..." Mr. Landon asks with a sarcastic tone.

"Grateful she has let me live another day, Mr. Landon," Eddy says while carrying the tray of drinks.

"Who knows what tomorrow will bring, Mr. Riley," I reply to him with a smile that he returns while handing me a glass.

28

As ever elusive, Margo has not provided a definitive answer about her being in love with a man in the country. Her attack in the library proved how she knew so much about intimate relationships, and her explanation about wanting Evey to have time to mature on her own was very moving. Yet, I cannot seem to shake the thought that there is a man who holds her heart.

I am a gentleman, an honorable gentleman. That is why I did not allow my lustful feelings to get the best of me in the rain. She may already love another man. *The pit in my stomach returns.* I would not want another man rolling around the grass in the rain with my future wife. It was the honorable thing to do, leaving her unkissed. At least unkissed by me, it is very possible she has kissed the lover I am convinced she has in the country.

Would Margo have let things move further? She certainly was not pushing me away from her at the moment.

Would she have kissed me back?

It does not matter. I have promised to assist in her search for a reputable husband in London society. After my time spent at Eton Cottage, I can consider Margo my friend once again. As a friend, I will assist her in her search for a husband. Margo and I seem to be doing well as friends. Perhaps we will find ourselves as close friends once again.

Or perhaps, even closer than friends...

No. I know better than to hope. My hand rubs against the spot on my neck, where I felt her warm breath while I held her in the grass.

How will I ever be able to see her on the arm of another man...?

Standing from my desk, I shift my attention away from Margo. Thankfully, I find myself with a distracting day ahead. Albert and Lily are to join us for the evening at Eton Cottage along with Mr. Landon's brother and family. An evening of socializing and what is promised to be another delicious feast. I make my way to the sitting room to join Evelyn and Margo. My sister seems to be distracted waiting for the arrival of our friends.

The sound of a carriage arriving fills the room and Evelyn is the first one to jump to her feet and head to the entryway. Margo looks at me, and I divert my eyes with a bow and wave my hand in direction for her to follow Evey. There is barely an opportunity for a knock before Margo opens the door, and we are greeted by a man even larger than Mr. Landon. I had not imagined that possible; there is no doubt this is the other Mr. Landon.

Margo greets her guests and then quickly turns to

begin introductions. Mr. Richard Landon is a shopkeeper in London. His wife, a tall and slender woman with fair blonde hair. Alice assists him in the shop, and he gives her the credit for the shop's success due to her vastly advanced knowledge of fabrics and clothing. This must be the woman responsible for those country dresses Margo insists on wearing in my presence. I'm not sure if I should scorn this woman or thank her for adding to the agony I have struggled with since seeing Margo in it.

Entering behind them are two sons who appear to have their father's builds, but their mother's light hair color. Arthur, the younger of the two, is clearly more reserved than his older brother, Thomas, who asks to be called Tom. I assume he was named for his uncle.

Handshakes and curtseys completed, our host leads us back into the sitting room. Mr. Richard Landon and his wife continue on to the back of the house to meet with Mr. Thomas Landon and Mrs. Emma Landon. Shuffling and squeals of laughter bring my attention back to the scene behind me. Margo is hoisted over Tom's shoulder and laughing while he walks past me, following in the direction his parents went. Evelyn is planted firmly on the ground by Arthur, who looks embarrassed by his brother's actions. He notices my reaction and tries to explain "It is tradition, Mr. Riley."

"Edward is fine." I look next to my sister. "Your feet are to remain on the floor," I command before either of them can get any ideas to follow in Margo's example.

Evelyn begins to blush. Arthur falls over his words, trying to offer reassurance. "Of course, Edward. This is between Margo and Tom." My eyes narrow at his use of the name I use for her. He corrects himself. "When we were younger and Tom would act up, Miss Eton would pick him up and carry him to the lake as punishment." That seems particularly cruel, especially if the boy was small enough for her to carry him.

"Was he able to swim?"

"Oh yes, sir. He just hated getting wet." He chuckles lightly to himself. "He promised that when he was bigger than her, he would take every chance to throw her in the lake." He shrugs slightly. As if to say she deserves it.

"Oh, I must see this." Evelyn runs quickly past me, and Arthur and I follow.

Both Landon couples are standing close to the cottage, watching Margo be carried away on Thomas's shoulders. I join them, particularly to see their reaction., Mrs. Landon gives me a knowing look. "It's a long story, Edward." Her husband chimes in, "But you should know she deserves it."

I am in shock watching this young man be so familiar with her, with her body. I feel so foolish, believing I have been the only man to feel her body so close to my mind. It seems it has been a regular occurrence for her to be so near to men. *Or could it be him, the only man she allows to touch her in such an informal manner?*

"Thomas Landon, you will pay for this!!!" Her screams are slightly muffled as she yells them into her abductor's back. Approaching from the right of the estate is Albert with Lily on his arm. She straightens her back and looks at the audience that has formed behind her. "Thomas, I have guests and a dinner to serve. *You must* put me down."

"Margo, you know that is not how this works." Tom

turns toward the crowd, giving everyone a clear view of Margo's backside. "Hello, Albert." One hand is still braced around Margo's legs while he uses the other to wave. "Lady Calderwood, what a pleasure to see you. Your timing is impeccable."

"Enough, Tom." Margo's legs start to kick, and he turns and continues his walk toward the lake. Her fight is unsuccessful, and they are only about fifteen paces from the lake; it seems Margo's fate is inevitable. Margo shifts, and it appears she is speaking to her captor, but they are too far away for me to hear. He stops and bends to let her stand in front of him. More words seem to be exchanged, and they both turn back in our direction. I believe I see a nod from Tom. They turn and begin to walk back to us. Evey and Albert both release a sigh of disappointment.

Lily and Albert use the time to greet everyone and come to stand next to Evelyn and I. Lily and Evey strike up a conversation and Albert notices my watchful eyes on Margo. "Margo is quite close with the Landon boys."

"So it would seem." I do not take my eyes off Margo. Could this be the man who has Margo's heart? He is a bit younger than her, perhaps closer to Evelyn's age. She was so excited by their arrival and seemed at ease in his presence. She places her arm through his, and they are laughing as they approach.

Albert leans close and speaks low, "You better learn to school your face a little better for when we return to London to find Miss Eton a husband."

"Any man who acts like that in London will be immediately removed from her list of suitors," I say as if my opinion would matter to Margo. While she was protesting being whisked away to the lake, it is obvious her only disapproval was the idea of getting her dress wet.

With a knowing head nod and an exasperated laugh, "We shall see about that, chap."

During our dinner, I pay close attention to both Margo and Tom, especially the interactions they have together. There are times when I can see affection in her eyes toward him, yet she does show similar feelings when speaking with his younger brother, also. At times, Albert catches me watching them closely, and he is right. I am concerning myself far too much; it should not matter if she does love this young man. She has agreed to find a husband in London. At least while courting the men in town, I will not have to watch her interact in such familiar ways. She did not avoid me during the evening, but we certainly spoke less than I have become accustomed to at this point. I must not be jealous—she has guests to entertain, but it seems she has forgotten that I, too, am a guest.

It is not until we move on to our card game that Margo selects a seat next to me. My excitement at her choosing to sit next to me is unexpected and frustrating. During my time at Eton Cottage, I have grown accustomed to her attention, positive or otherwise. Is this how life will be upon our return to London? Watching her share her witty mind, breathtaking smiles, and consuming laughter with other men, only to struggle to contain my elation when she returns to my side?

We have spent the entire day in each other's presence, but she is now sitting close enough for me to feel her warmth. I inhale the smell of her floral perfume and relax at the comfort that accompanies her.

"A pleasant surprise to be given the honor of sitting next to you, Miss Eton." I give her my best devilish smile.

"Your reputation as a card player is well known now, Mr. Riley." She leans toward me, never breaking our connected gaze. Her voice seems to drop just the slightest. "I am aware not to trust your words but to pay close attention to your actions if I wish to know your true intentions." Her words cause me to back up in my chair. Her dark eyes are still holding me hostage. She winks and then returns to study the cards that she has been dealt.

29

Another pleasant evening shared with our guests concludes late into the night, and I should be far more tired than I am. It is a cooler night than usual. I have been lying in my bed for more than an hour. As much as I try, I cannot find sleep. I decide to go for a walk. The house is quiet, and I do not want to risk waking anyone, so I take my leave from the back door to sit on the steps and admire the stars. With a chill in the air, I am thankful that I chose to wear my britches, one of Mr. Landon's longer tunics, and my housecoat, or it may have been too cold to sit out.

The night of the storm occurred days ago, and I have come to decide that it might as well have been a dream, and we shall never acknowledge it happened. Although Eddy said something that night, just one word, *years*. It could have so many meanings—the years it will take for him to forget he was that close to me, the years he has hated me, the years he feels that I have been wasting my life on the marriage market. Then, days later, he spoke another word that I did not understand the context of. Replaying my conversation with Eddy in the kitchen, I tried to understand the meaning of his *"relief"* in my answer to his question about being in love with a man from the country.

Why would he be relieved? He seemed to believe the things I said about Evey. He certainly could not be relieved on my behalf. If he were interested he would have kissed me during the storm. Perhaps he is just enjoying our rekindled friendship as I am, and if I were in love with another or to marry, it might interfere with that.

How will this friendship continue once we return to town? With my new outlook on the marriage market, I would hope that he would no longer act as he did before. Sharing negative gossip about me. I am sure my options of eligible suitors are small, to begin with. I do not need him chasing the remaining interested men away.

"Unable to sleep?" Eddy's soft voice carries from the door behind me.

Looking over my shoulder, I shrug. "You?"

"The same," he answers. "Would you like company?"

I take a minute to decide on my answer, then admit, "Please."

"Do you sit outside in the middle of the night often?" Eddy asks as he sits next to me on the steps. I am surprised he sits so close, our shoulders almost touching, but I'm not completely repelled at this closeness either.

I suppose I am starting to grow a fondness for his friendship. *Friends do not lie in the grass together, but he has not brought that up again so, it did not happen.* We have discussed plans for all of us while in London. Never having an older brother myself, I could appreciate how much he loves Evey, even if he does not know the proper way to show that love at times. When I remove the odd behaviors, the longing looks, and the mysterious moments of teasing, I must admit that I have enjoyed spending time with him these last few days. He is more at ease, similar to how he was when we were younger.

"Yes, I do it more often than I'm sure you would expect. And I know you are thinking, it is not safe for a young lady to be out by herself in the middle of the night." Giving him an accusatory look. He shrugs back at me but does not respond. "Well, you will take comfort in knowing I never encouraged such behavior in Evey, and Mr. Landon made me promise long ago that I would never leave the steps in the middle of the night. I am always close enough to run back in the house if needed."

"That man should write a book on raising daughters. He seems to have always been one step ahead of you." Eddy looks up to the night sky. "In the most loving way, of course."

"Yes, I doubt the Etons would have been able to handle my disposition in the same way the Landons did."

"What are your feelings on parenting? Having children of your own?" he asks.

I take a deep breath before answering. "I do not have any set plans, as we both know my future is extremely unclear. I believe I would enjoy children, exposing them to everything I had the privilege to experience. That depends on when I can finally trick a man into marrying me and then if he wishes to have children as well."

Eddy shakes his head. "And how do you envision this

unlucky man you plan to trick into being your husband? You must have very specific requirements for him before you plan to place him under your spell."

I begin to answer immediately. "I wish for a man that—"

Eddy cuts me off before I can finish. "Loves you, yes. That factor is a well-known requirement for you, but there must be others, more specific traits or features you are looking for."

"You are trying to make me sound shallow, Mr. Riley. You want me to comment on a man's appearance as a requirement in a potential suitor. I should ask you what parts of a woman's appearance would be most likely to tempt you in marriage."

"Fair enough, Miss Eton," Eddy answers with a small laugh. "Physical appearances aside. You must have some traits you are looking for in a husband."

"Yes, of course, and I will answer you, but I will expect your answer to this question as well." Staring him down with a look of challenge on my face. "I may have been informed that you are also being pressured to finally settle down. Maybe we can be of assistance to each other in finding a perfect match in London."

"I can only guess who shared that information with you, and I will be sure to thank her for that later. Yes, I will answer *after* you do."

"Fine. I would like someone who shares the same appreciation for family and intellect as I do. Someone who understands the demands of business in London but does not see that as the entirety of their lives, but only a part."

"You mean someone that hates society as much as you do?"

"It would not hurt." I smile with a shrug. "I'm not the only one who feels that way. It will not be hard to find someone like that. Mr. Berry, for example."

"Yes, but you are not going to marry Albert," he says with a huff.

I do not reply. I'm still holding out hope that he may be my best option if I cannot find a love match.

Eddy turns the upper half of his body toward me. "Margo, you cannot be planning to marry Albert." Eddy declares it in a statement. When I do not immediately respond, shock spreads across his face, "Is he the man you are waiting to return your affection? Are you confusing his friendship for something more? Do you love him?"

"Of course, wait, no, not like that. But as a very dear friend. I know my chances of finding love are very low." I sound like a child who just got caught in a scheme. "Well, he has yet to marry, and he has never shown interest in anyone romantically."

"Of course, he has not publicly shown interest to anyone." Eddy talks as if this is a matter of fact, and I should understand the reasoning.

"I'm not declaring my intentions. I just thought it would be an option if all else failed... I mentioned it to Lily—"

Again, I am cut off by Eddy. "You spoke with Lady Calderwood about possibly marrying Albert?" He lets out a mocking laugh in my direction. "What did she say?"

"I need to make an honest attempt at finding love for myself before admitting defeat and looking to Albert as an option. Please do not share this with Albert. It is not your business."

"I'm sure he is already well aware," Eddy says with certainty, then snorts again and shakes his head. "Yes, let's get back to focusing on finding you a love match."

It is confusing why he has such an outburst at my idea about Albert. I decide I have had enough of the attention in this conversation. "No, I believe it is your turn to share something you are looking for in a wife who will one day hold the esteemed title of Lady Riley."

"I would like a woman who is...kind."

"That does not count, Eddy. Everyone wants someone kind. No one enters marriage looking for someone who is intentionally cruel. That does not count as your answer. It is still your turn." Nudging him lightly with my shoulder.

He smiles and faces me. "For years, I have not believed a love match was possible for me, and I started to only think of practical qualities to look for in a lady."

"How unfortunate you feel that is your only option. And with such little requirements, you have not found anyone?" Surely, I can think of several shallow young women of my acquaintance who could fit that role.

"Similar to you, I must admit, I stopped looking years ago," he says with honesty and sadness in his voice. "I think our time of running from marriage is coming to an end, Margo. When we return to London, we must be prepared with what we are looking for in a marriage, so we do not make a mistake." His tone is very serious about this directive.

"Yes, better to be prepared," I reply with a swift nod.

"Aside from your basic requirements for a wife, is there anything specific you want?"

"Margo." He turns his entire body to face me and I mirror his movements. "So much has changed. When I arrived at Eton Cottage weeks ago, I was certain that I need not marry for love, but to simply find a respected woman to bear my children. I did not consider finding someone I could have shared interests with or admire as a person."

Looking down at my hands. "I understand the marriage prospect is much different from a man's point of view. You have mentioned that you will still have your freedoms in almost every way, and I understand you have no need for love. Please do not think I was trying to influence you personally or pass judgment."

With an exasperated sigh, Eddy places his hands in mine. "I'm grateful that you have opened my eyes in this matter. I now find myself reconsidering the qualities I seek in a wife. The possibility of spending my days with someone who can act as more than just my wife."

30

It is hard to believe this is the same man who stormed into my house a little more than a couple of weeks ago. The man who made no secret of his disapproval of my unwed status all these years. If it were not for his sister coming to visit, we may never have found this mutual understanding. "Eddy, you must be careful. You are starting to sound like a romantic."

Feeling proud of the progress he has made, I start to think about the woman who will become his wife. Something twists in my stomach. Jealousy? It could not be that. Maybe just that, another woman will have the chance to call Evey her sister. Yes, that must be it.

"The woman you select will be a very lucky lady indeed. We will just need to find her for you first." I think of Eddy courting and dancing with ladies—he is a fantastic dance partner. Possibly one of the best in London. I should compliment his dancing skills. "You will surely win over any lady's affection with your dancing," I say with a laugh, sounding nervous.

"You think I am a good dance partner, Margo?' he asks with a sly smile.

"Do not let me inflate your ego too much, Eddy. I think you should try with ladies who catch your interest when we return to town."

His voice turns serious. After a deep breath, he asks, "Would you dance with me, Margo?"

"We have danced plenty over the years, Eddy. I do not see any reason for you to waste a dance with me." I laugh at the question.

"It would not be a waste," he says, remaining serious.

"It would be taking away opportunities for us to dance with actual marriage prospects. You said to yourself, we need to get serious about marriage."

Eddy stands and walks down two steps, his hands on his hips when he turns back to me. "So this is not a product of our arguing or your anger. You truly are always this stubborn."

Offended, I immediately rise to stand, "Pardon me?" I shout back at him. Thankfully, the Landons and Evey's rooms are located at the opposite end of the house.

"You speak only of wanting to find love, but you have built so many walls around yourself you cannot even recognize it when it is right in front of you."

"In front of me, where?" I wave my hands to the open, empty field.

He takes the two steps he ascended in one stride and returns in front of me placing one hand on my hip and the other under my chin.. His gaze is wounded, his breathing heavy. I cannot pull away. I am not afraid he is going to hurt me. In fact, the closeness somehow settles my anger.

He bends his forehead down as close as he can to mine without breaking eye contact.

He whispers, "Here..." before his lips are on mine.

At first, I do not move at all while my mind tries to rationalize what is happening and process what he just said, but I cannot sort any of it. Eddy and I despise each other. Well, we almost kissed during the storm, but he stopped himself and refused to acknowledge his mistake for a week. Sure, we have not argued since then, but that does not mean he likes me enough to kiss me.

My thoughts are quickly drowned out by my body's reaction to Eddy's kiss. I can no longer hear my questioning thoughts. The warmth of his body is so close to mine that I feel myself melting into him. My arms find their way around his neck, and my lips push back onto his. The kiss changes when Eddy feels my response. I feel his body relax as one of his hands moves from my cheek down around my side to stop at my lower back. He pushes me closer to him as our kiss continues.

It is hard to tell how long he continues to kiss me, but disappointment washes over me when he finally pulls away. Both trying to catch our breath, we just smile at each other. My brain slowly begins to function again, and my body cools from the absence of his. The questions reappear in my mind and quickly escape my mouth. With my hands now on his shoulders, I ask, "Why did you do that?" His face quickly twists to confusion. I need to clarify I wasn't upset with him. "It was spectacular, Eddy. Really, more than I could have ever imagined a kiss would be, but why did you kiss *me*?"

His expression softens. "Margo Eton, you are easily one of the smartest women I have ever met, but you can truly be so obtuse sometimes." I do not reply, still waiting for an answer. He continues, "I kissed you because I wanted to. I have wanted to kiss you for...some time now." He must be playing a game with me. Does he think this is a joke? "I kissed you because, in this moment, I can no longer recall the words I have been longing to say, and a kiss was the only way to convey that message."

"Eddy, if this is a game you are playing, I want no part. If you did this so you can run back to London and tell them that you have compromised me. I will not stand for it."

"Margo! How can you think so low of me? Of course, I would never utter a word of this to anyone. Not my sister or even Albert."

My heart is racing, my skin is flushed, and my heart wants me to throw myself back into Eddy's arms, but I'm too bright for this. Edward Riley was my friend for years, and then he abandoned me, followed by public distaste for me. I let my guard down during his visit, and I will not forgive myself for it. He spent *years* hating me. This cannot possibly mean anything to him. "Are you simply lonely out here without your typical female companions from the city?" The only reasonable explanation for what happened last week and again tonight.

"Margo, I will not stand for your mockery any longer. I kissed you because I wanted to kiss you. I needed to kiss you! I do not care if anyone sees it because I plan to make good on our actions."

"You want to marry me?"

No, absolutely not. That cannot be true.

"Have we not put our past behind us? We were once friends who found a mutual understanding which I felt has progressed to rekindling our friendship. Marriage has been the main topic of conversation since I have arrived. We are both discussing getting married soon. Why is it so shocking that I would consider marrying you?"

I can no longer stand while I silently consider what he is telling me. I sit back down on the step he initially found me on when this conversation began. He knows I want to marry for love. I have made that clear over the last two weeks. He arrived hating me less than a month ago. A hate he held onto for years yet never made time to explain why he was so cruel to me. We have stopped arguing and have been civil, even flirtatious at times toward each other, but that does not make either of us in love.

This is absurd.

As much as I hate to admit it, he is too smart to think of himself in love after a few days of polite conversation. He has spent all this time without showing interest to anyone in town, but now he suddenly feels ready to commit to me? Evey did mention pressure from his parents for him to marry soon. A pressure that he has been pushing onto me since he arrived. At that moment, I meet his eyes, and everything becomes clear to me.

He places his hands on his hips, still standing beside me. "You are a frustrating woman, Margo."

"You need to marry soon. You have no interest in the women in London." Verbally connecting the puzzle pieces.

"That is all correct, but it is more than that," he says firmly.

"A surprising turn of events since days ago, you acted as if I were your sworn enemy. Since you've arrived, you've been reminding me that I, too, need to wed soon to secure my current lifestyle as well as my future."

"That is correct because I was concerned about what would come of you," Eddy answers, still standing.

"You stayed in my home and learned of my lifestyle and how dear it is to me. You were exposed to what my future husband is set to inherit. You are such a smart man, Eddy. You convinced me to start considering marriage."

"Be careful with whatever accusation you make next, Margo. I will not be forgiving if you dishonor me with your imagined excuses." Eddy's back is straightening as he stands taller.

"You said yourself. For years, you have only ever expected the basics from your wife while you can still have your freedoms. Who better to be that wife who stays out of your way and simply raises the children in the country but me? Not to mention the fortune you would be gaining."

"*Enough*, Margo! You shall make no additional judgments of my character or my feelings for you. You could not be further from the truth, but I will not stand here any longer and listen to you spin these lies in your head to justify the idea that you have cemented in your mind that no one can love you because of your fortune." He does not look at me again as he walks straight into the house and slams the door behind him.

I sit for a long time, looking at the stairs. Trying to process everything that happened since I stepped outside tonight. I also do not want to risk the chance of meeting him in the hallway. When enough time has passed, I return to my room.

31

The sky is showing signs that the sun is about to rise as I knock loudly on the main entrance to Lady Calderwood's estate. It would not surprise me if the staff were still asleep. I am prepared to sit here for hours before anyone realizes that I am out here. Even if it were raining, it would still be preferable over staying at Eton Cottage for another moment. To my surprise, the door cracks open.

"Good morning, Claire. My apologies for coming unannounced." I try to keep my voice low so as to not startle the maid who answers the door and hope she recognizes me from the dinner I attended last week.

"No need to apologize, Mr. Riley. Lady Calderwood insisted you are always welcome. I apologize, but both the Lady and her guest, Mr. Berry, are not yet awake. Do you need me to wake either of them?" She is careful not to insinuate that they are together.

"There is no urgent matter at hand, but if it is all right

with you, I would like to wait for them until they are available. May I wait inside?"

"Of course, sir. Would you like a room?" she asks in a welcoming tone.

"If you can just escort me to the library, I am sure there is more than enough there to entertain me for some time."

Claire nods and leads me to the library on the second floor. With my expressed gratitude she closes the door behind her and leaves me alone with my own thoughts. Speaking with her is a nice break from the agony I have been living with for the past twelve hours. Hopefully, I can find a book that will consume my mind while I wait to speak with Albert.

An hour of unsuccessful distraction attempts later, Claire returns with a tray of tea and biscuits for me. "With arriving so early, I assumed you mustn't have had the time to eat breakfast. I thought this may help. Is there anything else that I can get for you, Mr. Riley?"

"Claire, you are a gift from the heavens, but no thank you. This is more than enough." She smiles kindly at my thanks and leaves again. I contemplate calling her back for the company, but that would be selfish of me as I am sure the woman has responsibilities to attend to.

Hours pass, and I find myself surrounded by piles of books that I have pulled from their shelves in hopes that they would distract my endless thoughts of last night. My anger is getting the best of me. There are other emotions present, but I cannot process them at this time. No one else has a way of possessing my head, my heart, and my soul as Margo does. I begin pacing the library floor. It is as if I move enough that I will shake this feeling from my body. Perhaps I should go outside for a walk, fresh air might help. No sooner than I reach for the doorknob does it open to reveal Albert standing there assessing my disheveled appearance.

"Edward, has something happened? Evelyn? Margo? Is something wrong? I rushed to the library the minute Claire told me of your early arrival. Why did you not have her wake us?" Seeing the terror on my best friend's face made me feel foolish for acting so rashly in running away from Eton Cottage.

"Albert, please know there is no need for such concern. Everyone at Eton Cottage is in good health." I grab his shoulders to settle him.

Once he understands my words, he steps out of my hold and looks somewhat frustrated. "Lily would always welcome you into her home, but what was the reason for your early morning arrival?"

Feeling more embarrassed than ever, I turn and start walking into the library to the table in the center of the room. "You may want to sit down for this," I say, without turning my back to him but pulling out the chair opposite him from where I plan to sit.

Once we are both seated, he sits silently, waiting for me to explain. "I feel like a child for acting as such and running to hide here."

"Does this have to do with a particular young lady your sister is visiting?" Albert mocks.

"Indeed," I answer. "I shared my feelings with her."

Albert's jaw falls open so quickly that I am anticipating the sound of it crashing on the table. "And..."

"And she did not feel that they could be motivated by anything aside from her fortune and the ease of satisfying my family's demand of finding a wife. She added that I was only now interested since I have seen her way of living and, as such, would guarantee a wife that stayed out of my life."

Albert waits for me to elaborate, but I just cannot find the words. I am angry that she lets her fortune be the only reason she would assume that I would want to marry her. Not the weeks that we have spent together, fighting, laughing, arguing. Talking, coming to an understanding. Then, there is the hurt that I offered her my heart, my love, and my future, and she so easily turned me away. I cannot speak the words. I just let my face fall to my hands.

Albert speaks softly and steadily. "Okay, chap, we'll talk more when you are ready. Until then, we will just take it one day at a time. Firstly, does anyone at Eton Cottage know that you left or why?"

"I left Evey a note saying that I would be here this morning. I did not elaborate. Upon my departure, I ran into Mr. Landon. I told him that I forgot we had planned to hunt and to send everyone my apologies for the late notice."

With a deep sigh, Albert continues, "Okay, so you have some options. You are welcome to stay here until your return to London. When will you plan to return?"

While I would like to get as far away from Eton Cottage as possible this very minute, I know Evey would be highly suspicious of why I insist on an immediate departure for her as well. "I suppose I can stay until Evelyn is ready to return to London. No need to rush her."

"All right, then." He leans back in his chair for a few moments, clearly planning something I no longer have the capacity to do. "I will visit Eton Cottage today and relay that you will not be returning and fetch your belongings. We will need a reason for your sister and the Landons. Am I to assume that Margo will not be surprised by this news?"

"That is a correct assumption," I answer plainly. Will she ask about me? Will she insist on coming here when she knows I will be next door? Does she have any regrets for how she ended things last night? There is a part of me that wants her to ask about me, perhaps wants her to come see me here. I cannot linger on these thoughts. They will only lead to a truth that I do not want to acknowledge. I miss her already.

"All right, so they believe we are out hunting since dawn. I can head to Eton Cottage soon and tell them our hunt was ended short due to an injury on your part that will not allow you out of bed for a week's time?"

"That's fine."

With a mischievous smile, Albert asks, "What should this injury be?"

A broken heart. A slight huff leaves my nose. "I do not care, Albert. Whatever you think is best."

"Right, let's join Lily for lunch and share with her what has occurred. She can get you settled in a room while I'm gone."

"Thank you, Albert. I could not ask for a better friend in this life."

He nods and leads the way out of the library.

32

The sun begins to rise through my window. Things are different today than they were yesterday. I will never be able to go back to a time before Eddy kissed me and suggested we marry. I sat up all night, considering his anger when I questioned his motives. It is not to say there were not moments in the night that my mind drifted to thoughts of his lips on mine. It does not matter how much I enjoyed his kiss. I spent years convincing myself that no man would love me beyond my fortune. I struggle even now to recall the reasons he gave for wanting to marry me.

Could I have reacted too quickly?

Thinking over our exchanges since his arrival, even the positive ones surely cannot be enough to make a man fall in love with me after years of animosity.

I know better than to assume that we can go back to the polite conversations around Evey. Today, it all resumes. Out of what has become a habit and small hope,

I check the floor next to the door to my bedroom. It is bare, no letter from Eddy waiting for me.

If he seems amenable, perhaps we can speak further on the issue.

With a deep breath and my favorite dress, I turn my doorknob, ready to face the day.

The halls are quiet, and I find the Landons and Evey in the kitchen for what appears to be a typical morning. I have no intention of sharing last night's events with any of them. I look around for Eddy as I wish them each a good morning.

"That reminds me, Margo." Mr. Landon grabs my attention. "Eddy left early for Lady Calderwood's. He forgot to mention last night that he promised to meet Albert there for an early morning hunt. He sends his best." I attempt to keep my face unphased. If anyone could read my emotions, it would be the Landons. Mr. Landon continues searching my face for a reaction, but I simply act with the usual amount of pleasure at his departure. "He said he may be staying for the day and not to worry if he did not return for dinner."

"Perfect," I answer and turn toward Evey. "We could start our day off with a swim and then dry off in the sun?"

"Yes, that sounds wonderful," she responds.

My mind overthinking the events from the night before, I let Evey do most of the talking during our walk to the lake. "I very much enjoyed the visit from Mr. Richard Landon and his family, Margo."

Too distracted to truly contribute to this conversation, I try to think of a neutral response. "Yes, they are a wonderful family. Tom has a wild heart, but Arthur is a sweet boy. I'm glad you were able to spend time with them during your visit."

"Both very handsome young men." She stares off into the distance.

"Yes, I suppose they are. I still see two little boys when I look at them." Images of throwing Tom into the lake with Arthur trailing behind us snickering is a welcome distraction.

"I did not get to speak much with Tom, but Arthur was very friendly." Arthur has always been more interested in academics than his older brother. I can see why Evelyn gravitated more to him. Although, Tom was too busy carrying me to the lake to really make much of her acquaintance.

It is on our evening walk back to the house from spending the day at the lake that we are met by Albert.

"Hello, Ladies. Did you have a nice afternoon?"

"Yes, it was the perfect day for a swim, Albert. How was the hunt?" Evey asks.

Has he accompanied Eddy back to the cottage? I look around but do not see Eddy anywhere near us. He must be back at the house with the Landons.

"The hunt was thrilling today, Evey. So very exciting that your brother managed to twist his ankle." Albert gives me a stern look as the words leave his mouth.

"Oh my, is he okay? Where is he now?" she asks.

"Not to worry at all, my dear," Albert reassures her. "Your brother is a strong man and is currently being spoiled beyond belief by Lady Calderwood and her staff. A doctor has already come and gone and reported there will be no permanent damage, but he is to stay off his feet for a few days. I have come to collect his things for him while he rests at Lady Calderwood's estate."

A heavy feeling takes over, and I realize last night was more than just another argument between Eddy and me. How I wish I could believe Albert's story of Eddy's twisted ankle. I know it was I who ran Eddy from Eton Cottage, and now he no longer could face me.

"Shall I go to him?" she asks Albert and then turns to me. "Margo, would you mind?"

"Not at all, Evey. I completely understand." I squeeze her hand in support.

"Eddy knew you would want to rush to his side and asked me to insist that you stay and enjoy your holiday with Margo," Albert insists.

She nods in agreement, but it is clear she is still worried. We began our walk back to the cottage.

Albert addresses Evey, "I do believe your brother will plan to return to London after he is cleared to stand on his ankle again. He has asked if you would accompany him in one week's time?"

"Yes, of course," Evey answers with nothing but love in her voice.

"Splendid," Albert answers. "I will be by that morning to escort you to Lady Calderwood's where the Riley carriage will be to take you both home."

As we approach the house, Albert asks Evey if she would not mind giving him a moment to speak with me in private. She says her goodbyes to Albert as she runs toward the house.

33

Albert and I sit on a bench in the garden. I feel like a child who is about to be scolded. By the sheer miracle, Albert does not appear to be aware of last night's events. I am determined not to speak first in hopes of avoiding the unpleasant conversation.

"You did not show as much concern as Evey when I shared the news of Mr. Riley's accident." His statement is filled with judgment.

"Well, I am not his sister. It would be undignified to show more emotion than his family member." He gives me a knowing look. I continue, "Something tells me the accident is a fabricated story to cover why he ran from my home in the middle of the night."

"I will not confirm or deny your accusation," Albert answers. "Quite frankly, I am getting extremely tired of being in the middle of whatever it is that you two have going on."

"I can guarantee you, there is nothing going on between us," I answer with confidence.

"Enough, Margo." Albert is clearly exasperated.

"You are beginning to sound like him. He said those exact words to me last night when I realized his true intentions." An overwhelming desire to defend myself comes over me.

"Even after a night to sleep on the matter, you still feel that you were correct for accusing him of such things?" Albert asks, not raising his voice to me but clearly taking Eddy's side of things.

"So you have heard of the events? Keep in mind, Albert, you have only heard his side of the story."

"That may be true, and I will be happy to hear your side of the story but based on his brief recollection and my familiarity with you, I can only imagine he speaks the truth."

I roll my eyes and cross my arms in front of my chest. Before I can speak again, Albert turns to me. "Margo, we all know you are a brilliant girl, but you do miss things happening in your world more than you know."

"I find it hard to believe Albert. You cannot expect me to believe Eddy has suddenly fallen in love with me in just a few days."

"I will not speak on Eddy's behalf—that is for the two of you to work through one day, but I will be happy to provide evidence that you miss things that are obvious in your life."

"Such as?" I ask with sarcasm, certain he has nothing to tell me that I do not already know.

He squares his shoulders and sits up straight. "I am in love with Lily. I have been for years."

My world shatters. Not because I am upset that he

loves Lily or upset that this means he could no longer be a potential husband for me, but because I consider him one of my closest friends, and I never noticed. "Why did you not say something sooner? Did you not feel you could confide in me?"

He slides closer to me on the bench and puts his arm around my shoulders. "My dear, it was not done as an offense to you, but something I just wasn't ready to share with the world."

"Well, I suppose you are right. I did miss that, but if no one knew, then I cannot be blamed for not seeing it." I scramble to defend myself. "If Lily did not know, then how am I expected to have noticed."

"Lily does know. She has known for some time." Another confession that shakes me to my core. Why had she not told me? I have never kept anything from her and assumed she had done the same.

"What did she say when you told her?" I ask, knowing he has every right to deny me that information as it is not truly my business to know.

"I'm beyond happy to finally share with you that we have been in love with each other for almost two years now. We took things slowly at first but have been growing more serious with time. We planned to tell you after our return from London, but you invited Evey to spend the summer months with you at Eton Cottage. Lily did not want to intrude on her visit."

"Oh my, what I said to Lily about you when we were having tea!" I am so embarrassed for telling her I ever considered marrying Albert.

Albert laughs and gives my shoulders another

squeeze. "I heard about that, and I must say, I'm beyond flattered, Margo."

Heat rises to my face in embarrassment. I immediately cover it with my hands. Albert laughs gently, pulls my hands down, and turns my chin to face him. "It was not a horrible thought, my dear. Honestly, had I not fallen in love and found myself without prospects when you needed to marry, I would have done it. You made a valid point—when love is not an option, friendship would have been the second best choice." He pauses and waits for my reaction. I smile softly as he continues. "All I want for you, dear Margo, is to find a love like I have found. Promise me, you will try to open your eyes a little more once we arrive back in London to the prospect of falling in love."

"I promise, Albert. I truly am so very happy for you and Lily. I would go to her immediately and apologize for my comments, but I think your house guest is there to avoid me, so it will have to wait until he departs."

"Yes, it would be best to wait. But darling, due to Lily's circumstances and the Calderwood estate, we have not quite worked out how we plan to proceed with our relationship. If you could not make any reference to it when we are in London, we would greatly appreciate your discretion."

"Certainly, you have my word," I reassure him.

Albert begins to rise from the bench to take his leave when something occurs to me. "Albert, I still do not see how I was blind to your relationship if no one else knew."

He leans down and whispers, "I did not say no one knew. I said no one in London knew. The Landons figured it out a year ago. Even Eddy knew after spending one day in our shared company." My mouth falls open in shock. Albert leans forward and kisses my forehead. "Take care, my sweet girl. Enjoy the rest of Miss Riley's stay. I shall see you in a week when I come to escort Evey for her journey back to London."

And he walks off without another word. I sit on the bench alone for some time before Mrs. Landon comes out to sit with me. I'm not ready to speak about Eddy's suggested proposal, but she needs an explanation as to why I stayed outside by myself once Albert left. "What has your mind so occupied, Margo?" she asks as she takes the spot on the bench where Albert was sitting. "I cannot imagine it is your concern for Mr. Riley after Albert relayed the news of his accident."

With a huff, I answer, "No, that is not it. Albert was simply relaying that I have a habit of missing things that are happening in front of my face." I turn toward her. "He confessed his relationship with Lily. He said you knew for a year's time. You did not ever think to tell me?" I ask.

"Margo, it is your own fault you did not pay enough attention to the way they looked at each other, how they always seemed to sit or walk close to one another. At first, I thought you did know but were declining to mention it out of respect due to their situation. It was months later that I realized you did not even notice. It was never my secret to tell."

"I suppose you are right. Do you think they see me as a poor friend because I did not notice?"

"Not at all. I believe, if anything, they may be grateful that you did not notice. It allowed them both to maintain their friendship with you and develop their relationship without interference. The longer you did not know, the less strain on them to make the relationship work for your friendship."

"I suppose that is true. I still feel like a poor friend," I confess.

"Well, right now, you are playing host to another friend. I was informed she will be leaving in a week. I suggest you make the most of your time with her before she leaves, and then you will have plenty of time to work through things with both Lily and Albert."

"Of course," I agree, and we head back into the house.

Mrs. Landon places her arm through mine and pulls me close then whispers. "I do not expect it today or even this week, but I do expect you to share what happened that made Mr. Riley run from here and refuse to return."

I look at her with my mouth shut and a pleading face.

"When you are comfortable. Promise me."

"I promise." Thankful she was not demanding answers this minute. I do not know how I would explain it to her. I myself am questioning exactly what happened last night.

THE REMAINDER of Evey's stay is spent similar to our days prior to Eddy's arrival. By the end of her visit, I consider her one of my closest friends. We spend our days speaking about the books she reads during her stay, her reignited love of swimming, and much gossip on what we believe the important people of London must be doing to pass the time until the next ball.

While I make sure to give Evey my complete attention in her presence, when we part each night, my thoughts always drift to her brother. Most nights are spent trying to decide how I feel about the words spoken between Eddy and me that night on the steps. Albert was trying to expand my understanding when he shared about his relationship with Lily. I assume Lily wished to tell me herself, but she must have agreed with his urgency to share the information with me. Perhaps he was trying to tell me that Eddy was honest in his feelings. Yet, even if that were true, Eddy could not be trusted if he was so carefree with his feelings and judgments to declare he loved someone after a few days.

Other nights were spent thinking about his kiss. So many of my novels described a passionate kiss between lovers, but none of those descriptions came close to how Eddy's kiss felt. I find myself trying to remember what his hand felt like on my back.

I try to rid my mind of Eddy Riley, but nothing helps. By the end of the week, I find it difficult to concentrate on a new book without my mind drifting to him. Regardless of how much I think of him, I always come to the same conclusion. While I may not have handled the situation in the best way, the outcome was correct.

On the day of Evey's departure, Albert arrives to collect her with the Riley's carriage. He has a few letters from Lily in his hand. "These are from Lily. Mostly events and balls for you to attend in London. She wanted you to have the list so you can prepare."

"Thank you, Albert. Please send Lily my love. I will review these today."

We exchange pleasantries with Theo before he and Mr. Landon load Evey's luggage into the carriage. Evey says her goodbyes to the Landons with a hug for each and endless thanks for hosting her. They insist she returns as soon as she begins to miss Eton Cottage. She pleasantly laughs and answers, "If that is the case, we shall be seeing each other sooner than you would expect."

The time for her and I to say our goodbyes arrives. It will only be a few short weeks until we are reunited in London, but things will be different there. We both have different expectations of ourselves in London. "I will forever cherish the time spent with you here at Eton Cottage. I'm so thankful to have you as a friend, Margo."

"You have given me a friendship that I never thought possible, Evey. I look forward to our reunion in London. Please warn your parents that I will be expecting you as a regular guest at Eton Cottage."

"Certainly," Evey agrees, throwing her hands around me in a hug. I squeeze her tight, not wanting to let go.

Eventually, I do, as Albert holds out his arm to escort her to the carriage.

We wave from the door as they drive off in the direction of Lady Calderwood's home. It was a clear message that Albert came to escort Evey, and only after retrieving her would Eddy join his sister in the carriage... carefully avoiding seeing me.

The carriage containing Evelyn and Albert makes its way in the direction of the Calderwood Estate. I stand near the front stairs with Lily. She says quietly as if they might hear, "Do not forget to favor your left leg."

Immediately shifting my weight to my right leg, I hate the idea of lying to my sister, but it is the preferred alternative over including her in my mess with Margo.

Albert exits the carriage with my sister close behind him. "Eddy! How are you? I would have come sooner, but Albert insisted I stay with Margo until today." She barely finishes her speech before giving me a quick hug and looking down to check my ankle.

I knew she would be suspicious, so I made sure to bandage it this morning. "Almost completely healed, sister. It is good to see you now. Are you ready for the journey back to London?" She returns her gaze to mine with a look indicating she still is not convinced.

We each say quick goodbyes to Lily and Albert and

then begin our journey home. I knew better than to expect a quiet ride home.

"Tell me more about this injury that was so horrific you could not return to give your gratitude and farewells to the Landons and Margo yourself but instead sent them through Albert." My sister clearly has a speech prepared, likely one that will last the entirety of the ride home. I simply lift my pants cuff to display the bandages in response.

Evelyn is not convinced. "I know something else happened. Did you say something to Margo? Tell me!"

With a deep sigh, trying to hold in all of my emotions, I turn to my sister and give her the most honest answer I can bear. "If you wish to continue your friendship with Miss Eton and continue to visit Eton Cottage in the future, I will never speak against it again. You have my full support, as I have learned during my time that your friendship would only deliver positive results."

"Yes, I'm well aware of that. I certainly plan to remain friends with Margo. Why are you avoiding the question? I saw you both together as the days passed, and you seemed like friends yourself."

"Evelyn, my time at Eton Cottage has changed my opinion of Miss Eton from what it was before I arrived, but that does not mean anything aside from how it relates to you. There will never be any relationship, friendship, or otherwise between Miss Eton and myself aside from our shared affection for you." This is getting more and more difficult to speak about.

Evey sits back in her seat, utter confusion radiating off of her. I watch as she replays the events of my visit in her head. I am about to put an end to her torture, but before I can, she shares her thoughts. "Eddy, when Albert came to tell us of your *injury*, I was worried at first, but then I noticed Margo's face. She did not seem surprised at all."

"You mean she did not show any concern?" The snarky comment flew out of my mouth before I could stop it. Trying to mask my anger from Eveyln is not going as well as I would have hoped. I cannot help but be angry. Furious at Margo's dismissal of me and her accusation of fortune-seeking when she knew well enough that I did not need her title or money. Furious at the way her kiss haunts my dreams. And furious mostly at how she has damned herself to the life of an untrusting marriage.

"No. She seemed upset but simply not surprised at the news that you would not be returning. Tell me what happened. I know you did not have a hunting trip planned that morning. Why did you leave?"

Needing to deflect away from answering, I ask, "Did you batter Miss Eton with the same interrogation that you are giving me?"

"Of course I did, Eddy! But she did not give me any information and would only play into the story Albert delivered on your behalf. Even the Landons did not believe it. But Margo refused to discuss your departure."

Leaning forward toward my sister, I plead, "Evelyn, it was time for me to depart from Eton Cottage when I did. I can promise you that an injury on my part was the sole cause of that departure. Please let it go for now. We have a long journey ahead of us, and I would like to rest before we step back into our busy lives in London." I want to be honest with my sister, and every word I speak is the truth.

I just did not specify what my injury was. It was certainly not my perfectly healthy right ankle. It was my shattered heart.

She nods quietly and pulls a book out of her bag. We travel the remainder of the journey in silence. Again, I find myself consumed with thoughts of Margo. This morning was Margo's last opportunity to see me before we left. I certainly did not want to see her, but given our argumentative relationship, I expected her to show up at the Calderwood Estate to continue our argument.

An image of her in another one of those tight summer dresses comes to mind. The main doors would slam open with the force of the king's army only to reveal her standing in the entryway, her breath coming out in staggering huffs, her chest barely contained by that dress. Her face is stoic until our eyes meet, and then she unleashes a barrage of insults as she storms toward me.

Each time this scene plays out in my head, it ends with me grabbing her around the waist, pulling her in close, and kissing until I cannot remember my name as I did the last night I saw her. I knew at that moment that I wanted to spend the rest of my life making her mad, getting yelled at, and then resolving it with endless kisses.

Why have I been so cursed to love a woman that makes it impossible to do so?

In the week we have been parted, I have narrowed my numerous emotions down to two. I wake up angry and spend most of the day that way. It is only in the deep of the night before I find sleep that I miss her. Lying in bed, I replay every word said between us, trying to find something I misunderstood. While replaying these memories, I cannot help but recall the feeling of her under me the night of the storm. I knew it might never occur again, but I was hopeful it would. We barely spoke for years, and yet it took days for her to settle her soul back into my heart.

There was not a moment that I did not enjoy her company, her laughs, her arguments, her smart mouth. Then there was her love for my sister. How can I ever find a bride that is so close to Evelyn? It felt as though she were feeling the same toward me. That we were meant to reconnect. I have never felt more certainty in an action than when I kissed her, and she kissed me back. Could it truly be her stubborn mind stopping her from believing someone could actually love her with no care for the fortune attached to her?

35

It has been so quiet around the Eton Cottage since Evey left. That is not to say that I do not enjoy time with the Landons, but her departure was a sign of another upcoming trip to London with Lily. I try to focus on spending time with her, but I am not looking forward to facing Eddy again. We did not exchange any correspondence since he left for Lily's and conveniently twisted his ankle the following day. I am glad that when we are eventually reunited, we will be in a room full of people to distract us.

"Margo!" Mrs. Landon shouts as she bursts through the library door. "You must get dressed quickly."

"What is wrong? I am dressed." It hits then, not properly dressed, we must have unfamiliar company. Is it Eddy? What if he brought others from town to shatter my way of life? "Who is it?" I say as I quickly cross the room to meet her at the door.

She meets my eyes. "Lord and Lady Eton are here." For

as long as I can remember, Mrs. Landon has refused to address them as my parents.

Why would they come here? My suspicions must have been correct. Eddy must have gone to them to tell them of his disapproval or, worse, our interaction.

At least they would not be surprised at the Landons' lifestyle, but I cannot remember the last time they visited the country. "Did you say they are *both* here? They traveled together?" I stop in my bedroom's doorway. When were they last together? Something must be terribly wrong. I rush with Mrs. Landon's help to get a proper dress on and then we both run down to the sitting room.

Sitting with Mr. Landon are Lord and Lady Eton. Lady Eton is seated in a large chair, fixing her skirt, while Lord Eton stands and begins pacing past the windows. Both are dressed in their finest clothing, fit for an audience with royals. Their faces are as stoic as ever, which makes it difficult to guess what could be the reason for their visit.

"Father, Mother…is everything all right?"

"What a way for you to greet your parents, Margaret!" my mother screeches.

"Sorry, Mother. It is so nice to see you both. Have you decided to visit in the country with me?"

My father cannot stop himself as his face scrunches into a look of pure distaste at my last question. I would like to believe the distaste is his reaction to staying in the country and not spending time with me, but who could tell? He turns to me with a stern face. "I have terrible news to share with you, Margaret."

"Yes, Father?" I do not believe that I have ever been this nervous in his company. Panic is taking over my thoughts. Could he be selling Eton Cottage? Dismissing the Landons? Dragging me back to London for an arranged marriage?

"Do you recall my business partner and close friend, Mr. Ford?"

I remember the name, but I cannot recall much more about that man. "Yes." I feel that would be the safest answer.

"He died at the beginning of the week." My father says with such sadness that I am surprised by his irregular show of emotions. My mother sits unphased in her chair. She is obviously not as upset about this news as he is.

"Oh, Father, I am very sorry." I do not want to minimize my father's loss, but I still do not understand why this man's passing was a necessary reason for the two of them to come to the country. Could it be that my father suddenly decided to value the family he has? Want to spend time with his wife and only child?

"Mr. Ford's sudden death has forced your father to acknowledge his own mortality," my mother clarifies. "As you know, Margaret, if something were to happen to your father, it is up to you to maintain the family's position and lifestyle by marrying and providing a husband that your father can pass the estate onto." Well, that makes much more sense than the thought of my parents suddenly having an interest in their child.

The Landons remain quiet while my parents are in the room. I can be sure they will have plenty to discuss with me later, but for now, they are silent. Now that I know what they want, I can give them an answer that satisfies them, and they could be on their way back to

London in what I can only imagine would be a silent ride.

"Mother, Father...I have been giving serious thought to the idea of marriage since departing from London. I agree—I believe it is time that I start considering possible matches for myself when I return to the city. I have been visiting with Lady Calderwood, and she has planned a plentiful list of balls and parties for me to attend. I will be happy to write to you regularly on my progress. I am hoping within a year or two to find my husband."

My father and mother both look between each other and me with confused looks on their faces. I glance toward the Landons, and they appear just as confused.

"We were under the impression you just hosted Evelyn and Edward Riley here for weeks. Is that not correct?" my mother asks.

What does Evey's visiting have anything to do with the passing of Mr. Ford? "Yes, that is correct," I answer. Again, the confused looks continue between the two.

"Then why did you make plans with the Dowager Calderwood to search for suitors in London?" My father asks. I hate when he refers to Lily that way. As though she is less in society because her husband has died.

"I'm sorry, Father. I do not understand what the two things have in common."

"With Edward Riley visiting accompanied by his sister, I assumed you two finally came to an understanding. We are here to proceed with the arrangements," my father says with no emotion.

"Arrangements?"

"For marriage," my mother says, with little excitement in her voice.

I have no words—my mouth is open, but my voice is as silent as my mind.

"I understand you are both free spirits, but as you can see from our marriage, you can finalize the relationship and still retain your freedoms," Father says without judgment.

How is it possible that my parents are aware of Eddy's hasty suggestions of a proposal made in the middle of the night? Did he go to my father with hopes of overriding my refusal? "A simple visit from a young lady who was briefly joined by her older brother is enough for you to assume he proposed marriage to me?" I attempt to keep my tone even so as to not give anything away if this is just an odd coincidence.

"No, daughter. I assumed Mr. Riley sent his sister to get to know his soon-to-be wife, and he joined during her trip." His tone is firm, and it is clear his patience is wearing just as thin as mine. My mother is actively listening from her chair but has yet to interject.

"Just because a gentleman visited when his sister was staying with us, you assume it must mean we are to be married? You are both well aware Mr. Berry has visited both our home and that of Lady Calderwood. Did you assume he was planning to propose as well?"

My father straightens his posture as if I just said something preposterous. "No, I never assumed Mr. Berry was going to propose marriage because he never notified me of any intentions to marry you."

He did go behind my back. "And Mr. Riley has?"

Emotions of all sorts overtake me. I am angry with him for going directly to my father rather than coming back to speak with me directly. Among my frustration, I feel a slight sense of relief. Perhaps Eddy does want to speak with me again...more than speak with me.

"Yes, of course, Margaret. That is why we assumed you both finally decided to marry during his visit," he says with exasperation.

Thankfully, I am still close to the chair I was sitting in earlier. I grab the arm to make sure I fall into the chair and not onto the floor when my legs start to give out beneath me. My mind begins racing. "When?" It was the only word I could speak. I need to make sense of this information.

My father and mother look at my shock in surprise. My father answers, "Years ago, Margo. Why are you acting like this? Surely, you have discussed this with Mr. Riley."

"Years ago? How many?" So, it had nothing to do with his stay with Evey. I was right in thinking his hatred grew for me over the years. Why did he never come to me with his feelings? Was it before or after the announcement about my husband inheriting my father's estate? Although, I realize Eddy does not need my family's fortune. He was to become a Lord himself after his father's passing.

"Does it matter, Margaret?" my mother asks, clearly displaying her disinterest in this conversation. I do not care if she is bored. I need to know.

I repeat my question to my father. "How many years ago?"

"I believe it was your first year out in society. Is this

correct?" He turns for my mother to confirm. She just nods.

I lower my head into my hands. Eddy wanted to marry me in my first season. Why had he never mentioned this to me? Especially at the time? We were still on friendly terms then.

"Margaret," my mother speaks with a firm voice.

I lift my head, eyes catching the concerned looks coming from the Landons. "I...I was not aware of his intentions," I say to them, pleading in my voice. I turn back to my mother. "I never knew he felt this way."

As expected, my mother shows little interest in my current feelings. "Well, now you do know. Can we count on you to discuss this matter with Mr. Riley and move forward with the arrangements?"

Move forward? How can I ever speak to Eddy again after I all but ran him out of my house and accused him of being the worst type of man? Even worse, do I want to know why he decided not to marry me? I cannot worry about that yet. First, I need my parents out of Eton Cottage. I stand back up, addressing both parents.

"Father, I understand the urgency of this matter. I am again sorry about the passing of your dear friend, Mr. Ford. Mother, thank you for coming in support of both father during this trying time and myself, given the new developments. I cannot guarantee things will be resolved with Mr. Riley. I am almost certain he no longer feels that way toward me. I will find a suitable husband. Arranging a quick marriage will be my priority from this moment on." I remain standing, waiting for their response and hoping that they would take this answer as suitable and make their leave.

My father stays quiet at first, but my mother answers as she rises from her seat. "Thank you, Margaret. I will see you when you return to the city. We will be happy to start preparations as soon as you acquire another proposal." She looks back at my father, waiting for him to give his goodbyes.

He walks over close to me. "I am sorry to hear it did not work out with Mr. Riley. He is a good man, but I can understand why he would not find pleasure in a life like this," he says, looking around with the same disgusted face as before. It is certainly time for my parents to leave.

"Thank you, Father. Have a safe trip back to London."

My parents give the Landons brief goodbyes and head out the door.

"Now may be the time for you to explain what happened with Mr. Riley when he visited and be sure to include what happened the night before he left and refused to return," Mr. Landon says with his arms crossed over his chest.

I look at Mrs. Landon. "You will need to talk about this, darling. Let us help."

Beginning with the dinner Eddy and I attended at Lady Calderwood's, I explained that while the discussions were mostly heated, I was able to share my concerns in a way that I believed led us to an understanding and, at the very least, diminished his concerns for my influence over his sister.

"And what of the night before he left? We were all

together, and you both seemed to be getting along," Mrs. Landon asks.

"I could not sleep that night, so I went outside to sit on the steps. Eddy joined me."

"And you sat in silence?" Mr. Landon asks.

"No, we spoke. It started out innocently enough. Then, the conversation turned to the two of us needing to take the marriage market seriously when we returned to London. I teased him about his lack of interest in the woman he would marry. He then made a comment that he has changed his attitude toward this topic. I just assumed he meant he grew bitter with age, not that he was once so invested in a bride that he went so far as to ask my father for his permission."

"That still does not explain why he left," Mr. Landon reminds me.

"Let her continue, Thomas," Mrs. Landon says as she gives her husband a frustrated look.

"The conversation continued regarding what I may be looking for in a suitor and what he may be looking for in a bride. At one point, he…suggested we may be a good match." I cannot tell them about the kiss I shared with Eddy. I do not think that they would scorn me or force me to marry the man. I wish to keep it to myself.

The Landons do not speak, but their eyes grow wild and wait for me to continue.

"At first, I was shocked, unable to understand why a man I was sure hated me would suggest such a thing. I remembered Evey had mentioned weeks ago that her parents were starting to press Eddy to take a bride. That was when the argument happened. I accused him of spending his time here to deceive me into believing that I should marry soon and choose him. All so that he could get his parents off of his back and gain my father's fortune."

"Margo..." Mrs. Landon gasps.

"I know. I will spare you the details of how cruel I truly was. I panicked and became defensive...excessively defensive."

"Cruel enough that the poor man could not bear to face you the next morning," Mrs. Landon says.

I dip my head. She is correct.

"Margo, if you truly despise him and feel no regret for your actions, then I agree with what you have done. Any man who tries to determine your fate against your will deserves to be treated as such. Never apologize for standing up for yourself," Mr. Landon says as he leans from his chair in my direction.

"No, it was not that. I do feel guilty. I felt guilty that night and even more so now," I admit. "Where do I go from here?" I ask for guidance. "Father just admitted that Eddy wanted to marry me eight years ago, but that certainly has changed in the past years. Yet, why would he revert to feelings of interest toward me now?"

"Because of the time you have spent together, I'm sure of it," Mrs. Landon states with confidence. "As for what you do next, that is up to you."

"How do you feel about him now, Margo? Have your feelings changed since he arrived?" Mr. Landon asks.

"I suppose they are not what they were when he arrived." I take a moment to consider before continuing my answer. "I'm embarrassed to say I wish I never dismissed him. How will I ever correct this? Do you think he will forgive me?"

"Only time will tell, Margo. Maybe it would be best to speak with Albert and Lily on the matter. Being they are acquaintances of you both, they may be able to offer advice on the best course to move forward."

"Thank you both. I think I would like to retire to my room. I have much to consider."

"Of course, darling, we will fetch you when dinner is ready." Mrs. Landon says with a smile that Mr. Landon matches with his own and a head nod.

36

Two weeks have gone by since we returned to London from the country. Trying to distract myself with my father's business has proved to be a useless attempt. Evenings are spent with family dinners and keeping to my room, trying to undo the damage done at Eton Cottage.

While Evelyn has stopped inquiring about the events of that night, she has moved onto encouraging me to write to Margo. Her suggestions opened my wounds in a way she could not possibly understand. At first, I ignored the idea. Then, as days go on, I decide that it might help to release some of the feelings that I cannot seem to shake. The first few letters are far crueler than any I had written at Eton Cottage. But the more letters I write, the less cruel they become. With no intention of mailing the letters to Margo, it helps to finally address all the emotions that have clung to me since her refusal.

My mother's most recent interference has been to invite

her friends and their eligible daughters to join us for dinner. In my room before this evening's meal, I contemplate leaving for the night to avoid the entire charade. There is a knock at the door, and without waiting for an answer, Evelyn enters. "Mother has requested you downstairs to welcome our dinner guests," she says with very little enthusiasm. Clearly, she is also getting tired of these games.

"I think I will stall for just a few minutes more. Care to join me?" I ask as I make my way to the small tray in the corner of the room.

"Why do you think I offered to come to fetch you, brother?" Evey steps beside me, pointing at a bottle. I grab a glass and pour her a small drink. This is a new occurrence that has become more regular since our time at Eton Cottage. I suppose I have Margo to thank for bringing my sister and me even closer than we were. She takes a sip and continues, "That girl downstairs is barely my age, and from the sounds of it, she has her life planned with you already. She is bragging to Mother about how she would make a perfect wife." She looks at me with a worried face. "Is that truly something gentlemen find appealing?"

"No, sister," I answer too quickly, thinking only that I would not find it appealing. "That is to say, unless it is a gentleman who has no interest in knowing their wife and just needs someone to fill the role." The more that I think about it, it is clear that I will eventually become that type of man. "As fun as this is, it will do us no good sitting up here wallowing in the knowledge it will be a boring evening. We may as well get this over with."

With a half smile on her lips, she says, "The sooner we go…"

"The sooner we can leave," I answer and hold my arm out for her.

If Evey and I spent hours preparing for this dinner it would not have been enough. Lady Harris and her young daughter, Miss Harris, are determined to make an impression tonight. They want my mother and I to be fully aware of how well-suited the young lady is to be my bride. Interestingly enough, there is no evidence that I am expected to prove myself a suitable husband for her in any way. I am barely expected to open my mouth since they have yet to stop talking since we sat down. I look over to my sister, and when she notices, she acts as if she is falling asleep. I smile, and Miss Harris takes it as a reaction to whatever she is going on about.

"I am so glad to see you are pleased by that, Mr. Riley," she says with great enthusiasm, as it is the only smile I have allowed this evening. "It would be a great honor to continue to please you, sir." This woman is starting to get on my nerves. I nod and return my attention to my meal.

"Edward, dear. This is an excellent opportunity for you to become better acquainted with Miss Harris. I recommend you take full advantage of it." My mother has authority in her tone.

With a sigh of resentment, I address Miss Harris with little interest showing in my features. "Tell me, what are some hobbies you enjoy?"

Lady Harris speaks before her daughter can. Quickly rambling on about Miss Harris's accomplishments, including speaking multiple languages, playing instruments, singing, and so on. All things she has mentioned multiple times since I joined their company. "Yes, quite impressive, Lady Harris." I turn to her daughter. "But what is it that you enjoy doing, Miss Harris?"

The young girl's back is straight, and it is clear that she has practiced this response many times in the mirror. "I enjoy learning new languages so that if my husband has international business associates, I will be able to act as host for any ladies or children in the party."

"How considerate of you, Miss Harris," is the most diplomatic answer I can think of at that moment. She opens her mouth, but I cannot bear to listen to any more prepared lines. I cut her off by turning the conversation to my sister. "Evelyn, perhaps you can speak with Miss Harris about the best languages for young ladies to learn?" At first, my sister gives me a look that indicates that she is not happy to be dragged into this conversation, but with a slight plea in my features, she understands immediately that I need her assistance.

I will always be thankful to be blessed with the perfect sibling.

"Yes, please, Miss Harris, I'd love to hear about the languages you've learned and which you would recommend," Evelyn says with fake enthusiasm.

Not long after the plates are cleared away, we move into the sitting room for conversation. I have no intention of enduring Harris's company for much longer. After a few minutes have passed, I stand to address the room. "My apologies, but I am not feeling well. Please excuse me." Without making eye contact with my mother, I bow and bid goodnight to Lady Harris and her daughter. Before I reach the staircase, Evelyn catches up with me.

"Eddy are you all right?" she asks with concern.

"I will be as soon as I put a healthy distance between myself and our dinner guests."

Her gaze falls as she gives a slight nod of understanding. I turn to climb the stairs when she grabs my arm. I turn back, and Evey quickly shares, "I miss her too." She does not wait long for me to respond before she drops her hold on me and returns to the sitting room.

I suppose I never thought about it much, but I realize I have never considered anyone as a potential wife aside from Margo. I knew it eight years ago, and it is just as clear tonight. How could I when I have been in Margo's presence since childhood? How could I find myself attracted to anyone less interesting than her?

AN HOUR LATER, a knock comes at the door, and Evelyn enters again without invitation. I give her an exasperated look. "Do you ever wait for an invitation or do you only reserve these poor manners for me?"

"It is not just you. I did it with Margo, too," she says so matter-of-factly. "I think she quite enjoyed it. I cannot imagine what it would be like to grow up without a sibling. Although, you would probably understand as you were half grown by the time I was born."

My mind floats to memories of Evelyn and Margo together. "I want you to know I'm thankful you both found a strong friendship with each other."

Evelyn takes a serious pause and asks, "You still feel that way, even after what happened during your time at Eton Cottage?"

"Of course, sister. Margo cares for you and gives you support as a young lady that I simply cannot offer. I will always be thankful to her for that." I do want their friendship to continue, and I ignore the pit in my stomach when I thought that friendship may lead to forced proximity with Margo in the future. That is a problem for another time.

"Well, that is great. I think you should tell her yourself." Evelyn pulls a card out from behind her back that I did not realize she was hiding.

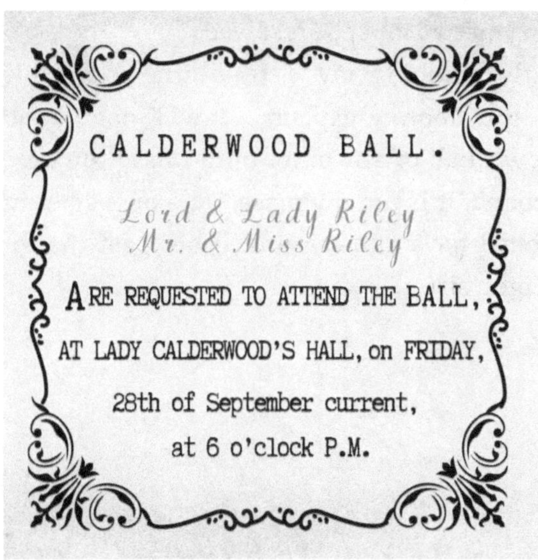

"When did this arrive?" I ask my sister.

"This afternoon. I did not want to give it to you before dinner." There is a hint of apology in her tone.

"Well, it seems Miss Eton has finally decided to find a husband. I suppose her friend is wasting no time introducing her to England's most eligible gentleman." My world begins crashing around me. I have no one to blame but myself. If I had not stomped my way into Eton Cottage this summer, Margo might not have changed her outlook on marriage, at least not yet.

"Yes, and I believe you will be the most handsome, eligible gentleman there!" Her smile is so wide that it touches her eyes.

"Please send Lady Calderwood my best and Miss Eton my wishes that she finds a very suitable match."

"You are not going?" She is shocked. "Eddy, you must go. You need to speak with her. Whatever happened between you two must be resolved."

Gently grabbing my sister's arm and walking her toward the door, I explain, "I will not be attending tomorrow's ball or any other until Miss Eton has secured her husband. It is not my place." She opens her mouth to argue, but I have already guided her past the threshold. "Goodnight, sister."

37

The Landons have been respectful of the time I have been spending contemplating how I would like to proceed. This particular rainy afternoon, I find myself wandering around Eton Cottage, stopping at the door to the room Eddy occupied during his stay. I push the door open and enter with caution as if a ghost will jump out at me.

No, it's worse.

The memories of Eddy's visit are far more terrifying than a ghost. Not much is out of place, the bed is made, the window closed—the one that he saw me running to the stables on the night of the storm. The night he held me so close in the grass as the rain fell on us. This is not doing any good—I should leave.

As I make my way to the door, I notice that the desk is covered with parchment. It seems most are written on. Some look as if they were crumbled and then flattened again. I lean over to take a closer look when I notice my name on the first one.

Margo,
I'm sure the doctors of your medical journals would love to study the muscles in your arm, as I am not familiar with many women who could throw such heavy books with your accuracy. Perhaps we should share this skill with the eligible suitors of London.

Your decision to ride a horse as a man does is completely off putting. Please do not encourage this behavior in my sister.

Miss Eton,
Your exceptional card playing skills are unbecoming for a young lady of your status. Should I assume you frequent pubs and gambling halls in your spare time?

While I would like to continue as usual, I have nothing cruel to say today. I enjoyed your company.

You are being far more cruel now than I could have ever imagined, Margo. Your smart mouth and wicked words, while alluring, do not cling to my soul as your laughter and smiles do. How will I live without them?

Margo,

How will I ever be able to apologize for my actions over the last eight years? You gave me the gift of your friendship at such a young age and I did not value it as I should.

Please let me explain my actions.

I have been in love with you since our childhood. I was determined that I would never find a woman more accomplished, intelligent, kind, and beautiful than you.

I was young and foolish to think that you shared my feelings and even more foolish to meet with your father before discussing my intentions with you. I was prepared to make you an offer of marriage after a short courtship that started at your first ball.

During our first dance, I did not get a chance to speak before you declared yourself uninterested in marriage. You spoke of your displeasure with the men in the room who saw you as a bride and not an individual. It was at that moment that my world came crashing down.

My heart was broken.

Over the next several years, I tried to maintain a distance from you, without an explanation with the hopes of mending my broken heart. It was only after your father's announcement that your husband was to inherit his title that my feelings resurfaced. I no longer held out hope of us being together, but I still felt protective over you. The way the gentleman began talking about you was just as you saw them during our first dance, and some even worse. The men who planned to win your hand had no care for you or your happiness, they only wanted the money. I had to do something. So I began to say things I did not mean, tried to make you and the idea of marrying worse than gaining the Eton fortune. The bitterness became a companion to my broken heart, and at some point, I began to believe the horrible lies I told about you.

While I railed against it at first, I am so thankful for having the chance to visit with you and find myself again. I do not know if we can be friends again, but I will do anything I can to make that happen. I do not deserve your trust, but I hope you can find it in your heart to forgive me. I realize the reason I never married during this time was that my feelings for you have never faded. No other woman has been able to gain my love.

My heart has always been yours.

THE NIGHT before our return to London, I find myself determined in my course of action and how I must attempt to win back the affections of Mr. Edward Riley. Being aware of my own temper and uncontrollable smart mouth, I find it best to write to him.

Mr. Riley,

I am positive that you are surprised by my correspondence since I have not attempted to contact you during your stay with Lady Calderwood. I would apologize, but if I am to be honest, I am not apologetic. It was for the best that I was able to have distance from you while processing the events that occurred on the final night of your stay at Eton Cottage.

After much reflection, I realized that I needed the distance from you to recognize that I was unable to think clearly in your presence. You may think the remainder of this letter is a tirade about the anger you invoke in me, but I can guarantee that is not the entirety of it and insist you read until the end.

Your presence at Eton Cottage evoked every possible emotion I could experience. At the beginning, the most common emotions were anger and, honestly, sometimes jealousy, as I have no rights to the freedoms you experience as a man. Yet, as your stay continued, those emotions changed. Admiration developed as I witnessed the devotion you showed toward your sister. Enjoyment was often present when we would share a game of cards or a meal with our families. I found myself curious to discover your motives for your kind words or sweet smiles. The desire that started with an innocent brush of our hands grew greater each time and continues since the kiss we shared, and I cannot forget it. Lastly, the emotion I felt I was unable to cope with was surprise. Surprise when you hinted at an interest in me and complete shock when you mentioned that we would be a well-suited match.

It was my greatest mistake to act in such a cruel and defensive way to you that night. You must believe me when I tell you, it was a result of my personal doubt in myself to ever find true love. I have spent the weeks since our separation stepping away from my stubborn insecurities.

Please do not be cross. My father has recently shared with me that you met with him many years ago to ask his permission for my hand, years before his fortune would be my dowry.

We were great friends as children, and you have grown to be one of the most exceptional men of London. You made one thing very clear to me on the last night we met. I stressed that I wanted to marry someone who truly loved me. There is no other man who is as aware and as adapt to be by my side for the rest of my days.

If there is a possibility you would be willing to give me a chance to regain your affections, or at the very least, your friendship, I would like to begin doing so at the ball Lady Calderwood will be holding this evening.

If your feelings are not what they were three weeks ago, I will understand and wish you well.

Yours,

Margo

I found the letters, the ones you wrote to me, and left on the desk.

- Perhaps the reason I never considered another suitor is because my heart was already claimed... by you.

THE NEXT MORNING, Lily's carriage arrives before the sun is barely on the horizon. We need to travel early as she is holding a ball that evening. It will take at least three hours to travel to town, and then we need to change into our gowns. Lily will be frantically running around checking that all preparations are completed with expert precision,

This ball has not been planned for months as most are, as this was decided when I went to visit Lily to share news of my father's visit. Lily was happy for me and insisted on holding a ball so I can make my intentions known to Eddy.

With hugs from the Landons and insistence that I keep them informed of what happens tonight, I get in the carriage, and we are on our way.

I pull the letter out of my bag and hold it out to Albert. "Albert, you are sure that you will find him before the ball tonight? He did not respond to the invitation. What if he has left town?"

"I am sure I would have been notified if he had left town, Margo." Albert places the letter inside his coat pocket.

"His mother and sister have responded that they will be in attendance," Lily reassures me from her seat next to Albert. They do not hold hands, but they sit closer than society would find suitable.

"Do you think he told them what had happened?" I ask nervously.

"I do not think that they would come if they knew what had happened between the two of you," Lily answers.

"When I saw them off for London, Eddy maintained

his twisted ankle tale, so much so he pretended to favor it as he climbed into the carriage," Albert says.

I nod and look out the window, trying to distract myself. The nerves are getting the best of me. It is obviously clear to my traveling companions as well. Lily reaches over and holds her hand out for mine. When I place my hand in hers, she gives it a squeeze. "There is nothing that can be done right now, Margo. You will do no good by making yourself sick with worry. Try to close your eyes and rest."

"Thank you." Tipping my head back against the seat, I close my eyes. Trying to ignore my worries and focus on my breathing helps me to fall asleep.

ALBERT WAKES me as we approach Lily's townhouse. Our luggage is taken from the carriage to our quarters, as we share a small lunch and tea in the sitting room. Once we are able to retire to prepare for the evening, Albert says his farewells and is off to find Edward to deliver my letter. Taking a deep breath, I watch him walk down the front stairs. There is no turning back at this point. What happens now is up to Edward Riley.

Lily comes up beside me and says, "You are worrying."

"Yes," I answer.

"Well, stop." I turn back to her, and she continues, "We do not have the time for worrying, there are far too many other things to do. You are not allowed to worry again until everything else has been completed. We must focus on the ball we are hosting tonight."

"I believe that the invitation states Lady Calderwood is hosting a ball, and it does not have the Eton name anywhere on this invitation, Lily." I point it out to her with sarcasm.

"That may be true, Miss Eton, but everyone in London knows we are never apart. You will be expected to help with the hostess duties."

I roll my eyes at her.

"Before you go to your room to prepare for this evening, I have made a list of things that I need you to attend to." She hands me the list and turns on her heels down the hall.

"Where are you going?" I yell at her.

"I have my own list to complete. See you shortly," she yells over her shoulder, never once stopping her stride toward the kitchen.

WITH MY LIST of preparations for this evening complete, I return to my room, anxious to get out of my travel clothes.

A warm bath did nothing to help settle my nerves, and now I find myself lounging on the bed in nothing but a robe, not ready to dress for the evening yet. There is a knock at the door to pull me out of my self-wallowing.

"Come in," I yell, looking away from the woman in the mirror. She is a little more familiar than the last time I was here but certainly more nervous.

"Margo, your face is so pale. You need to relax, dear," Lily says as she rushes over to me.

"I know Lily. Have you heard from Albert? Is he here?"

She gives me a strong look as if to remind me not to say anything compromising about her and Albert. "No, dear. Why would he come here so early? He is to arrive with the rest of the guests this evening."

"Of course," I say, being sure not to mention him again.

38

With final checks in the mirror, we decide to head downstairs to the ballroom. Lily pulls me over to the trays filled with glasses of wine. She hands me two. "Drink one down now, for your nerves, then work on the other as you are greeting our guests. It will help. I promise."

I do as she says. It does little to help until the doors open and guests begin to enter Lily's home. I am able to breathe with more ease, but my stomach is still flipping from the nerves. Once the initial crowd has made their way into the party, panic strikes. I search for Lily to tell her the news. Edward has not arrived and clearly has not forgiven me.

"I have yet to see Lady Riley or Miss Riley enter," Lily says.

"They are not here," I clarify.

"Well then, do not stress yet, Margo. He may arrive with them at any minute."

At that moment, they arrive without Edward. Lily

stays by my side as they approach to greet us. Reminding myself we are no longer in the country, I stop myself from hugging Evey as soon as she is close enough. We all bow to one another in greeting and then exchange pleasantries.

Lily is first to ask, "And how is your family, Lady Riley? Lord and Mr. Riley are well?"

"Yes, thank you, Lady Calderwood. They are doing very well," Evey's mother answers.

"That is wonderful. Please enjoy the evening." Lily waves her hand toward the dance floor and begins to move so they may pass us.

"Thank you. I do not think I could have asked about Eddy without showing my emotions."

"Of course. Stay close, Margo. I will not leave your side." Lily's support is both comforting and concerning. She only feels the need to stay by my side since the arrival of the Riley ladies. It is obvious she takes this as an indicator that Edward will not be attending the ball. Adding to the concern is Albert's lack of attendance as well. I know what my fate would most likely be, but I must admit, I spend the entire evening with a watchful eye on the entrance, hoping that he will arrive late.

"Apologies, Margo dear, but I have a few things to attend to," Lily whispers into my ear. I turn to her with panic on my face. I do not want her to leave. "I found an alternative guard while I'm away. I think you will be safe." She turns us, and Evelyn interlocks her arm on my other side as Lily walks off.

"Did I hear her correctly—the tough Margaret Eton needs guarding? Who am I protecting you from?" Her chest puffs out as she is proud to take this role. "Do not fear. You are safe with me, dear lady." I squeeze her arm in thanks.

"Oh! Did you find the letter?" I freeze at her question. She sees my reservation. "I know Eddy wrote those letters to you. And he threw some of them away, but I grabbed them from the bin and left them on the desk." She watches my cool face melt at the mention that she read those letters. "It is okay, Margo. I know how he feels, and by the look on your face, I can guess how you feel, too. I assume you read them. Is that why you included him on the invitation?"

Before I can answer, we are interrupted by Mr. Harold Grange. "Miss Eton, Miss Riley. You both look beautiful this evening," he says with a wicked smile. We both offer a polite smile and attempt to continue with our conversation, but he is insistent. "Miss Eton, may I have this dance?"

Harold Grange is the last man I want to be around at the moment. "I apologize, Mr. Grange. I injured my ankle recently." Evey tries to hide her laugh with a cough. "I have no intention of dancing this evening."

"Well enough, Miss Eton, can we perhaps take a stroll? I met with your father today, and I believe we have much to discuss." My heart sinks to my stomach. I feel the panic spread through my body. As much as I would like to storm away from him, I need to know what he spoke with my father about.

I pull Evey close. "Get Lily," I whisper into her ear. And more loudly, "I shall find you soon, Miss Riley." Turning back to Mr. Grange to follow him to the outer part of the ballroom.

"As you are well aware, Miss Eton, my affections for you have been unmoving for years." Yes, five years, to be exact, since my father made his announcement. "I have made it a regular occurrence to ask your father for your hand in marriage, but he always declines. I was never discouraged as it was clear that it was not due to any other suitor but perhaps waiting for you to come around on the idea of marriage." My head is starting to hurt. "You can imagine my surprise when I went to him this morning and asked again but was finally met with approval. I could not wait to come to tell you the good news."

The room is starting to spin, and it is getting harder to breathe.

Harold takes this opportunity to wind his hand around my waist to hold me up. "No need to swoon, Margaret. You will be my wife soon enough, then you shall never need to contain your passions for me. I have gone ahead and made the arrangements for us to be married next week."

I am no longer able to hold myself up. I cannot fight him off anymore. His hand caresses my cheek, and he says something in my ear, but I cannot make it out. I hear Lily's screams before everything fades to black.

I WAKE to the sound of Evey's calmly calling my name and repeating, "It's all right, he is gone." I feel a cool, damp towel on my head, and I open my eyes. I'm in a chair off in the private parlor of Lily's townhouse. Evey embraces me and then yells to someone over my head.

Lily comes rushing in, and her arms replace Evey's. As she is squeezing me, she mutters "Where is Albert?"

It all comes rushing back. Harold Grange. I am to marry him. The panic returns to my body, this time accompanied by an endless stream of tears. This is my fault—Eddy was right. I waited too long, and now I'm destined to be married to the horrible Harold Grange.

"It is all right, Margo. We will find a solution." She is at eye level with me now, "You will never marry that awful man."

I try to calm myself to avoid losing consciousness again. "Is he still here?" I ask with a shaky voice.

"Certainly not. I had him removed and warned to never return to my home." I am so thankful for Lily. "You do not need to return. Please feel free to stay here and rest."

After my dramatic event, the evening has come to an early end. Evey's mother comes to bid farewell. She turns to me. "I hope you find a way out of this, Miss Eton. Being married to that man is a fate I would not wish on anyone."

When the last guest takes their leave for the evening, my heart sinks to my stomach. I feel my breath catching as the result of this evening is finalized. Lily approaches with another glass of wine and hands it to me. "How are you doing?"

I keep my eyes on my glass and shake my head. I know if I look at her, the tears will return. "It's time for you to rest, Margo. Take your drink up and prepare for bed. I will be up shortly to say goodnight," Lily instructs.

I nod again and head straight to my room without looking at her. Once I am out of that uncomfortable dress and my hair is down, I enter the bath, still clutching my wine close to me. Between sips, I scrub my entire body, trying to remove the memory of Harold Grange's touch. When my skin is red and beginning to sting from the roughness of my efforts, I give up and make my way to bed.

There is a knock on my door. "It's just me," Lily's voice comes from the hallway. I rise to let her in. We walk back and sit side by side on the end of the bed. She puts her arm around me and says, "You are a strong woman, Margo; you will get through this. We still do not know what kept Edward from attending. Albert has not yet returned, so he may have not found him yet. As for this Grange business —Albert and I will not allow it. I will go to your father myself at sunrise tomorrow. We will convince him to change his mind. And, if we cannot...you will marry Albert."

"Lily, I could never. You and Albert are together. It is you who should be marrying him."

Lily shakes her head, "I am not sure if that was ever in our future, Margo. It is far more important for us to keep you away from Grange. That is a life that we will not allow for you. I know Albert would agree to this."

Holding my arms around her neck, the tears finally return. "Thank you, Lily. Thank you for everything. Perhaps we can change my father's mind." That is all I am able to say. Exhaustion and the wine are finally catching up to me.

She holds me as I cry a little longer. Once I stop and we

separate, Lily pushes the hair from my face, saying, "Get some sleep. We will get things straightened out in the morning," and kisses my forehead. With one last gentle smile and nod from me, Lily leaves the room.

It does not take long for me to fall asleep that night, I find I do not need a book. I just watch the stars out the window until rest takes me.

39

The day begins with a loud banging on my door.

"ENOUGH!" I yell harsher than I should speak to my sister.

"Eddy! Why did you lock this door? Are you all right?"

I roll over to spot the empty bottle of brandy I opened last night after hearing of the ball this evening at Lady Calderwood's.

"EDDY!" My sister is not going to stop until I let her in.

"Yes, sister. Give me a moment." I rise to my feet, swaying while trying to find my balance to stand straight. I salute the empty bottle and cautiously make my way to let Evelyn in.

As soon as I open the door, I turn to make my way back to my bed. The location I plan to spend the rest of the day or at least the next few hours.

"Are you ill?" she asks as I throw myself back into bed. "Or should I ask, have you made yourself ill?" she adds as she picks up the empty bottle.

"Can you just be helpful and order food to be sent up here for me?"

"Sure, brother. Any requests?" she asks with sarcasm.

"Bread. And meat." She makes a face at my answer but walks out the door for a brief moment, then returns.

"It will be here shortly. Now, I wonder what would drive such actions... Could it be that you were absolutely enamored with Miss Harris last night and that you cannot bear to spend time separately and that you turned to the bottle to help soothe the pain?"

I lift my arm from my face to give her a look that demonstrates she is mad for even suggesting that. When I return my arm to its place over my eyes, blocking out the sun, she continues, "Could it be due to the invitation we received last night about the ball at Lady Calderwood's?" I ignore her. "That's what I thought. Eddy, you can go. You are doing this to yourself. If Margo did not want you there, she would have exclusively invited our mother and me." I let out an unintentional huff but otherwise ignore her response. "Is this really that bad, Eddy? Even when you hated her, you tolerated balls that she was in attendance, but you cannot tell me you still hate her."

How could I tell my sister that I did not hate Margo, that I was completely in love with her without her trying to interfere?

I chose to stay silent.

"Tell me what happened, Eddy. I can help."

"I am not in search of assistance in the matter. It has been resolved, and I am simply going to enjoy the day by making myself as numb to recent events as possible."

"And what should I say to Margo tonight when she

asks about you? Should I tell her that this news has brought you to a state where you can barely function?"

I sit up faster than I should, and the room begins spinning. After a moment to regain my balance, I look at my sister with an attempt at an intimidating tone, but it comes out more like a plea. "You will simply tell her I was unable to attend, and I wish her the best in her endeavors to find a suitable husband."

"Fine, and if she inquires more about you?" If Margo was interested in me she would have reached out by now. Instead, she will hold steady and stubborn until her final days.

"She will not. I promise you," I confirm it with my sister.

A knock comes at the door, accompanied by the smell of food on the other side. "Please come in," I yell. As they enter, I turn to Evelyn. "Thank you for your concern, sister. I hope you enjoy your evening."

As I continue to pour myself another drink, I attempt to write Margo another letter. After multiple failed attempts at starting the letter and wasting the remaining paper I have in my room, I decide to write on the backs of the other previous letters I have written. I make an even bigger mess of my desk than it was when I started searching for them. I try to remember the words I wrote in the letter I left at Eton Cottage, yet in this state, my memory is failing me. I chug down the remaining contents of my glass, refill it once more, and head in the direction of my bed.

After hours of sulking and the pain growing, the alcohol intoxication from the previous night fades, and I decide that I can no longer stay here. I know that I do not want to give Evey another opportunity to persuade me to go this evening. I leave the house without a destination and see where the night will take me.

The sun is beginning to set as I take to the streets of London. I look around, deciding where I should go. I cannot think straight so I decide to start walking. Quickly, I come upon a pub Albert likes to frequent. This should be a good place to start. As I walk in, familiar men wave in greeting from the card tables. They wave me over in hopes I will join their games, but I am now sober enough to know if I did sit down, I would walk away without any money to my name.

Sitting at the bar, I order another brandy and begin my slow descent into a night of self-pity and loathing.

By the time I enter the third pub, I am oversharing with strangers the woes of my heartbreak. I make sure to keep her identity to myself, but I am not shy about most of the other details. It is easy to learn of their experiences with love. The responses are equally split between those telling me to fight for her or forget her.

It is easy to keep moving from one pub to the next. As soon as one of my audience members suggests anything foul about Margo's intentions with me, I move myself straight out the door to ponder on her intentions until I step into the next bar. She has admitted multiple times that she never believes any man will seek her out for any reason other than her fortune. How a woman can have all of the confidence that she carries around but still think so little of herself and her alluring personality is beyond comprehension. Any man would be lucky to have such a wife and partner in life.

As I take my seat at the next pub, I keep the details of my heartache to myself and simply ask the other patrons what they think of love. Most answers make it clear they feel love and lust are one and the same. Do not get me wrong, I believe the two are very connected, but I do not believe that one is required for the other. I have only ever loved one woman, and while the physical attraction is like a magnet's pull, it is not at all the sole reason for my love. On the opposite end, I have engaged in sex with women with whom there was a mutual understanding, and we had no fantasies about loving each other.

I stay longer at this bar than the others and drink more than I should. I order more food to combat my poor decisions, which makes it difficult to move on to the next. I should begin heading home, as it is well into the night. Looking up at the moon, I wonder if Margo is staring up at it as well with one of her lucky suitors from this evening's ball. The realization grips me at my core. How did I end up back here, where I swore I would never be again? I worked so hard to banish every drop of love I had for her. Within days of being in her company, she tore that hate away, and I fell even more in love with her than before. Just for her to crush my soul again.

As I stumble into the next bar, I am not sure how many this is as I have lost count. I burst through the doors loud enough to gain the attention of most of the patrons. My resolve is set—I will never forgive Margo for breaking my heart...twice. I will find a wife—one who would love me, even if I can never love her back. "A brandy!" I yell at the barkeep as I hold onto the bar to help me settle on the open stool. Raising my glass to the crowd, "Love is for the weak." They burst into cheers.

Exactly.

I down the contents of my glass in one gulp. I will drink away my feelings for her and wake up a new man tomorrow. "Keep them coming," I say with a slam of my glass on the counter.

40

BOOM! BOOM! BOOM!

I am startled awake by loud banging sounds followed by muffled yelling.

BOOM! BOOM!

I jump out of bed, grabbing my housecoat and pulling it on as I run down the hall. I am met by Lily. Before we can speak, the banging continues.

BOOM! BOOM! BOOM!

Muffled voices are a slight bit clearer, almost sounding familiar, but I cannot make them out. It becomes clear that the banging is coming from the front door. We head to the front window and pull it open with hopes of identifying the culprits.

BOOM! BOOM!

"MARGO!!!"

We stop to look at each other before we have the chance to look out the window. Why is someone yelling for me in the middle of the night? We poke our heads out, hoping to see them but not be seen ourselves.

Albert is pacing at the bottom of the front stairs. We are able to make out his whispered pleads. "You must stop. I insist. You are going to frighten them out of their wits."

"Mr. Berry?" Lily says in a loud whisper, hoping to grab his attention. It works. He sees us and throws his hands up.

"Lady Calderwood and Miss Eton. I am so sorry for the disruption, my frie—" Albert is caught off guard by a figure running down the stairs toward him. I hear him before I see his face. "Margo!!!" Eddy yells from below. He is close enough for Albert to grab him and cover his mouth to stop him from yelling anymore. Albert then says something only Eddy is able to hear because he stops fighting to get out of Albert's hold.

"Ladies, my greatest apologies for the late-night intrusion, but I was unable to convince my dear friend to come at a more reasonable hour," Albert says as quickly as he can.

"Stay there," Lily says and pulls the two of us out of the window. She leads the way down the stairs to the front door.

"What are you doing?" I ask.

"Letting them in. It seems Mr. Riley is insistent on seeing you. I want them inside so as not to cause a bigger scene," Lily answers.

No sooner has Lily opened the door than Eddy runs in. Albert is quick behind him. I am lighting candles as they enter. I carry the stands to the end tables throughout the sitting area where Lily is guiding the men. Albert pulls Eddy down to sit next to him on the loveseat. Lily and I each sit in chairs. Albert looks exhausted, still in the clothes he wore during our travels. I take a quick look in Eddy's direction before looking down into my lap.

It takes what feels like hours but must be only a few seconds for me to find the bravery to look at Eddy. It is as if he ran here—his breathing has yet to settle. I notice his hair is wet, just as it was that day he arrived at Eton Cottage. Instantly, I notice he is gripping something in his hand.

My letter.

My body goes rigid. I cannot so much as move my gaze from the letter crunched in his strong hand. After this evening took that distracting turn of events, I have not given much more thought to Eddy's reaction to my letter. Given our conflicting feelings toward one another over the past few weeks, I cannot be sure how he feels about what I wrote. It would not be out of the question for him to have shown up just to berate me and scold me for how I treated him. I would deserve it and would gladly restate my apologies.

Yet, I must allow myself a small bit of hope that he is here to renew our friendship, or could it be even more? I must face my fate and learn what it is that Edward Riley has rushed here in the middle of the night to tell me. There will be no return from this point on. Collecting every ounce of courage that I can, with a deep breath, I force myself to move my gaze from the letter and up to his face.

When we make eye contact, his hand squeezes, and the crinkle of the paper is heard clearly in the room filled with silence. I do not look away, trying desperately to read Eddy's face.

"Margo…" My name is spoken so softly as he rises from his seat. I do not say anything, but I keep eye contact, waiting for his next word, but it does not come. He takes large but slow steps toward me. I am frozen in my seat. Once he is directly in front of me, he kneels on one knee before my chair.

"Eddy…" I need to say so much more, but all I can get out is his name. I am overcome with the happiness I feel from his proximity.

As if in response to his name, he smiles. His face is no longer unreadable. He reaches for my hand with his free hand, still gripping my letter in the other.

"May I have this dance?" Eddy asks.

Confusion washes over me. We are in a dark room hours after the ball has ended. I do not want to dance, I want to talk. I want to say everything that I was too afraid to write in that letter. Then the music begins playing, and I look up and see Albert and Lily at the pianoforte. They look back at me with smiles, and Albert makes a nudging motion in the direction of Edward. I turn back to the man on his knee in front of me. "Of course," I answer. Eddy quickly rises to his feet then lifts me from my chair and into his arms. There is no formality here but a simple dance with our arms around each other.

"My greatest apologies for missing the ball this evening, Miss Eton. I want you to know the moment I finished reading your letter, I rushed directly here to you."

"When did you receive the letter?"

"A little over an hour ago." He must note the confusion

on my face. Before I can continue my questioning, he answers, "You see, Albert had a difficult time finding me today. From what I gathered, your party arrived in London early in the afternoon. After dealing with matters at his residence, he began his search for me. I did not make it easy on him. I never told anyone where I was going and did not stay in the same location very long. I have been rather absent from my home lately."

A small drop of water leaves his hair and drips onto his forehead, but he does not seem to notice. "Why is your hair wet?"

Eddy looks up as if he is checking that his hair is wet. "Ah, yes. I must confess we did not come directly here. It was on Albert's wise counsel that I stop to refresh my clothes and body. I could not very well show up smelling like the pub. I also could not be reasoned with to come tomorrow morning. This matter is of the utmost urgency."

"Is something wrong?" I mock him.

"Why yes, Margo. My heart was broken...for the second time...by the same woman."

"Eddy...I'm—" He stops me.

"Tonight, I found myself in less desirable places with hopes to forget the woman I have spent most of my life loving. Everywhere I found myself, I could not stop my mind from thinking of you, so I would change locations. Unfortunately, by the time Albert tracked me down at the pub, we had missed the ball." He spins me as we dance. "I was surprised to see Albert but even more surprised when he handed me your letter. Poor man could barely keep up with me as I ran out of the pub to find a horse to get to you. I could not wait until tomorrow to see you."

"I'm so glad that you did not wait. Although, I apologize that I am not properly dressed." I say, hoping to lighten the tension.

"You look more like yourself at this moment than I can guess you did at that ball. Honestly, I'm surprised I did not find you in britches."

"Mr. Riley, they are only for the country. I am a lady and would not dare bring them to London," I answer with a laugh.

"Then I suggest we get you out of this town immediately and back to the country with your wardrobe of britches and those tantalizing country dresses that flatter you so well," he says as he pulls my body closer to his. We were no longer in a traditional dance stance but still swaying to the music with our arms wrapped around each other's bodies.

"I would love nothing more than to return to the country, but unfortunately, I have some upsetting news to share." I stop dancing, but Edward does not remove his hands from my waist. Lingering in his embrace, I turn to Lily and Albert.

Lily understands, "I think we should all sit down to discuss this." Albert and Eddy look at each other nervously that neither knows what will be said. I place my hand in Eddy's and squeeze it for reassurance as we sit next to each other. Lily continues and shares the evening's events as I feel myself shrinking into myself. Recalling the feeling of Mr. Grange embracing my body and how it became numb with the news of his plans.

"Lily, Margo." Albert is looking back and forth between us. Both of us are clearly holding back tears in our eyes. "I should have been here. I'm so sorry that I was not."

Edward pulls me to his side, "It is my fault, Albert. If I had not made myself so hard to find, we could have been here before the ball began." He leans into me. "I'm sorry." I give a slight nod.

This is too much. I need to sort things out with Eddy without the threat of Harold over my head. I turn to Eddy. "I will go to my father first thing tomorrow. I will fix this," I promise him.

"My dear, Margo. Do not spend another moment worrying about Mr. Grange. I know I will not. I have had your father's approval for nearly ten years' time." His voice is calm and soothing but also firm and resolved. Pulling me into his arms, he turns and nods at Albert and Lily, who quickly understand their direction and leave the room.

Once we are alone, I can finally give Margo the attention I have so longed to share with her. It is not like Margo to be so shaken. I must fix this. Separating from our embrace just enough to tuck my fingers under her chin to lift her gaze to meet mine. "Miss Eton, how can I settle your nerves."

"There is so much to say, so much to discuss, Mr. Riley. Could you truly forgive me?"

"You are forgiven. We are both guilty of horrendous actions against one another. Fortunately, I believe we will have years to make it up to each other."

"*Years*?" she teases me. Of course, she repeats the word that I whispered into her ear that night in the rain. "Eddy, does that mean...are you sure you want to...after everything..."

She does not need to question my intentions, but I do love to see her so bothered. "Miss Eton, do you have something you'd like to ask me?"

She stands just as if we are in the middle of an

argument, increasing the distance between us. Her hands on her hips and her feet planted firmly on the floor. "Mr. Riley," her face is growing flushed. "Do you... Would you... like to marry me?"

There is not a single thing in my life that I am surer of than wanting to be Margo's husband. I'm certain she knows that too, but watching her fingers fidgeting in front of her shows there is room for me to tease her. "Margo!" Her chest is rising, and her gaze is locked on mine. I stand and begin to walk toward her. "To think, if word got out that you, Miss Eton, famous for refusing marriage and tradition, asked a gentleman for his hand in matrimony."

"If you think this is a joke, Eddy." She takes a step back as I close the distance between us.

My hand finds its place on the small of her back, and I pull her toward me. Leaning down to close the distance between us, I stop a breath away from her lips. "I have never loved another, Margo. You and only you have held my heart. It would be my honor to marry you."

She exhales in relief, and I do not let another moment pass before my lips are on her. Reminding myself to be gentle, she had a difficult night with unwanted touches from a scoundrel. Just the thought of Grange near her causes me to tighten my arms around her. I vow to myself in that moment, that he will never get close to her again.

All thoughts of Grange are banished from my mind as a quiet moan escapes Margo's mouth at my embrace. It's as if all the restraint I was clinging to suddenly snaps, but I have to be sure—I cannot push her too far. I pull away, checking her face, searching for approval. "Margo..." I gasp, waiting for a response.

One side of her mouth curves up, her eyes are filled with lust, her voice low and seductive. "Eddy…" I can barely hold my composure. I move to take her to her bed and demonstrate just what she has been missing these past eight years when I realize that I am not sure where her bedroom is located in Lily's townhouse.

A soft giggle escapes her lips, and she immediately covers her mouth.

"Lead the way, Miss Eton."

She grabs my hand and quickly begins to run up the stairs. "Right this way, Mr. Riley."

At the top of the stairs, I can no longer wait, I pick her up in my arms. "Which room?"

Surprise and excitement cover her face, "Last on the left." She takes advantage of my concentration on getting us into that room as soon as possible by placing soft kisses on my neck. I pick up the pace. Thankfully, she left the door slightly ajar, and I nudge it open with my foot. I lay her gently on the bed and connect in a kiss much deeper than before. My hands have a mind of their own, exploring every inch of her soft body.

As my attention moves down her neck, Margo starts to moan my name "Eddy…Eddy." My body is pulsing with the need to make her repeat it until the sun rises. "Door… Eddy… *Door*!" I jerk my head up and notice the door to the bedroom is still wide open.

To my displeasure, I stand and move to close and lock the door. "I suppose we do not want to wake the entire house with your screams of ecstasy."

She laughs.

"Are you questioning my abilities again, Miss Eton? I

do believe you have made a few very outlandishly false accusations about my experience with women." She looks a little nervous. *Oh yes, darling, you are in for a long night.* "I feel it is my responsibility to defend my honor."

I return to my place on top of her, picking up where we left off. Our skin is heated, and our breath is rapid as I kiss my way down her neck just to return to her lips. She wraps her arms around my neck and quickly follows with one of her legs around my waist, unable to move the other due to the ridiculous amount of fabric from her nightgown. *This will not do*, bunching the fabric up her legs, freeing them to move around me, but I do not stop there. I keep pulling it up until she is forced to unlock her arms from around my neck as I pull it over her head.

With lust in her gaze, she is a vision. No signs of shyness in her gestures, just pure want and need. This is the trance she always held over me—her beauty, every curve, every blush of her skin. I plan to worship this body for the rest of my days. Beginning with tonight, I start by pulling a leg up to my shoulder, never breaking eye contact as I kiss my way toward her center.

Her breaths are heavy as I get closer to her hips. She should know I prefer her to be frustrated and on edge with me. I move from her hips, continuing in my exploration up her body in the direction of her opposite shoulder. I should be spending additional attention on her chest. Her glorious chest, which, before tonight, I have only admired contained behind her tight dresses. But now I have an unobstructed view.

I break for a moment to end this half of my journey at her shoulder, only to cross sides through her collarbone as

I make my way to her other shoulder. She is growing impatient. Her body begins to move with mine, and her hand grips the back of my head as she pulls on my hair. I moan in response and nip at her shoulder, and she responds with another pull on my hair.

When she realizes my plan to travel down the opposite end of her body, she attempts to gain control. "Eddy..." she says in that low voice. She is quick in her action as she finds the bottom of my shirt and begins to pull it out from my britches.

Who am I to deny this woman her wants?

Her hands explore my bare chest before she pulls me back on top of her. She was seeking this contact, this connection. Her hands move behind my neck, and she brings me back to her mouth. The kiss is more intense than before, our tongues exploring each other. Our bodies create friction against each other; she grates against me, and my body responds to her movements with only my britches separating us.

Her hands moved down to remove the final barrier. "Eddy..." This time, it is a plea for more.

"Margo..." I say, trying to convey my reassurance as I back away and fall to my knees. I hear her intake of breath at my new position. Lifting one leg over my shoulder, my other hand caresses her stomach to ease her nerves. Just as her hips began to relax, I began to express my devotion to this flawless woman. I do not cease when her hips start to buck, and her cries are barely audible.

This is my opportunity to show her she is making the best choice in a husband. Her legs begin to shake, but I continue on until her body shudders around me with my name on her lips. Her body seems to melt into the bed as I rise to my feet before her.

She sits up to kiss me, her kiss frantic and needing. This time, I allow her to push my waistband off my hips. As the fabric falls to the ground, I step out of it and stand before her. She studies me from top to bottom as if she were in a museum. This only adds to my eagerness. She can look more later, I cannot wait.

I climb in front of her, forcing her to back up until she falls backward onto the bed. One arm behind her head, another locking her leg behind my back. "Margo, I love you," I say with my last bit of restraint. I do not expect her to say it back, but I want her to know how I feel.

Her eyes go wide beneath me, "I love you, Eddy." The tightness I have held in my chest for eight years shatters throughout my body as my mind attempts to catch up to the admission I never believed I would hear from the beautiful lips of Miss Margaret Eton.

My kiss is urgent, but the rest of my movements are gentle. Our initial connection must be soft. I watch her face, willing to stop the moment she shows discomfort. When she moves her hips to respond to mine, my world explodes. Our bodies are joined just as our souls are. We both allow our true personalities through. As the movement becomes regular, I feel the need to slow, waiting for her frustration to roar through her body. I roll us over, placing her on top of me. I'm met with glorious and unexpected results. She meets my challenge, controlling our rhythm. Urgent and demanding, just like her. I could die a happy man with this woman above me.

Unable to relinquish complete control to Margo and

feeling myself approaching my limit, I pull her back under me. Feeling her pulsing, I know she is just as close to her end as I am. I lean in to kiss her neck and whisper, "Let go, Margo," as my movements are rushed and erratic. Her hips meet mine with urgent need.

Release shatters through her body as she screams my name. I follow quickly with a growl and my final deep thrust. Both panting, trying to catch our breaths, I wait a moment before separating us and moving to lie beside her.

She turns her body toward mine, curling into me. Her wild, curly hair falls in a mess around her face. I move the strands away to look into her eyes. "My Margo." My beautiful, fierce, strong-willed, intelligent, kind, and stubborn Margo. I pull her into an embrace and pull the covers over us.

She picks her head up to kiss my cheek. "Your Margo," she whispers before curling into my shoulder and falling asleep.

42

The bright sun enters the room with the sound of curtains opening, and then I am wrapped in strong arms and pushed against Edward's strong body. "Good afternoon, Margo," he says sweetly into my ear.

"Afternoon?" How late did I sleep?

"Yes, my bride, it is just past noon."

"Why did you not wake me earlier?" I ask.

"Because I thought you would want to be well-rested on our wedding day."

I shift in his arms to face him. "What did you say?"

His smile is larger than I have ever witnessed it. "Well, I have waited almost a decade for you to reciprocate my love, and now that you have, I do not see any reason to delay our wedding any further."

Holding the blanket over my chest, I sit up and take in the view of this breathtakingly handsome man in front of me. His growing beard is a new look for him that I very much appreciate. As if the fresh-faced Eddy is a man of the past, the one standing in front of me is to be my husband. He is already dressed, but after last night, I have some ideas on how to change that.

"I can think of a reason to delay. Surely you do not need to leave at this moment. Perhaps I can entice you back into bed with me?" My question is barely finished, and he is now looking between the sheets covering my naked body and back to my face. His gaze is heated as if he can see through the blankets.

He drops the robe he is holding on the bed and begins to crawl his way up to me. His lips meet mine, and my body blazes from the heat of his kiss, remembering what came after a kiss like this last night.

Before I can pull him under the sheets with me, Eddy takes control of my arms and pins me to the bed. He lowers himself to hover just above my body. "We will have plenty of time to revisit last night's activities once we are wed, Margo. Now, you need to dress for the day and prepare for the journey back to Eton Cottage."

"Eton Cottage? We are returning there today?"

"Margo, I am aware of your distaste for London. I would never dream of holding our wedding here." My heart swells at his words. "I spent the morning making arrangements. We are to marry at Eton Cottage this evening." As if I needed any more reassurance about marrying Eddy, but now I am more certain than ever. I lift to kiss him deeply.

He pulls back and releases my arms. "Enough with the distractions, my bride. I have many more arrangements to see to. Get dressed." He leaps off the bed and leaves me in the room to bask in my happiness.

ONCE I AM DRESSED, the disappointment of Eddy's earlier departure begins to fade as Lily comes to fetch me for our journey back to Eton Cottage. She is also in high spirits this morning, and I can only assume she had a similarly exciting evening with Albert.

She hugs me. "To think you've only spent one day in town and already secured a husband, Margo."

"A perfect husband," I add. "Oh, Lily, how stubborn I have been all these years."

"Yes, that is true, but everything happens for a reason, and at the exact moment it is meant to, Margo." Of course, she is right.

Our bags are already packed as they had never been unpacked since our arrival yesterday. In our traveling attire, we decide to have a quick breakfast before beginning our journey. Passing through the foyer, we notice a guest coming through the main entrance.

Lily and I freeze as if we are seeing a ghost. Harold Grange has not crossed my mind since Eddy's reassurance last night. While I know more than that must be done, I truly have not considered this man again.

"I am here to see my bride." He pushes past Darcy, Lily's butler in town. Darcy attempts to stop Harold but is met with a physical confrontation. When Harold catches sight of me, he makes his way to me. As if something shifts inside me, I think of Eddy and that I will be marrying him this evening. There is nothing to fear from this man any longer.

"Margaret, my beautiful." He steps directly in front of me and brings his left hand up to touch my cheek.

Absolutely not.

I repeal back and use my right hand to slap his hand away from my face. "Do not touch me, Harold."

He grabs my wrist tightly and turns me around, using his arms to hold mine down while he pulls my back against his chest. The many lessons with Mr. Landon should have prepared me for this very moment, yet they are useless as I cannot swing to punch him, so I resort to kicking him. He squeezes me tighter and lowers his foul-smelling mouth to my ear. "Glad to see you have come around to addressing me informally, Margaret." He lowers his head to place a kiss on my neck before returning to my ear. "I always knew you had a fight in you. I cannot wait to see how this comes out in the bedroom."

"You disgusting old man, let me down," I yell, but it just seems to delight him.

"You let her go," Lily yells just in time for me to see her swinging an umbrella at Mr. Grange's head. I duck mine to be sure that I do not distract from her target. I hear the thud as she makes contact with his thick skull. He loosens his hold on me, and I break from his hold. She hits him once more, causing Harold to bend forward, seemingly losing his balance.

"Good swing, my love." Albert's voice is like a sound from the heavens. I look to see him behind Lily, kissing her on the cheek and pulling the umbrella out of her hands. She whispers something, and they both look at me. She nods and comes to my side.

Eddy comes running up behind Albert. He looks over at me, assessing my body from head to toe and back again.

Albert walks closer to Harold as he begins to straighten, only to be met with another blow of the umbrella. This time, it's clear to do more damage than both of Lily's swings. Grange is hunched forward with his hands on his knees for support. After dropping the umbrella, Albert slams his knee into Harold's stomach. "You are finished, Grange."

Harold turns his now red face in Albert's direction; he must seem confused as Albert elaborates, "Edward has not addressed you yet; that is how I know you're finished. Before he knocks the life out of you, here is your warning. You are never to look in the direction of these women again. And if you do, I will be sure to find you and end you." Albert gets in one more punch before moving behind Harold and kicking his knees, causing him to kneel on the ground.

Eddy is still entirely focused on me until he takes a quick look at Lily and then returns to me. "Are you both all right?" We nod in unison.

Without notice, Eddy turns and delivers blow after blow to Harold. I never considered Edward Riley a fighter, yet the precision of his hits and the strength behind them is evidence of the contrary. Seeing Eddy in this unhinged state makes my skin warm and flush as I stare in admiration of my powerful man. Grange's face is starting to become unrecognizable from the bruising and swelling. He deserves far more for his behavior. I'm not sure if he's even conscious at this point, but then he mutters, "Riley, she is to *be my* bride." With what I can only assume is an attempt at a smile.

How arrogant and foolish can this man be?

Eddy leans low, "She was never yours, Grange—she has always been mine."

He quickly looks back to meet my gaze and winks. Edward Riley, who is covered in another man's blood, winks at me, and now my knees are weak.

He turns back to Harold. "We were married this morning." How could I love this madman more...

Grange begins to stutter his words, "No, i-it can no-not be tr-true."

Eddy's wicked grin spreads across his face as he stands tall in front of Grange, "Yes, it is. And she and I are to become the lord and lady of two of the most prominent estates in this country. More power than you can dream of."

Eddy turns back to me, extending his hand for me to join him. I'm unsure of what to do until he addresses me, "Wife?" A smile covers my face with the affectionate title. I walk to the man who is as good as my husband, placing my hand in his as we stand before Harold Grange.

Eddy asks, "What would you like done with him?"

Kill him.

This man needs to be removed from society so that he can never turn his unwanted attention on a young girl again. However, I cannot have my new husband wanted for murder, so that is not a reasonable request.

Yet, I want him as far from the young ladies in town as possible. No woman should be subjected to the likes of him for a husband. "Take him to the outskirts of town; leave him there."

Eddy kisses the back of my hand. "Right away, love."

Grange begins to mumble what sounds like derogatory words in my direction, but it's hard to make out. Apparently, Eddy understands and gives him one last punch, and Grange falls unconscious to the ground.

With assistance from the butler, Albert and Eddy remove Grange's limp body from the townhouse.

43

Albert and Eddy originally planned to travel ahead of us to Eton Cottage, but due to the unexpected visit this afternoon, they decide to travel with us. Throughout the journey, we do not speak of Harold Grange again and I hope that name never crosses any of our lips again. As we are nearing Eton Cottage, Theo takes a different road that would take us directly to Lily's estate.

"Are we not going to Eton Cottage?" Before I can finish my question, I notice no one else seems to be surprised by this.

"You'll be preparing for the ceremony with me, Margo," Lily begins to explain, and Albert continues, "And I shall be by shortly to escort you two back to Eton Cottage."

"And where will you be?" I ask my groom sitting next to me.

Eddy leans in, pretending to whisper, but is loud enough for the entire carriage to hear, "I am about to marry the most demanding woman in England. There is still much I need to prepare if she is to agree to this marriage."

Laughter fills the carriage, "I suppose, but what about Mrs. Landon? I'm sure she would like to help me prepare for my wedding."

Eddy answers, "This schedule was her idea. She has sent a selection of dresses to the Calderwood Estate for you. She sends her best and looks forward to seeing you shortly."

The gentlemen assist us with exiting the carriage and bid us goodbye. Lily and Albert move to the other side of the carriage, out of sight for us. Before I realize it, I am in Eddy's embrace.

"This morning, waking up next to you was better than I could have hoped. Tonight, we will have our first dance as husband and wife. I expect the rest of our days to start and end exactly as today." Before I can beg for different afternoons, his mouth is on mine, and I am wrapped tightly in his arms. He parts with one more gentle kiss and then he joins Albert in the carriage.

Watching the carriage pull back onto the main road, I pause to enjoy a brief moment of quiet. My fingers linger on my lips, which are still warm from Eddy's kiss. I never truly recovered from losing his friendship all those years ago. With a satisfied sigh, I bask in the comfort that I will never long for Eddy's company again. Bringing my hand from my lips to my chest, I can feel my heart fluttering underneath.

The carriage is finally out of view, most likely arriving at Eton Cottage now. The next time I see Eddy, we will be husband and wife. I allow myself a quick dance to let out some of the nerves and excitement and then run to the front entrance of Calderwood estate.

Lily and I get straight to work preparing for our evening, starting with baths. Then it is time to choose my dress. After seeing the choices, it does not take long to pick the right one. Of course, Mrs. Landon would send this over. It was not made for me. It's a bit outdated and considered out of fashion with the light blue large and flowing skirt and the matching tight corset tops with flowing sleeves. Surely, no one from town will be here, so I may as well dress as it pleases me. Preferring my hair to hang loose, Lily styles it away from my face with a modest tiara she wore during her wedding.

As we make our way to the foyer, I begin to worry that I will regret my decision to wear this gown that exposes so much of my neck and back when a chill from a window hits me.

"I have just the thing for that." Lily seems elated with herself. There is a small box near the entrance. I open it up and recognize it immediately as Mrs. Landon's shawl. She keeps it in a chest in her bedroom. Her mother made it for her wedding day. Tears well in my eyes as I wrap myself in the shawl.

Albert arrives to escort us back to the cottage. After greeting Lily with many flattering compliments, he turns to me with a tear in his eye. "Dear, sweet girl. I wish I had more time to prepare for a day as important as today, but it came as such short notice." We both chuckle as tears fill our eyes. Lily is already wiping her tears away beside us.

"Watching you grow over these past years has been an

honor I will never forget. I am so proud of you, and I cannot wait to accompany you into this next chapter of your life." I throw myself into his arms. Without the words to express how much his friendship has meant to me, I attempt to show it with my embrace.

"Enough of all these emotions—it is time for us to go, Margo." He holds out his arm to me and does the same with his other arm for Lily. Once we are settled in the carriage, Lily pulls something out of her bag, and Albert explains, "Margo, dear. Your groom has requested you wear a blindfold upon your arrival to Eton Cottage."

And Eddy says I am the controlling one. "What about my hair?" I ask.

It seems that is why Lily is the one holding the scarf because she says, "I will make sure that your hair will stay just as it is." Begrudgingly, I agree.

The carriage comes to a stop, and the first voice I hear when the door opens is Mr. Landon. "My beautiful daughter!" He helps me out of the carriage, with Lily and Albert assisting from within. They say their goodbyes as I am moved into the cottage.

As my blindfold is carefully removed from my hair, I smell the delicious aromas within the kitchen. After hugs and tears, I take a few minutes to settle and Mrs. Landon moves onto the topic of my dress. "I just knew you were going to pick this one!" I hug my hands around my dress. "And my shawl complements it so well. Thank you for wearing it, Margo. It means so much to see you in it."

Next, it is Mr. Landon's turn to discuss a very important matter. "Margo, I know you are here and dressed, so it seems you are planning to go through with this, but I need to hear it from your mouth. Is this what you truly want? Is he who you want to spend your life with?"

"Yes, I am more certain of this than anything else, Papa."

"Then you have our blessing," he confirms with a grin and pulls me into his arms once more.

Bells begin to sound from outside. "That's our signal." Mrs. Landon moves to one side of me while Mr. Landon stays on the other side. As we make our way through the door, thankfully without a blindfold this time.

As the ceremony begins, music plays, sounds of a soft violin and I recognize Arthur Landon at once. He is seated next to where the vicar stands, surrounded by baskets of wildflowers. Chairs were brought into the yard from all over the cottage and filled with familiar faces. Seated behind two empty chairs, Mr. Landon's brother is here, accompanied by Arthur's mother and brother, Tom.

On the opposite side are Lily and Albert, with Lord and Lady Riley and an ecstatic Evelyn Riley. She gives me a knowing look, which I return with a mischievous smile. Then, I notice movement in front of the vicar.

There stands Mr. Edward Riley, my husband, my Eddy. Devilishly handsome, standing strong in his dark blue formals that complement my dress perfectly.

I barely take notice of what is happening, my gaze and attention held by the man before me. I know the vows are exchanged as the sun sets behind us, and we promise to love, cherish, and antagonize each other for the rest of our days. Eddy's playful smile melts my heart at the additional promise he requested the vicar to include in our vows. We are named husband and wife and are kissing as our friends and family cheer around us.

With night rising among us, we make our way inside. The cottage has been decorated with flowers and candles to match the outside. It is beautiful. It is perfect. I will not cry. I am so happy.

Evelyn is first to congratulate and interrogate us. I learned that she did not hear about the wedding until she woke up this morning. Apparently, when Eddy went to notify his parents, she was still asleep. "How could you not wake me, Eddy?" she pleads with him.

"Given the bruising and tongue-lashing I have received from you on numerous accounts in the past while trying to wake you, I knew better than to attempt that today, sister," he mocks her.

"This is not the same," she scolds him, then turns to me. "And you! Margo. How could you not tell me of your feelings for him?"

Eddy replies for both of us, "It was to be a surprise, Evey." Her mouth drops open. "You were surprised, are you not?"

"Not too surprised, brother. After reading those letters you left on the desk here at Eton Cottage, I knew that you loved her. Especially after pulling out the one you crumpled and threw in the bin." She pauses to watch her brother's shock cross his face. "And when I left them on the desk for Margo to find, I was sure you would both finally find your way back to one another." She winks at me. "Who is surprised now, brother?" Then she hugs us each before disappearing into the crowd.

"I cannot believe that you were able to pull all this

together in a day's time," I say, squeezing his arm and looking among our loved ones.

With a sigh, he apologizes, "I am sorry I was not able to get Lord and Lady Eton here. I went to them both this morning, but they had previous commitments," he says, the latter with anger in his voice.

I must say, I haven't thought of them much since arriving back in the country. "That is quite all right. My true parents are here, and that is what is most important." As if they knew we were speaking of them, the Landons are next to approach us and offer their congratulations.

Next, Lord and Lady Riley find us, offering a more formal set of congratulations than we received from the Landons. Lord Riley seems much happier with his son's choice of bride than his wife. While I do not believe Lady Riley was ever particularly fond of me, she seems to find me an adequate match for her son. "Congratulations, Edward and Margaret. As unexpected as this was, I must say I am glad this matter is settled. I have been waiting years for Edward to finally settle down."

Eddy is quick to defend us, "A lesson that I have learned is that love does not always arrive when we would like it to, Mother. Some things as important as love are worth waiting for." His mother seems indifferent to his declaration, but I am moved by it.

The celebration continues after dinner with drinks, desserts, and card playing. Perhaps in the future, we can make this an annual event for our anniversary. Have our guests over for an evening of dining, drinking, and card playing. I will be sure to share this idea with Eddy later.

The Rileys are the first to take their leave. I assume our

guests will be staying at Eton Cottage, but Lily whispers to me, "Everyone will be making their way to Calderwood Estate. I have offered to host them for the next few days."

Lily's house is typically empty, and I am moved that she would offer to host so many guests.

"That is not necessary. I do not want to impose. I would be happy to have everyone here," I reassure her.

With a knowing look, Lily lowers her voice, "Trust me, Margo. You will be much happier to have Eton Cottage to yourself as newlyweds." She winks and then turns to start ushering her guests into the carriage.

The carriage makes multiple trips between the two residences, especially to transport all the Landon's to their destination for the evening. Albert and Lily elect to take the last ride when Arthur and Evelyn meet us at the entrance to Eton Cottage.

Lily and I exchange a knowing look and then back to Evelyn, her cheeks blushing. Luckily, Eddy is too distracted in conversation with Albert to notice. Perhaps young love is in the air.

The final four of our guests ride off in the carriage toward the Calderwood Estate.

I turn to Eddy, whose attention is completely on my dress, before slowly moving up my body to meet my gaze with heat in his eyes. "Well, husband. Whatever shall we do now?"

He closes the distance between us, "Library."

Interesting. "Looking for me to throw another book at you?" I ask coyly.

His lips pull into a tight smile, and then he lifts me into his arms. "Since that night, I have been planning far more pleasurable activities for us to enjoy in that library, and I plan to enjoy each one of them this evening with my wife." My toes curl at his words, and my mind begins to conjure what exactly my husband has been fantasizing about doing with me. I begin to kiss his neck as he leads us through the cottage.

Edward Riley was my adversary for so long, which made him the perfect husband. I will not change to become his delicate wife. We will continue to face the world just as we were, but united instead of opposed.

ACKNOWLEDGMENTS

This page is not long enough to express the endless gratitude I have for those who have supported me during the *years* I have spent writing Eddy and Margo's story.

To the guy playing guitar in the room across from me, thank you for always keeping your endless support close by and providing the soundtrack to my author journey.

To my beta readers/author friends, Taryn and Cait. Your kindness and support have given me the confidence to move forward on this journey. I do not have enough page space to share how much that has meant to me.

To my editor, Cassie. Thank you for your patience, understanding, and guidance through this process. With your help, this process has become more exciting than I could have ever imagined.

To my family and friends, thank you for putting up with my endless ramblings about this couple. Being able to talk through different scenes and ideas with you allowed me to bring this story to life.

ABOUT THE AUTHOR

E.G. Verot spends her days in the world of education but spends her nights reading, writing, and loving books of all flavors and spices. She has a TBR list longer than she cares to admit. She has been longing to share the characters from her daydreams with you for many years. She lives in the Northeast and looks forward to the winter weather all year. When she is not reading, she can be found spending time with her pets, crocheting, and enjoying her life with loved ones.

For more information on E.G. Verot, her social media accounts, and the Hostility and Heartstrings playlist, please visit https://linktr.ee/e.g.verot